Perseverance

Perseverance

A novel by

Robin Lehman

FOGDOG PRESS

PERSEVERANCE

Cover design by Robert Aulicino

Library of Congress Control Number: 2009907077

ISBN 978-0-9841469-0-1

Printed in the United States of America

FOGDOG PRESS
Box 3510
Lawrence, KS 66046

www.fogdogpress.net

Acknowledgements

My thanks to the Baranof Hotel in Juneau, Alaska, for allowing me a crucial behind-the-scenes look; to Larry Welch, former director of the Kansas Bureau of Investigation and 25-year veteran of the Federal Bureau of Investigation, who gave my Fibbies a greater level of authenticity (any lingering shortcomings in that department are mine, not his!); to Sandra Baxter Dunn and Karen Jacobsen Hansen, my lifelong Alaska pals who enthusiastically helped me reconnect with the elements of my hometown that show up in this novel; and to Jerry Harmon, owner of AJ Mine/Gastineau Mill Enterprises, who gave me access to the now-defunct goldmine that plays a prominent role in the story.

Last but not certainly not least, my heartfelt thanks to my family: my sister, Susan Henderson, who bravely read every single draft of *Perseverance* (way too numerous to count) and lovingly fanned my confidence; my daughters, Lindsay and Regan, extraordinary women whose innate wisdom inspires me; and my husband, Pat, who has stood beside me through every version of myself and whose faith in me has never, ever wavered.

For my parents,
Joseph and Carol Waddell,
who gave me the gift of an Alaska childhood
and an imagination as wild as the Taku wind.

Perseverance is more prevailing than violence;
and many things which cannot be overcome
when they are together, yield themselves up
when taken little by little.

— **Plutarch**

CHAPTER ONE

THE SOUND of impending doom is often faint at first, like a deadly storm that growls in the distance before it inches in and unleashes its wrath. Or like a woman's voice, softly pleading for mercy.

"Please don't be angry with me, Paul ..."

A mere whisper, barely audible above the traffic on the bustling Georgetown street, but tinged with a tone that caused Regan's skull to prickle.

She shot a glance at the couple seated two tables away on the outdoor patio; they appeared civilized, not on the verge of violence. Regan returned her focus to her book.

The words swam on the page like fish dodging a net. Regan sighed, again shifting her gaze to the couple.

The woman possessed a fragile beauty, like delicate china adorned with dainty flowers. Decorative, breakable. Her eyes were locked on the man, fingers nervously toying with her necklace.

Did the woman's tiny stature make her feel insignificant, like she needed Paul's permission to breathe?

Regan knew plenty of dinky women who would rip your heart out and throw it at you if you dared to cross them. It wasn't the size of the body; it was the size of the attitude.

The man pulled some sort of document from the inside pocket of his jacket and skimmed it, seemingly indifferent to his companion's distress.

Regan studied him: tan suit perfectly tailored, chic patterned tie, saddle brown Italian leather loafers. His complexion and tawny hair hinted at time spent outdoors when he wasn't wherever it was he went in his pricey suit.

He had a certain quality … what was it? *Allure.* That was it. And a hint of something else: cruelty. She saw it in his dismissive air, in the way he glowered when he bothered to look at the woman at all.

But none of it was her affair. Regan had a rare bit of leisure time; she planned to lose herself in a good book and let the evening breeze fondle her skin while she sipped wine and enjoyed her dinner. She commanded herself to concentrate on the page.

"Babe, I hardly know him," the woman said in a low voice. "He wasn't even there five minutes." She tucked a wisp of wheat-colored hair behind her ear and waited.

The man kept his eyes on the papers, but Regan saw the tells: rigid jaw, flared nostrils, lips compressed into a thin line. Free hand clenched into a fist.

She moved into a state of readiness, like quietly removing the safety from a loaded weapon.

The woman flicked a glance in her direction before looking forlornly at the salad she'd barely touched. She rubbed her arms like she was chilled, even though the heat of the day had diminished only a few degrees.

The waiter stopped at the couple's table to collect the man's empty plate. "Can I bring you anything else, Congressman Slade?"

Congressman? *Oy.*

"The check," Slade snapped.

"I have it right here, sir. I can take —"

Slade snatched the leather holder from his hand and jammed a couple bills inside. The woman visibly jumped when he sprang from his seat and seized her arm, pulling her onto the sidewalk.

Regan fished cash from her Louis Vuitton knockoff and threw it on the table. She charged after the dashing congressman and the woman in his clutches, who was struggling to run in three-inch heels.

Wait. Regan came to an abrupt halt. *What are you doing? They're having a tiff, that's all. Butt out.*

She shook her head and reversed direction, thinking if she hurried she could get back to the table before they cleared away her own half-eaten salad. Salvage her leisure plans before they were completely in the tank.

She gave the couple a final glance, just in time to see the congressman stop and turn toward the woman, his face contorted into a vicious sneer. Like a prize fighter moving in slow motion, Slade pulled his arm back.

Regan broke into a sprint. Before she could get to him, he delivered a knockout punch.

He was eyeball-to-eyeball with his bloodied companion before he knew what hit him. "What the hell —"

Regan had her knee in his back as she pulled cuffs from her bag. "Think you *own* her, huh, Congressman? How *dare* she speak to another man, right?"

"Get off me, bitch! I'll have you arrested!"

"No, it's Agent Manning, FBI. And *you're* the one under arrest."

సా

"WAIT UP, Manning," said Nick, jogging to catch up with Regan as she headed for the classroom building. "I heard about your takedown last night." His eyes twinkled with admiration.

"Yeah, I was up in Georgetown, grabbing a little leisure while I could. Thought I'd have some dinner, read a book ..."

"Read *people*, more like. I know you."

"Nope, you're wrong, Nick. I was totally into Elizabeth Berg's new book when I heard this tussle going on. I couldn't very well ignore it."

"No, you couldn't. But a *congressman?*"

She stopped and turned toward him. "What, you think because he's an elected official he should get a pass?"

"No, I ... of *course* not. I just —"

She resumed walking. "But I should have moved quicker. Gotten to him *before* he punched her."

"How could you know what he would do? You're not psychic." He paused. "Come to think of it, maybe you are."

"Not psychic, just observant."

"*Hyper*-observant."

Yeah, well, she had her dad to thank for that.

"Whatever, but it was obvious that Slade sees himself as a powerful man, and she made him feel insecure. He wasn't going to let her get away with it."

"But right out in public? Did he seriously think it wouldn't end up in the news?"

"He *wasn't* thinking. He was too consumed with rage."

"Well, at least we've got him on aggravated assault," said Nick.

Regan nodded. "That should give Congressman Pretty Boy a nice stretch of quiet time to reflect on how he just sank his political career."

"Think he'll actually do time?"

"I don't know ... he might prefer to be locked up than at home with his very-pissed-off wife."

"How's she doing? Is she going to be okay?"

"Oh, the woman he hit wasn't his wife. That was his personal assistant. And mistress."

Regan had chatted with Kate at Georgetown University Hospital. "She'll be okay physically. The broken nose and bruises will heal pretty fast. It's the emotional part that's going to take time." The gruesome injuries to that lovely face hadn't masked the shame, the self-loathing. She'd given Kate her card, told her to call if she wanted to talk. Or learn a little self-defense.

Regan picked up the pace so they wouldn't be late for class. "So, Nick, you ready for the training to be over?"

"Yeah, I'm glad it's the last one. Hostage negotiation isn't my bag."

Regan stopped and looked at him. "You mean you aren't going to put in for the Crisis Negotiation Unit with me? C'mon, Jenesco, we're a *team*."

"We'll still be a team. You talk, I'll aim."

"Oh, I get it. Negotiation's too touchy-feely for a manly man like you, right?"

"Nah, I'm okay with touchy-feely, as long as you make it quick. Negotiation takes too damn long."

She shouldn't have been surprised; it was the same theory Nick employed with relationships.

Her cell phone beeped. "Hi, boss."

"I'm moving up your deployment," he said. "We're getting word the protests up there could get ugly."

Regan felt her stomach constrict; she'd expected to have a couple more days to psyche herself up. "When do we leave?"

"Wheels up in two hours."

❧

DREAD WEIGHED on her like a coat of thick mud, dulling the usual thrill. Even being tapped mission team leader wasn't enough to shake it off.

The Bombardier Dash 8 turboprop bucked and bounced as it cleared the last layer of clouds. Rain streamed in horizontal stripes along the windows, distorting Regan's view of the rippling waterways below.

Everything looked gray. Just like it always did.

"Man, it's beautiful up here," said Nick, peering out at the snow-capped peaks. His eyes were bright, one foot bopping in anticipation.

Regan envied his excitement, his lack of connection to the place they were headed.

The rest of the team chattered like magpies, grating on her nerves. The plane hit an air pocket; someone said, "Whoa, hang on to your hat!"

"It isn't usually this bumpy coming in," Regan announced. A wave of nausea hit, something she seldom experienced flying, turbulent or not. She pressed a hand to her lips.

Nick said, "How long since you've been back?"

"Five years."

Not long enough.

"Five years? Why so long?"

She shrugged. It was easier to chase other people's demons than face her own.

There were few signs of life below. Just tree-shrouded mountains and pewter ribbons of water stretching in every direction as far as the eye could see.

A mental image snuck past the gatekeeper in her brain: trails strewn with pine needles, the way the tree canopy cast an emerald glow and made the forest seem magical. Playing hide-and-go-seek, her favorite childhood game.

Funny to think she'd made a career of it.

Regan closed her eyes and locked her thoughts on the mission checklist until the aircraft was on final approach, traveling north along Gastineau Channel.

As they skirted past Douglas Island on their left, Regan gazed at her old stomping grounds. She felt a stirring in her chest and put a hand over it, as if to snuff it out.

Mount Roberts loomed on their right, almost close enough to touch. She looked for the familiar landmark on its side, the multi-leveled carcass of the old goldmine. But it was gone, imploded so it could no longer lure people who were too damn dumb to comprehend the danger of entering an abandoned mine.

She absently rubbed the scar above her left elbow.

The team reveled in the birds-eye view of Juneau, pointing and babbling like school kids on a field trip. Regan stared at the bulkhead in front of her.

Minutes later, they touched down. The turboprop taxied past an Alaska Airlines plane, jetway cupped at its side, and came to a stop on the tarmac, twenty yards from the terminal building.

Regan took a deep breath and plopped an FBI cap on her head, pulling her auburn ponytail through the opening in back. She slipped into a Bureau-issue windbreaker, as though the attire would somehow restore her Regan-as-agent equilibrium.

It's just another mission, she told herself.

Too bad her stomach wasn't buying it. She closed her eyes and took another deep breath.

Do NOT throw up. It is unprofessional.

Nick reached over and squeezed her hand. "Welcome home, partner."

Ten seconds later, they heard the explosion.

CHAPTER TWO

P IPE BOMB exploded in a field near the airport right after we landed, boss," Regan said in a quivery voice. The attack rattled her, made her feel like something malevolent had followed her home.

"Any injuries?" Al Rinehart asked, his voice calm. He rarely, if ever, displayed emotion, which made him good at his job, freakin' terrible at relationships. He had three divorces under his belt to prove it.

"No, just total chaos in the terminal building. It's the height of tourist season. Planes are grounded while they sweep the aircraft and the fields close to the runway."

"Okay, good. Glad you guys are there to assist."

Regan glanced at the other members of the Critical Incident Response Group milling around a short distance away on the tarmac. The team relied on her instincts, on her legendary composure. She couldn't let them think she was knocked off her game less than five minutes into the mission.

"Al, do you think the bomb was timed to coincide with our arrival? 'Cause if it was, how'd they know our ETA?" He wouldn't have the answer; she was simply thinking out loud, attempting to make sense of it.

"Don't know, but watch your back."

"We will. What about bomb techs? Can you send —"

"They'll be there tonight."

☙

"IT'S THE Baranof, for cryin' out loud, not Attica," grumbled the hotel's general manager. His nose curved downward into a beak, reminding Regan of a parrot. His carping only reinforced the image.

"I thought you said the security measures would be nearly undetectable." He pointed to the screening device erected at the front doors. "You call that undetectable? It's a gigantic eyesore, that's what it is."

He was right, the contraption didn't exactly complement the wood-and-brass lobby of the historic hotel, but they had a member of the president's cabinet to protect. Energy Secretary Ella Vargas would arrive the next day, along with an entire assortment of lawmakers, oil execs, energy analysts, academics, and environmentalists attending the Alaska Energy Summit.

Police Chief Pat Lamont tried to placate the hotel manager. "It's temporary, Reuben. We'll all get out of your hair next week and give you back your classy joint."

Reuben flapped his arms and stomped away.

The chief turned to Regan. "C'mon, let's go sit a minute," he said, pointing to the lobby. "Catch up a little."

They plopped down in overstuffed chairs. Regan noticed that gravity had started to take a toll on her former boss; his face seemed longer, jowlier, and his barrel chest had slid south.

"Reuben's right, that screening device does make this place look like a prison." The chief's forehead was creased in a scowl that made his eyebrows look bushier than usual, like a pair of woolly worms glued to his face. "That bomb, Regan – it makes me damn uncomfortable."

"Me, too, especially since we don't know who or why yet. But this is what we do, Chief. My team has it covered."

Had she sounded confident enough? Because right now, Lamont wasn't the only one who needed convincing.

"So whose brilliant idea was it to finalize the energy plan in Juneau? I don't know about you, but that strikes *me* as pretty idiotic."

Regan nodded. "Somebody's delusional if they think Alaskans are going to let a nuclear waste facility be built up here without a fight."

"Well, I'm just glad you guys are here to help out. Especially you – my favorite Fibbie," he said with a wink.

Regan raised her eyebrows. "'Favorite' is not the *f*-word you usually pair with 'Fibbie.' Does that mean you've seen the light?"

Lamont chuckled. "Now that the Bureau has you as one of its own, there's hope for those bastards."

Regan laughed. She felt a rush of affection for the man who not only had been an amazing boss but also a friend who helped her through more than one rough patch. "How's Marian?"

"Champing at the bit for me to retire. She wants to join the other snowbirds in Arizona during the winter."

"Sounds nice," said Regan, knowing the chief would hate it. "You'd come back here during the summer?"

"Don't know ... Marian said something about traveling during the summer." He looked like a convicted man awaiting sentencing.

Regan decided to change the subject. "Speaking of travel, I saw five cruise ships in the channel this morning. It's a wonder they all fit."

"Yep, we pack 'em in like sardines. Thirteen thousand visitors on our fair streets today. I oughta stick around here and open a souvenir shop."

Regan smiled at the mental image of the chief hawking wares to the tourists down on South Franklin Street. If he was half as popular with them as he was with the locals, he'd be rich in less time than it took to say, *We have some dandy gold nugget watch bands, in case you're interested ...*

He said, "You been to your mom and dad's yet?"

"No." The smile evaporated.

"Spend some time with them, Regan. I know things haven't always been smooth, but they're awfully proud of you. Your dad talks about you all the time at coffee."

She gave a bitter snort. They hadn't spoken in two years, ever since he came to D.C. for a mayors' conference. Regan invited her parents to stay with her, had armed herself with resolve not to fight with her dad. *No matter what.*

It lasted less than a day. *Adios Regan, hello Hilton.*

The chief wanted to help heal the rift. Devlin Manning was his best friend, and Regan was like his own daughter. But he didn't know how deep those Manning family secrets ran.

For a few moments, they quietly watched the bustle in the hotel, unshed tears making Regan's eyes burn.

"What about Danny?" she said finally. Might as well go ahead and get it all on the table at once.

"Lead detective now."

"Still with Susan?"

"He is. Their marriage seemed to survive the … uh, setback."

The familiar guilt washed over her. Could she avoid seeing Danny while she was here?

Chances were about as good as a southeast Alaska drought.

"Get to play much basketball back there at Quantico?" the chief asked.

"A little," said Regan, relieved to talk about something less charged. "We play pickup games whenever we can."

"You should be playing in the WNBA, not chasing murderers and drug dealers."

Regan rolled her eyes. "You're the one who talked me into being a cop when I got out of college. Besides, I'm not *that* good a player, Pat."

"The hell you're not … just ask anybody in this town. They'd give their eyeteeth to be able to watch you again. And I recruited you *after* you decided not to pursue professional basketball. I wasn't going to let good talent go to waste."

"Or pass up a chance to increase the diversity of the department."

"That, too."

Nick came into the lobby. "Okay, the cameras are up and everything's been checked and re-checked. This place is tighter than a girdle on an elephant. You two wanna grab some coffee?"

"Okay," said Regan, standing up. "Chief?"

"No, you guys go ahead," he replied, dragging himself up from the chair. "I've got to get back to the station. Keep me posted, though."

"I will," said Regan, squeezing his arm.

"Seems like a good guy," Nick said as the chief moved off.

Regan watched Lamont smile and wave at the front-desk clerks on his way out the door. "He's the best," she said wistfully. She'd trade Devlin Manning for Pat Lamont in a New York minute.

They entered the coffee shop, empty except for a middle-aged couple studying excursion pamphlets, and slid into a booth.

The waitress sauntered over, eyeballing Regan, straining to place her. Regan and Danny used to stop in for lunch occasionally, and the waitress – named Gail, according to the plastic name tag pinned to her mustard-colored uniform – practically purred when she talked to Regan's handsome partner. And look, here was Regan with *another* one.

After Gail scooted off to get their coffee, Nick said, "No bigger than this hotel is, it seems like we've got cops tripping over each other."

"I know, but AR wants to make sure we've got things plugged up tight." The team found endless amusement in their boss's initials, given how anal retentive Al Rinehart was.

The waitress slid two cups of coffee in front of them and gave Nick a saucy smile. "Let me know if you need anything else, hon."

He smiled back. "Thanks." When she was out of earshot, he told Regan, "If *you* need anything else, hon, let me know and I'll have Gail get it for you."

"Right," she said, watching Nick perform the usual ritual of stirring three creams and four sugars into his coffee. She didn't mention she was used to Gail's tricks.

"Are the officers in place to check IDs on the top three floors?" she asked.

"Yep." He took a slurp of the thick brew. "So what happens if some poor schmuck gets mixed up and presses seven instead of six? We shoot him?"

"Check the shoes," Regan quipped. "If he's wearing white tennis shoes, he's a tourist. You can let him go."

"Eco-terrorists don't wear white tennis shoes?"

"No. Neither do assassins. Violates the dress code."

"I'll be damned," said Nick. "I musta missed that chapter in the agent handbook." His smile lit up his face.

Regan gave an inward sigh. When it came to the whole being greater than the sum of its parts, her partner was the poster boy. Individually, his features were unremarkable – smallish hazel eyes, chestnut hair short and ruffled in the front, like it hadn't seen a comb in months, if ever. Nose on the large side, slightly crooked teeth, stubbly chin. But somehow it all added up to ridiculously sexy.

Not that it mattered one way or the other; the *last* thing she'd do was hook up with her work partner. Only needed to learn that lesson once.

Regan half-listened to Nick's animated story about something he found in a hotel room. Her mind drifted to what the chief had said: *He talks about you all the time at coffee.*

Ah, the two faces of Mayor Manning. A strapping Irishman with a personality as big as Alaska. Boisterous and funny, a lovable bear of a man.

In public.

At home he was surly, especially after a toddy or two. He preyed on the meekness of her mother and younger brother, Colin, like they existed simply for his own amusement. Regan spent her youth defending them. The pint-sized protector, the cop-in-waiting.

"You okay, Reegs?" said Nick.

"I'm sorry … what were you saying?"

"Nothing important. You look a little funny, that's all."

"I'm okay," she sighed. "Just ready to get back to Quantico."

"You're ready to go *back*? We've only been here a couple days. Besides, we haven't been to the famous Red Dog Saloon yet."

"The *real* Red Dog Saloon isn't even here anymore," Regan huffed. "They built a new one that's just a tourist hang-out."

"Well since the VIPs don't get here 'til tomorrow, maybe tonight you can introduce the team to a little of the Juneau night life. Show us the *real* spots." Nick tweaked his eyebrows suggestively.

"No!" she blurted. "I mean, you know, 'cause we're on duty."

"Whoa," he said, holding his hands up, his face registering surprise. "Then we'll drink Shirley Temples. You know, you've been acting a little weird ever since we got here. And you keep looking at the door.

What's up, partner? You got some old flame you're afraid of running into?"

Regan vaulted from the booth. "You know what, Nick? Sometimes you just need to mind your own friggin' business."

CHAPTER THREE

R EGAN PLOWED into a man entering the restaurant. He was rock-solid, like a punching bag with arms. The collision nearly knocked her off her feet.

"Hey, you okay?" he said, hands on her shoulders. She spotted the Glock 22 perched above his right hip, an FBI shield on his left waistband.

"Yes, sorry," Regan said, collecting herself.

"Guy at the front desk said to look for red hair and green eyes." He pointed toward the coffee shop. "Unless that's a clubhouse for redheads, you must be Agent Manning." He didn't crack a smile.

She nodded, unsure if the remark was meant to be funny.

He shoved his hand toward her. "Mark McKee, ASAC from Anchorage." Short for assistant special agent in charge of the FBI's Anchorage Field Office, but it sounded like he said "a sack from Anchorage."

She reached her hand out tentatively, expecting a vice-like grip to match his brusque style. Instead, his handshake was flaccid, like grabbing a dead trout. It gave her a chill.

"I'm Regan," she said, enunciating the long *e* out of habit. People usually pronounced it Raygun.

"Good to meet you, Raygun. Those are my guys over there." He pointed to five agents standing to the left of the front desk. "So where's the command post?"

"This way," she said, rolling her eyes as she turned away from him. She introduced herself to the four men and one woman, then led the group down a wide hallway. "We're right across from the Treadwell Ballroom, where the energy summit will be held."

24

They stepped into the Douglas Room, which was twittering with activity. "The team is getting things set up," said Regan. "Hey, guys," she said in a raised voice. All eyes turned toward them.

Regan introduced McKee and his officers to the group. "The Anchorage Field Office's jurisdiction covers all half-a-million square miles of Alaska," she explained.

McKee pulled his shoulders back and put his hands on his hips, ready to expound.

The agents nodded in reply, waved, and went back to what they were doing. Punching Bag looked a little deflated.

Regan beckoned him to a large whiteboard that contained notes and headshots of the summiteers. "Our VIPs. We've run background checks on them; we're in the process of digging deeper, see if anything hinky pops up. We don't want any surprises, especially with several hundred protestors on our doorstep."

"Okay, good," McKee said, as though she needed his approval.

Nick came in. He introduced himself to McKee and the others, then leaned toward Regan and whispered, "Sorry to stick my nose where it didn't belong."

She squeezed his arm in apology for her huffiness. She was better now; the command post was beginning to feel like a mini-Quantico.

"Here's the conference schedule," Regan said, handing McKee a folder. "We have tight containment when attendees are inside the hotel, so our biggest challenge will be to keep it that way when they're taken out for excursions. They have one each of the three days of the summit."

"Advance done on all three?" He squinted at her, his brow furrowed.

He's trying to intimidate me, take control.

Nothing new.

"Yep," she responded without a trace of rancor. "We've created operational plans for each one. They're in your folder."

McKee opened it and read aloud. "Let's see ... Mendenhall Glacier, Mount Roberts Tramway, Perseverance Salmon Bake. I don't see too much problem."

"Yeah, nothing too crazy logistically. I'm just glad they're not loading everybody onto floatplanes and flying them out to the Taku Lodge or someplace like that."

"You know the area?"

"She grew up here," Nick said proudly. "Former Juneau cop."

"That right?" said McKee. A quizzical expression crossed his face, like he was about to embark on a game of forty questions.

She rushed on. "My primary concern is with Perseverance. I don't know how familiar you are with Juneau, Mark, but there are a lot of trails up in that area. The conference materials invite attendees to take a hike after the salmon bake if they're so inclined."

Nick smiled at her pun.

"How'd that get past you guys?" said McKee.

"It was apparently a last-minute addition to the program," Regan replied. "Otherwise, we'd have squelched it. We still might if the situation warrants." The bomb at the airport weighed heavily on her mind.

Nick said, "Or we could casually mention that bears roam all over up there. That'd be enough to keep me from taking a hike."

Regan glanced at him and smiled. "Let's make sure we're all wearing our hiking boots, just in case some of those summit people are more adventurous than you, Agent Jenesco."

One corner of McKee's mouth curved upward into something resembling a smile. "Bears are a fact of life for us up here, son."

Nick smiled indulgently. "I'm just saying —"

"Hey, that's okay, we'll protect you." He winked at Regan and gripped Nick's shoulder, giving it a hard squeeze.

Nick flinched; his face lost all hint of amusement.

"Oh, don't worry, Mark, a bear won't be able to catch my partner," said Regan. "He runs like a deer. And I just need to be able to run faster than you."

CHAPTER FOUR

I'M NOT sure you can mix political parties to this degree and expect it to work," Landry Ness grumbled. "We have some major philosophical differences." He'd just finished reading the latest draft of President Eli Sanford's proposed health care plan.

"I know what you mean, Mr. Vice President," Macauley Holman said dutifully. The chief of staff really wanted to say, *You knew that when you signed on, sir. Sanford's bipartisan pledge is what got him elected.*

Ness yawned and stretched. "When does the energy summit get under way?" He straightened the black marble pen and pencil cradle on his nearly empty desk. The gold-plated writing instruments stood like missiles ready to launch.

"Tomorrow," said Mac.

"Have we heard from Bob?" Ness was referring to Axis Oil CEO Robert Carney. The VP hardly took a pee without discussing it with the oil man.

"Not yet, sir. I'm sure he'll check in with you when he gets to Juneau this afternoon."

"He's got his work cut out for him with that bunch, Mac. Like mixing oil and water." He wasn't being ironic; he was never ironic.

"Yes, but they're all being asked to support the president's primary focus on nuclear energy, first and foremost. Who knows, perhaps they'll all oppose it and end up united despite themselves." Mac chuckled.

"Well, the bugaboo is deciding where to store the nuclear waste," said Ness. "That could take up the whole summit. They might not even get around to the part of Vargas's plan that really stinks: the

27

timeline for reducing foreign oil imports. She's hell-bent on cutting off oil and pulling troops and funding out of those regions sooner rather than later, but it could be disastrous for national security."

For a minute, Mac thought Carney himself had materialized in the room. But no, it was just his minion, the vice president of the United States.

"Well," said Mac, "Bob and his oil buddies are going to have to convince some of the others if they're going to have a prayer of changing her mind on that. Vargas won't give in on *anything* Carney wants, and the other oil execs will likely suffer guilt by association."

Ness shook his head. "Bob's paranoid when it comes to Ella. First woman he's ever met that he couldn't charm the socks off of."

Or the rest of her clothes, thought Mac. Carney's fourth marriage was about to end after his wife caught the massage therapist they kept on staff doing more than rubbing the boss's back. According to Ness, his friend couldn't help it – women threw themselves at him.

"Frankly, I can't see why the president named Vargas to the cabinet," Ness continued. "She doesn't have a deep enough knowledge of foreign matters – doesn't understand that there has to be some compromise on oil imports, that the leaders in the Middle East have to be handled with skilled diplomacy."

"Umm," Mac said noncommittally. His boss had shared that view with him at least a dozen times. Personally, he'd always found Ella Vargas to be intelligent and quite likable, even if she *was* a little too defined by her populism.

"I hope the president can be persuaded that her timeline is completely unrealistic – that we need to look at import diversification instead," said Ness. "Tap the regions outside the Persian Gulf before we abandon oil for some of these untested fuel sources. Not every American is ready to run out and buy a hybrid, for godsakes."

Ness ranted daily about this or that, but he was careful not to criticize Eli Sanford. Despite their difference in political tilt, the president and vice president respected each other. Ness admired the president's razor-sharp intellect, his ability to size things up in an instant, his poise under pressure. Sanford saw his VP as the consummate gentleman, if a bit old-school; he relied on Ness's foreign policy experience and the trust he'd built with government officials all over the world during his reign as chairman of the Senate Foreign Relations Committee.

The only thing that threatened to sour the relationship was the vice president's fierce loyalty to Carney. If push came to shove, would Ness support the president over his friend?

Mac wasn't so sure. With Carney scrambling to make back-room deals before a new energy policy could take effect, Ness would be well-advised to distance himself. Finish out his political career with dignity, not servitude to an oil magnate. Even if they did go way back.

"The environmentalists will be a problem for Bob," said Mac. "They'll agree with the secretary's timeline on foreign oil."

"Pfft," muttered Ness, flapping his hand. "Bunch of drama queens. Vargas stacked the deck with them because she knows they'll squawk about anything that comes out of Bob's mouth."

No, sir, Vargas included them because she shares their beliefs.

"Well, all I can say is it's going to be an interesting summit. Especially with Alaskans up in arms at the prospect of a nuclear storage site in their back yard."

"I know, Mac, but I agree with the president that the site does make sense. Alaska's one of the least populous states in the union and has a ton of land area. Vargas isn't keen on sucking more oil out of the state using Axis's new recovery tool, but that's what it'll take to get Alaskans on board. They want that revenue."

Mac hoped his boss was right. Otherwise, the administration had a big problem on its hands. One that translated into a stalled energy plan and major delays.

The vice president stood and pulled on his suit coat, tugging his heavily starched shirt sleeves so the monogrammed cufflinks showed. "I don't envy Bob," he muttered. "That summit's going to be a giant slugfest."

࿊

THE HEADLINE in the *Juneau Empire* caught Regan's eye as she passed through the lobby: Former JD High Star Heads Up FBI Team.

She scooped up the paper and skimmed the story. It recounted her high school basketball career, calling it "stellar," then went on to mention that she was a starter all four years for the University of Washington Huskies … spent four years as a Juneau police officer … now beginning her sixth year with the Bureau, she was heading up the FBI team responsible for security at the Alaska Energy Summit.

Where had he gotten his information? No reporter had tried to reach her.

"We're proud of our daughter. It'll be good to have her home, even for a brief visit," read the quote.

Thanks, Mom. So much for flying under the radar.

Regan tossed the paper back down on the side table, feigning annoyance, but she was secretly pleased. Everyone liked a little positive press.

Inside the command post, Regan's team and the Anchorage agents yukked it up like they were at a cocktail party. She saw Nick engaged in lively conversation with the only other female agent besides her, a curly-haired brunette.

"She's from Maine, too!" he exclaimed when he saw Regan. "Lindsay grew up in Brunswick – twenty miles from me."

"Awesome," said Regan, moving off so they could talk about *lobstuh* and *beeah* in private.

McKee stood apart from the others, flipping through a folder. "Looks like everyone's playing nicely," Regan said.

McKee glanced around. "Yeah, I guess. Back of the hotel covered?"

"Uh huh, they're in good shape. And the local agents are working with JPD and state police on the search for our bombers."

"What do we know about the device?"

His tone was interrogatory, but she refused to get ruffled. That's what he wanted.

"Our bomb techs said its signature is similar to some IED's used in a Seattle bombing a few years back." First case Regan worked fresh out of the academy. "Do you recall the Mariner Mall bombing?"

"New mall under construction at the time?"

"Right. Three bombs detonated, one didn't. Gave us an intact specimen."

"Green Globe Defense League, right?" McKee's eyes narrowed.

"Yep."

"They might be forming a splinter group in Anchorage. Not too organized so far – mostly just a website."

"Yes, SIOC informed us of the possible link," said Regan. The Strategic Information and Operations Center at Bureau headquarters was a twenty-four-hour clearinghouse for crisis management.

"Then why didn't you inform us?" McKee snapped. "If they're planning —"

"Hold your horses there, cowboy," said Regan, fed up with the macho routine. "We contacted your S-A-C a couple hours ago. You were en route to Juneau."

McKee's shoulders came up and his head dipped slightly, revealing his sudden discomfort.

So he's one of those guys that keeps pushing until you push back.

"The bomb signature is close to the specimen but doesn't appear to be exact," Regan went on, her tone even again. "The techs are still tracking down the source of the components."

"Those Green Globers at the Mariner Mall – weren't they convicted?" For the first time, McKee sounded conciliatory.

"Yes, but not then," said Regan. "Two years later, we linked them to the bombing of a logging truck in Oregon. Exact same signature. Just one guy – the group's leader – went down for that."

"Still behind bars?"

Regan nodded. "He's serving eight years at Monroe Correctional Facility north of Seattle. His name is Randall Strathman."

"You think Strathman might be reaching out?"

"Could be," said Regan. "Your boss mentioned that a longtime environmental extremist from the Anchorage area could be helping them get a foothold up here."

"Right," said McKee. "A self-employed mechanic named Herschel Baker."

CHAPTER FIVE

HERSCHEL BROKE into a grin when he saw the sign-toting crowd outside the Baranof. The proposed nuclear waste facility had finally raised the stakes enough to rouse people off their butts.

He had a message for Secretary Vargas, and he planned to deliver it in person. The former congresswoman from Colorado liked to hear from voters, especially those most affected by proposed policy changes, and by God *he* was affected by poisoning Alaska with radioactive waste.

He would tell her why ripping up the Coastal Plain to extract more oil was a travesty, too – even if most Alaskans didn't see it that way. All they saw were the dollar signs.

Herschel spotted the screening device at the front door, glad he'd left some items behind at the motel. He went to the front desk. "Excuse me ... can you tell me if Secretary Vargas has arrived? I have a meeting with her." Never mind that she hadn't exactly been informed.

The desk clerk gave him a practiced smile. "Oh, I'm sorry, sir – I'm not at liberty to say."

He gave her a withering look and stepped back.

A young man in a tailored pinstripe suit came off the elevator and breezed up to the counter, casting a dismissive look at Herschel. "I'm Trevor Wolf, chief of staff to Energy Secretary Ella Vargas," he proclaimed to the desk clerk. "She asked me to take a look at the room where the summit convenes tomorrow. Could you direct me, please?"

Herschel's hope surged. Maybe he'd just found a way.

ॐ

REGAN MOVED over to the front desk.

The desk clerk chirped, "Good afternoon, ma'am! How may I help you?" Her cheerfulness bordered on manic.

Regan displayed her ID. "I'm Agent Manning with the FBI. I saw a man talking to you a little while ago – he had a whiskery face and was wearing a flannel shirt, dark green pants …"

Seeing the badge made the clerk even chirpier. "Oh, yes, ma'am. He asked if Secretary Vargas had checked in yet. Said he was supposed to meet with her."

Regan felt her pulse quicken. "What did you tell him?"

The clerk smiled proudly. "Said I wasn't at liberty to say."

"Do you know if he's one of the hotel guests?"

"I'm not sure. If he is, someone else checked him in."

"Okay, thank you, Miss —"

"Potts. You can call me Patty, though."

Regan nodded in slow motion, fighting to keep a straight face.

The desk clerk shrugged. "I know," she said, her cheeriness dipping slightly. "What kind of mother does that to her child, right? Anyway, is there anything else I can do to help, Agent Manning?"

"Not right now, Potty. Patty. Sorry – I haven't had much sleep." Regan could feel hysterics creeping up. "You've been very helpful."

She glanced at the lobby to see if the whiskered man had decided to stick around.

It was empty.

CHAPTER SIX

TREVOR WOLF surveyed the room. The tables were arranged in a large square; it was his job to assign seats, make sure cohorts didn't clump themselves together. The secretary wanted to mix them up as much as possible to keep the dialogue open and flowing.

He turned when the door clicked open. A scruffy-looking man, the one he saw at the front desk, stepped into the room.

"Sorry, sir," Trevor said brusquely. "This is a secure area. You can't be in here." He moved toward the man, flapping his hands like he was shooing chickens from the yard.

"I'd like to see Secretary Vargas," the man said.

Trevor almost laughed. "Absolutely not," he snapped. "Now please leave."

The man's eyes hardened; he held his ground. "I know the secretary likes to hear from people with in-depth knowledge of the issues. That's what makes her different from other politicians. It's Ella Vargas's hallmark."

And a ridiculous one at that, as far as Trevor was concerned. People like this joker thought they knew the issues, but they had no clue what it took to get a bill through Congress – the compromises that were necessary, the relationships that came into play.

"Yes, well, her time on this trip is simply too limited, sir."

Trevor froze as the man moved toward him.

æ

REGAN STRODE toward the Treadwell Ballroom. Before she got there, the suit-clad young man who'd been at the front desk burst from the room.

"Where's the head of the security detail?" he blurted.

"That would be me," said Regan. "Agent Manning. What's the problem, sir?"

"What the hell kind of security allows a terrorist to march right in to the site of the summit and *threaten* me?" His pale, freckled face was suffused with color.

"Is he still in there?" she said, hand on her gun as she moved toward the door.

"No," Trevor said angrily. "When I threatened to call security, he left through a door near the front of the room. I don't know where it leads."

Regan dashed into the command post to summon agents to help. Nick and a half-dozen others spilled into the hall.

Regan blurted, "A man came into the ballroom and made threats to … I'm sorry, sir, what's your name?"

"Trevor Wolf. Chief of staff to Secretary Vargas."

"Mr. Wolf said the man escaped through a door leading off the ballroom," said Regan.

Nick and the others took off.

"Let's have a seat in the lobby," she said. "You can tell me what happened."

Trevor recounted the story.

"Did he display a weapon?" said Regan.

"No."

"Did he attempt to touch you?"

"No, but he got too close. Made me uncomfortable. And he shouldn't have been in the room at all."

"I agree, Mr. Wolf. I'll get officers stationed at the door immediately. As for your visitor, I guess I'm not understanding the exact nature of the threat."

Looks to me like you're crying wolf. She stifled a laugh.

Trevor sighed loudly, perturbed at her ignorance. "He demanded to see Secretary Vargas. I said no. He said it was his right. I said she was too busy. Told him to write a letter expressing his concerns and I would see that she got it. He said he'd write a letter and see that it got shoved up my you-know-what."

Regan could see how Trevor might have that effect on people.

"What made you think he was a *terrorist*? I believe that was the word you used."

"He looked like one."

Regan smiled. "I think you'll find, Mr. Wolf, that many Alaskans dress and act differently than people you encounter back in D.C. It's kind of the frontier spirit of the place."

"Don't patronize me, Agent Manning. It wasn't just his clothes – it was something in his eyes."

Regan bristled at his arrogant tone. Trevor's type was a dime a dozen in Washington, clutching politicians' coattails and hoping to catch a whiff of their power.

"Well, if he's still on the premises, my team will find him. Now let's go have a talk with your boss."

҂

THEY RODE the elevator to the ninth floor, flashing ID at the grim-faced officers standing guard. Trevor knocked on the door of the corner suite. "Madame Secretary? I'm here with Agent Manning of the FBI."

The door opened. Regan was surprised at how striking Vargas appeared in person. She wore an aura of confidence as evident as her sleek outfit – white silk blouse tucked into a straight black skirt, string of pearls at her neck. And some *fabulous* shoes.

"Hello – I'm Ella Vargas," she said with a warm smile, extending her hand. "Please come in."

Vargas seemed apathetic about Trevor's adventure. "I would like to hear what the man has to say," she said. "But Trevor's right, my time is too limited on this trip. The letter was a good idea." She flicked a smile at her chief of staff, who perched on the edge of a wingback chair nearby. He responded with a tiny, officious nod, his expression sober.

Something seemed a little off; Regan wondered if the secretary's praise was simply a pat on the head, meant to remind Trevor of his place.

"If he delivers a letter to the hotel, Madame Secretary, we'll screen it and make sure you get it," she said.

"Excellent. Coffee, Agent Manning?"

"No, thanks." Her cell phone vibrated on her belt. It was Nick. "Excuse me a moment," she said, moving over near the door to take the call.

"The man's not on the premises, unless he ducked into a guest room," said Nick. "We've covered every square inch of the hotel's public areas, and also the kitchen and laundry. We'll take a look at the security tapes."

Regan returned to the sitting area and joined the secretary on the sofa. "Whoever the man was, he seems to be gone." She glanced at Trevor; scorn was written all over his face.

Regan wanted to smack the little twerp.

She ignored him and ran through security procedures for the summit. "As a result of the pipe bomb at the airport two days ago, we've added more personnel on-site, guards at every entrance, security cameras."

"Comes with the territory, I'm afraid," said Vargas. "President Sanford is attempting something truly ground-breaking, both with his administration and with this energy plan. I know many Alaskans don't support the nuclear waste facility, but once we've had an opportunity to explain the minimal threat it poses, we believe that will change."

"What if it doesn't? Will Alaskans' opinions be given consideration?" Regan's question had more to do with loyalty than security.

Vargas smiled. "My job – *our* job – at this summit is to sell the president's energy plan in its current form. We simply need to work out the details for implementation."

"So that would be a no."

Vargas's surprise at the flippant remark registered in her eyes. "Of course we'll listen to Alaskans, Agent Manning. But I've learned that most people's first instinct is to oppose something they don't understand. We'll make sure they do understand that this facility is state-of-the-art, non-polluting, and won't adversely affect wildlife. I think they'll get on board."

Regan didn't share that view, but it wasn't her place to argue. She'd leave that to the protestors outside, who appeared to be multiplying like bacteria.

"Do you expect much controversy at the summit table?" she said.

"Let's just say I expect an extremely robust discussion," Vargas replied. "It's necessary and healthy for what we're trying to accomplish."

"Which is?"

"Swift action rather than endless rhetoric. Initiatives starting in three months, not three years."

"What happens after the summit?" said Regan. "Will Congress act on the president's plan?"

"Yes. We're fast-tracking this. It'll go first to the House Energy and Commerce Committee – which I used to chair – then to the whole House for a vote. Same process in the Senate, then to the president – assuming it isn't materially changed on the Senate side. If it is, the two chambers will have to work out the differences first."

"Expect much opposition?" said Regan.

"I think we'll be in pretty good shape. The committee's new chair is an absolute dynamo at lining up votes and holding things together."

"That helps," said Regan, once again coveting the secretary's shoes.

"Yes, it does. We're going to rely heavily on Congressman Paul Slade."

CHAPTER SEVEN

F OR THE thousandth time, Robert Carney cursed the
president's choice of energy secretary.

"Madame Secretary, you aren't hearing me," said Carney, his voice
peppered with frustration. He wanted to scream at her, penetrate her
implacable shell.

"I hear you loud and clear, Bob," she responded coolly. "You're
telling me your company isn't going to meet the deadline, despite your
repeated assurances that it could."

Pompous bitch.

"Development costs for the tool have exceeded projections," he
said, keeping his voice as even as he could. "We had no way of
predicting that. This is a brand new, cutting-edge device, never before
produced. It will revolutionize the oil industry. I think we can afford
the extra time it takes to bring it on line."

Vargas got up from the sofa and moved to the window of her suite,
arms crossed, shoulders stiff. After a pause, she turned to face him.

"I'm not sure the oil industry needs a revolution. Maybe it simply
needs less focus."

Fury coursed through his veins like red-hot lava. How *dare* she
suggest companies like his were becoming irrelevant.

She's just egging you on. Say nothing. He bit his lip.

"Nevertheless," she said, "do you recall why Axis is being allowed
to take the helm as project leader in Alaska? Why we gave the nod to
you at the expense of the other oil companies?"

Because we will preserve the American way of life, whatever it takes. He
remained silent.

"The tool, Bob. The rotary steerable device you said you'd deliver according to the president's timeline. Phase one emphasizes our ability to extract more oil domestically, and it's slated to ramp up in September. You've known that from the beginning."

"Oh, c'mon, Ella. Delaying until spring isn't going to make a noticeable difference." He twisted the diamond-studded Harvard class ring that adorned his right hand, smiled his most charming smile.

He should've known better. Her face got even stonier, if that was possible.

"Believe me, it would be noticed. President Sanford put his trust in you."

"I realize that, and I —"

"This is about *synergy*, Bob. And this summit brings valuable PR to the new technology – in its ability to extract previously unreachable domestic fossil fuels while we build more nuclear power plants and develop renewable energy sources." She laced her fingers together. "Everything works in sync. Beginning in September."

She was trying to back him into a corner, make him think he was about to run the president's entire energy plan into the ditch. All he was asking for was a little more time.

"I can't help it. We need an extension in order to secure additional funding." He braced himself.

Vargas's jaw dropped. *"What?"*

Carney held up a hand. "Axis has made major investments in those renewable energy sources. In case you've forgotten, Ella, it all takes massive amounts of capital."

"In case *you've* forgotten, Bob, oil company profits have been at record highs for more than five years. You've invested six times as much in stock buybacks and dividends than renewable energy. And by the way, the investments you *have* made came with hefty government subsidies."

He bit back a nasty reply. They'd been through this dance before. Too many times.

She went on in a reproving tone. "You of all people ought to know that the political situation in oil-producing nations is putting us at enormous risk, especially with the wild price fluctuations making our suppliers nervous. We don't have unlimited troops to send in and secure every spot in the world sitting on top of oil."

Unlike her, he'd seen those spots for himself. Smelled the danger mixed in with the crude.

"But things aren't going to change significantly between September and May," he said again.

Vargas's eyes hardened. "We don't know that. What we *do* know is that the longer we wait to start demonstrating our self-reliance, the harder it is for this administration to take meaningful steps to reduce the threat to national security. The clock is ticking."

Carney abruptly stood. "I understand. But the situation is what it is. Ask President Sanford to delay drilling until spring. If you don't feel like you can do that, Madame Secretary, I'm sure I can get someone else to step up."

For an instant, she looked like she'd been doused with a bucket of water. Then she gave him a sardonic smile. "Ah, yes, I'm sure your old frat brother would throw himself on the sword for you. Tell Landry Ness it won't be necessary, at least not yet. I will convey your request to the president and let *him* decide whether Axis Oil still has a part to play."

CHAPTER EIGHT

THE PHONE jangled her out of a dreamless sleep. It had taken forever to drift off, disquieting thoughts wafting through her brain like noxious fumes.

"Manning," she croaked, glancing at the clock. Three-ten.

"Regan, it's Pat. There's been another bomb."

She sat up so fast it made her head spin. "Where?"

"Mendenhall Glacier."

Regan felt like she'd been sucker-punched. The glacier was as familiar to her as her own back yard. "How bad?"

"Remember that big rock just to the right as you're facing the glacier?" said the chief. Regan could hear frenzied voices in the background.

"Yeah, of course," she said, reaching for her clothes. "That's the way we always gauge how much the glacier has receded."

"Right. Well, we won't be using it as a gauge anymore."

Another punch to the gut. "What about the observatory?" The building sat above and back a ways from the rock.

"Damage doesn't appear to be too extensive at this point, but that could change when they get a closer look. A chunk of the glacier is gone, too."

Regan sighed. "Okay, Chief, I'm on my way."

❧

IT WAS light out by the time Regan and Nick arrived at the glacier just before four. She stared in horror at the craggy hole, an ugly pockmark on a face whose beauty had been, until now, timeless.

42

The summer solstice allowed only a couple hours of total darkness for someone to plant the pipe bomb undetected. The webcam in the observatory picked up movement near the rock before the explosion, but it was hard to distinguish it as a human being, much less determine identity.

She shook her head slowly back and forth, fighting back tears. "Why the glacier? What's the message?"

"I don't know," said Nick. "How the hell do we respond to it?"

"We'll come at them with guns blazing," Regan growled, hands clenched in fists at her sides. "We have to stop them, Nick. Before one more pebble of this town is disturbed."

Nick looked surprised. Usually he was the reactive one, not her. "Do we have the manpower? I mean, you know the area better than I do, but look at all these woods," he said, gazing around. "It'll be like finding a needle in a haystack. No, worse than that. A needle in a hay *field*."

"I'm pulling some of our agents out of the Baranof. We have more than enough officers to keep the conference people safe. The rest are going to go out and cut these guys off at the knees."

"But what if that's their strategy? Maybe they're trying to lure us away from the Baranof. Increase its vulnerability. Should we get AR to send reinforcements?"

Regan paused to think, to calm the swell of emotion. "I'll have McKee request additional agents from Anchorage. They can be here in less than two hours. In the meantime, Chief Lamont will assign some of his officers to back us up at the hotel. We should be able to keep things contained there – as long as Secretary Vargas cooperates."

❧

THE SUMMIT was set to begin.

Robert Carney caught himself staring at Vargas with contempt; it took some effort, but he forced himself to look congenial.

"It is truly my pleasure to welcome all of you to the Alaska Energy Summit," the secretary said in a spirited voice. "I want to thank Governor Tom Larson for hosting us here in Alaska's beautiful capital."

"We're glad to have you here," replied Larson. But Carney thought he detected a bit of discomfort behind the governor's words.

"Folks, we have before us an extraordinary opportunity," Vargas continued. "President Eli Sanford has asked us to come together to forge a powerful new plan – to check our labels at the door, along with our preconceived notions, and to open our minds to exciting new possibilities."

Carney glanced around. A few, mostly the environmentalists, were eating it up; others didn't bother to disguise their skepticism.

One guy in particular looked like he had something on his mind. The cardboard name tent in front of him said DR. WILLIAM PRINCE. Carney looked at his roster and saw Dr. Prince was a professor at the University of Alaska.

"It seems fitting that we finalize this plan here in Alaska," Vargas was saying, "in a state integral to the nation's energy policy, where the pioneer spirit is a way of life. I might also add that it's fitting we hold the summit in the Baranof Hotel, which has served for years as an informal branch of Alaska's capitol."

She shifted her gaze to Carney; he knew it was her clever way of acknowledging the recent scandal involving a group of Alaska legislators who took bribes from oil industry executives in Suite 604 upstairs. Regrettably for them, the FBI was watching. Indictments and ugly press followed.

Axis wasn't implicated in the debacle; two of the other oil companies at the table were. But Vargas was looking at him like *he* was guilty. He was sure of it.

He met her gaze, his expression neutral.

The secretary looked around the square, smiling at the expectant faces. "Ladies and gentlemen, as we begin our discussions, remember that the key word is *balance*. The president seeks to achieve a delicate balance between …"

Balance, my ass. It's about forcing people to buy into a nuclear waste dump and unproven, unreliable energy sources. To turn their backs on oil, the very substance that made this country what it is.

Carney tuned her out and checked his watch. Forty minutes until he needed to excuse himself to take an important phone call. A call that could make all the difference in the world.

CHAPTER NINE

REGAN RUSHED into the command post.

"How bad?" said McKee.

"Bad enough that we have to stop them before things get any worse," said Regan. "This town is going to go nuts. I need you to call the Anchorage office, Mark – have them send down every agent they can spare."

McKee crossed his arms. "I don't know if my boss will —"

"Just do it, McKee."

McKee shrugged and pulled out his phone. A minute later, he said, "He can round up nine or ten and have them on a charter flight in an hour."

"Good. Chief Lamont is assigning some of his officers to help us out, too. Anything new here?"

"We looked at the security tapes. The man who harassed Wolf *was* Herschel Baker."

"Have you alerted our people?"

He nodded. "Used a photo from the database and distributed it to our people and hotel staff. If he comes back here, we'll nail him."

"Have you made any attempt to locate him in town?" asked Regan.

"We're checking area motels and rental car agencies. If we get a hit, I'll send someone to have a chat." He added flippantly, "If you concur, that is."

"I do. Thanks for handling it, Mark." She forced herself to smile, show appreciation.

McKee nodded, his eyes skimming her body.

"Good God, McKee, don't be rude."

His face turned crimson, but he tried playing dumb. "What?"

She ignored the act. "Have you found anything else?"

He cleared his throat. "Uh, maybe." He turned to Lindsay, who was staring at the laptop in front of her, trying not to laugh.

"Fill her in, Agent Pryor," McKee said gruffly.

Lindsay lost the smile and straightened in her chair. "Dr. William Prince is one of the academics attending the summit," she said. "Professor at the University of Alaska in Fairbanks. Area of expertise is resource economics. He's either a member of or a sympathizer of the Alaska Separatist Party."

Regan knew of the group that pushed for Alaska's secession from the United States. Its logo was a sinister-looking snake; at first, it perplexed her that they'd chosen a creature not found in Alaska – until she realized it graphically represented their acronym, ASP. Those clever separatists.

"Wow," she said. "Makes you wonder if Prince is somebody we really want crafting the country's energy policy."

"We haven't been able to confirm that Prince is a bona fide member of ASP, but he's a fairly regular speaker at their meetings," said McKee. "At the very least, he's considered a 'friendly' among them. And ASP is vehemently opposed to the nuclear waste facility."

Lindsay turned to look at Regan. "Their website says, 'Alaska is not the nation's dumping ground.' It calls on all members to do whatever it takes to keep the facility out of this state."

"Like blowing up Juneau landmarks, maybe?"

Lindsay shrugged.

"There's another site you need to see," said McKee. He gestured to Lindsay again, who hit a key on the laptop and popped up another website.

Regan could see a large headline splashed across the screen: *UNLEASH THE MEAN GREEN IN JUNEAU.* She knew whose it was without asking. "Well well, Green Globe strikes again. Find out who registered that domain."

࿏

CARNEY'S HANDS shook; waves of nausea pummeled his insides. He sat on the side of the bed in his hotel room, elbows perched on his thighs, head in his hands.

He sat up and poked a number into his cell phone. It took four rings before his party answered.

"Yes?"

Carney said, "The Caspian deal ..."

"Yes, what about it?" said the voice on the other end.

"They upped the amount." Carney's voice quivered.

"What do you mean? I thought you'd already reached an agreement."

"We did, but they reneged. Now the, uh, principals in the deal want a larger, uh, investment. Said if the rumors are true that the U.S. plans to pull military support out of the area, they'll have to fund security on their own. If we want unfettered access to the new pipeline, we have to pay more."

"Aren't they jumping the gun? The energy plan isn't even finalized."

"I know, but they said they had a better offer. Either they're lying or one of my competitors is one-upping me."

"Gee, Bob, seems like you've already put an awful lot of eggs in that basket ..."

Carney felt a flash of irritation. "For good reason. The return on investment is enormous."

"So what's the problem?"

"Cash flow, pal. Cash flow. Vargas is leaning on me to get the new tool finished, but I'm having to divert funds to this other deal. Now it's going to require even more, which means the rollout of the tool will be delayed that much longer." His armpits were damp; his skin felt clammy. "I'm getting in a hell of a bind."

If the Axis shareholders found out, he'd find himself back on the oilfield crew. Or someplace with steel bars for doors.

There was a pause on the other end of the line. "Here's something else to think about. What if you pay up and then they turn around and expose your, uh, investment?"

Carney could feel his breakfast coming back up.

"Gotta go." He hung up and raced for the bathroom.

᠅

THE ELEVATOR door opened and Robert Carney stepped off. His tanned face looked ashen, his slicked-back hair a little wonky.

"Good morning, Mr. Carney. Everything okay?" said Regan. She'd never met him, but his face was on TV with such regularity that she felt like she knew him personally. Reporters, female and male alike, loved the ruggedly handsome oil man – especially when he tossed them juicy tidbits. He knew just how to keep their interest in him piqued.

"I ... yes ... I'm fine. Just needed to make a call." He flashed bleached teeth at her, but his usual swagger seemed to be missing.

"Has Secretary Vargas adjourned for the morning break yet?" Regan needed to fill her in on the explosion at the glacier.

Carney glanced at his watch. "Should be any minute now." He floated toward the Treadwell Ballroom.

Regan followed, planning to catch the secretary as soon as they broke. She wanted to avoid pulling Vargas out of the meeting and arousing concern among the summiteers. They had to be keyed up enough with the swelling crowd of protestors outside.

The double doors opened and Carney's colleagues spilled into the hallway. Regan swam her way through the crowd and into the ballroom. She spotted the secretary standing near the table, listening intently to Trevor.

As Regan got close, they both turned and stared at her accusingly. The secretary's lips were parted, her dark eyes flashing.

"What have you done?" Vargas said.

Regan was startled. "What are you talking about?"

"What did you do to Congressman Slade?"

Regan felt like she'd been hit with a wrecking ball. "What did *I* do to *him*? I'll tell you, Madame Secretary. I stopped him from beating an innocent young woman half to death. I only regret that

I didn't get to him before he broke her nose and bloodied her face."
Her hands were shaking.

"Do you have *any* idea how vital he is to the passage of President
Sanford's energy plan?"

Regan's jaw dropped. "You condone his hideous behavior just
so you can get a stupid piece of legislation passed? This is a human
being we're talking about, someone who —"

"*A stupid piece of legislation*? Get out," the secretary hissed. "Get
out of my sight."

CHAPTER TEN

REGAN'S PHONE tickled her hip.

"Hi, Mom." She struggled to sound calm after her run-in with Vargas.

"Hi, sweetheart. How are things going?"

"Okay. Is something wrong?"

"I'm just worried about you, that's all. Everyone's upset over those bombs."

"I know, Mom, but we're handling it. We'll get whoever's doing this." She hated the wisps of uncertainty that swirled behind her words.

"Why would somebody want to blow up the glacier, Regan?" Her mother's voice was plaintive.

Regan sighed. "I wish I knew. Try not to worry. We'll get it taken care of."

"I know you will, honey. Can you come for dinner?"

"Not tonight – I'm a little busy. I'll call you as soon as the summit wraps up, okay?"

Nick came around the corner into the lobby.

"I've gotta go, Mom. Talk to you soon." She hung up and turned to her partner. "Well? How'd Vargas take the news?"

"She's too pissed at you to even care about bombs exploding." He shook his head.

"Amazing," said Regan, still in shock over Vargas's outburst. A young woman's injuries, not to mention the destruction of treasured natural landmarks, took a back seat to Ella Vargas's ability to maneuver politically.

"And inconvenient," Nick said. "This gets a lot harder without her cooperation. You know, maybe we should think about shutting this thing down."

"What, the energy summit?"

Nick nodded. "Get these people out of here so they aren't sitting ducks."

No way. She would not leave this town in defeat again.

"I doubt we'd get support from the top if we tried to do that, Nick. And Vargas would throw even more of a fit. She's intent on getting this plan finished, bombs or not."

"Well, I just hope she understands the level of risk." Nick leaned forward in his chair. "All right, let's lay it out. If the bombs are tied to the energy summit, then it suggests the perpetrators are trying to scare Vargas and the rest of the energy planners into leaving – to stop what they're doing."

"Or back off at least part of the plan," said Regan. "The most controversial thing in it is the nuclear waste dump."

"Do you think some of your fellow Alaskans are motivated enough to build homemade pipe bombs?"

"Maybe, but the question is, could they pull it off? I think it has to be people who know what they're doing – and that brings us to the two groups we know have expressed the most volatile opposition to the energy plan. Green Globe and ASP."

"I'd put my money on Green Globe," said Nick. "We already know they're big fans of explosive devices."

Lindsay came around the corner. "I have the name of Green Globe's domain name registrant. It's a guy named Cory Winslow."

"Cory Winslow?" said Regan. "That's Strathman's half-brother. He was arrested at the same time as Strathman, suspected of being Green Globe's bombmaker, but there wasn't enough evidence to convict him. Where is he now?"

"Lives in Portland."

"Thanks, Lindsay. Contact the Portland police and have them get a bead on Cory. If they can't find him, it may be because he's up here. Distribute a picture of him to our people."

Lindsay nodded and headed back to the command post. Regan said, "Nick, as soon as the Anchorage agents arrive, you and I are going to make a quick trip to Seattle – if AR says it's okay."

"To see Strathman?"

"Yep. Maybe this nuclear waste facility has him so fired up he's dying to spill his guts to somebody."

પ્

HERSCHEL LOST himself in the crowd of picketers, fishing cap and sunglasses masking his face.

Write a letter? *Jesus.* He wanted to *talk* to the secretary, not be her pen pal.

Herschel had spent twenty years trying to light a fire under people, get them to protest drilling in ANWR and to stop the logging that threatened to destroy Alaska's forests. Mostly he protested alone on the Anchorage streets, the other so-called environmentalists too uncommitted to join in.

But now they were here! It was a thing of beauty: strength in numbers, voices demanding to be heard. Men, women, and children, a mix of races and backgrounds, Alaskans shoulder-to-shoulder with environmentalists from across the country, all united for a common cause.

THE LAST FRONTIER – NOT THE PLACE FOR NUCLEAR WASTE read one sign, and it said it all.

Was Ella Vargas getting the message?

Herschel glanced up at the corner window on the top floor. Ella Vargas stood there, gazing at the crowd below.

CHAPTER ELEVEN

RANDALL STRATHMAN looked more like a serial killer than a treehugger. His scalp was shiny beneath the buzz cut; his eyes displayed a frightening intensity.

"How would I know what Green Globe is doing?" he snarled. "It's not like they hold their monthly meetings here." Lack of sun had sallowed his complexion; orange definitely wasn't his best color.

"Who's their new leader?" said Regan.

"Don't have a clue."

"They holding the spot open 'til you get back in, what is it, five more years?" said Nick.

"It's not about some damn spot. I will fight for the environment until I die," Strathman said dramatically, leaning forward. "Doesn't matter if that means being part of some group or going it alone. Somebody has to care enough to halt the destruction of our wilderness areas, to stop letting them screw with the ecosystem." He thumped his finger on the table for emphasis, causing the six-inch tree tattoo on his right forearm to ripple.

Regan stared at him, intrigued. *Seriously ... he looks like a psychopath, not a warrior for the environment.*

After a pause where nobody said anything, he started in again. "What are we doing to our children and grandchildren? There won't be one square inch of backwoods left for them." He was on a roll, eyes flashing, playing to his audience.

"You're probably right, Randall, but that really isn't the point, is it?" said Regan. "It's the way you and your pals choose to fight for the environment, like you have some God-given right to destroy property and risk injury and maybe even the deaths of innocent people. Do you have less regard for human life than you have for trees?"

"Innocent? You think those people are *innocent?*" The intensity in his eyes almost made Regan shiver.

Maybe Strathman was a psychopath. You had to have a screw loose to justify killing people to save the environment.

"How 'bout that nuclear waste dump they're talking about?" said Nick, cranking up the heat. "That's something, isn't it?"

Strathman looked ready to burst into flames.

Regan slid a piece of paper across the table. It was a print-screen from the Green Globe website. "What do you think this means? 'Unleash the mean green in Juneau'?"

Strathman studied the message, then leaned back and said, "Don't have a clue."

"C'mon, Randy," said Nick. "Bombs going off in Juneau and you're saying you know nothing about it?"

"It's Randall, not Randy. And like I said, I don't exactly have the boys over for a beer." He crossed his arms and clenched his jaw.

"But you post on Green Globe's online forum, right?" said Nick. "I'd say that's the electronic equivalent of a beer with the boys."

Strathman shrugged.

"I understand you've been taking vocational classes in here," said Regan. "Want to tell us about that?"

Strathman straightened, clearing his throat. "It's a way to pass the time."

"Didn't you earn a degree?"

"Just an associate." He moved his hands under the table; Regan could tell from his shoulders and arms that he rubbed his palms along the top of his thighs. Leg cleansing, it was called. Happened when someone was really nervous.

"Congratulations. In what?"

"Uh, computer support specialist."

"I'll be darned," said Regan. "So did you learn how to build websites, things like that?"

He did a nod-shrug that was meant to say, *Yeah, no big deal.*

"Brother Cory help you get a domain or two to play around with?"

Strathman blinked but didn't answer.

"Did you build Green Globe's website, Randall? Did you post that headline?"

"Nope." He blinked again, like maybe it was a fib.

"Who's Green Globe's bomb guy, Randy?" said Nick. "Is it Cory?"

Strathman looked like he wanted to jump across the table and grab Nick by the throat. He didn't answer.

Regan said, "Last chance, Strathman. We're walking out of here in two minutes."

Strathman clamped his lips together and said nothing.

"Okay, fine," said Regan. "Since you have some time on your hands, here's a little something for you to mull over. If we discover you played any part whatsoever in the Juneau bombings, you won't set eyes on a live tree again until you're too damn old to care."

CHAPTER TWELVE

THE BUS carrying the summiteers pulled into the parking lot at Mendenhall Glacier. Officers swarmed around it, shielding the passengers as they stepped off the bus.

Regan parked the Suburban nearby and got out. She winced again at the sight of the gaping hole on the edge of the ice field; it was a wound that would take time to heal, both for the glacier and for her.

Secretary Vargas looked at it, then cast a glance at Regan. Her face showed more reproach than regret, as though it was somehow Regan's fault for not catching the bombers before they struck again.

Regan's temper flared. She marched over to Vargas. "Madame Secretary, as Agent Jenesco told you, we decided it was important to keep to the summit schedule – not let the terrorists gain the upper hand. If we keep you locked up in the Baranof, they could become bolder and step up their aggression."

Vargas listened without looking at her.

Regan continued in a curt tone. "The brush surrounding the path to the observatory and the building itself have been swept for explosive devices, and you and your colleagues will be under heavy guard the whole time you're out here. The area has been sealed off, closed to the public, so you should be able to enjoy the view in safety. Do you have any questions?"

"Just one." She turned to face Regan, her eyes steely. "Are you willing to get the aggravated assault charge against Congressman Slade reduced to simple assault?" It would mean the difference between years spent in prison and a slap on the wrist.

Kate's battered face swam before Regan's eyes. She glared back at Vargas. "No, I am not."

Vargas spun around and walked away.

~

THE AREA around the Mendenhall Glacier may have been closed, but at least one creature hadn't gotten the message. A black bear ambled along the edge of the water, searching its depths for a juicy salmon.

He caused quite a stir among the visitors, even though the clatter of their cameras didn't produce even a backward glance from the bear. The sound was probably as familiar as the chirping birds.

The group babbled excitedly as they headed back to the bus. Regan watched them with amusement until she spotted Vargas. The woman put on an animated performance, as though she actually cared about the bear or the glacier or something besides her damn energy plan.

One of the other summiteers also caught her attention. Robert Carney held himself apart from the group, like the tour was beneath the dignity of an oil magnate. He surveyed the area as though he were contemplating the development of a hotel/casino smack dab in the middle of the Tongass National Forest.

The phone on her belt beeped. "Manning."

"Regan, it's Pat." Something in his voice set her on edge. "We just found another bomb."

"Where?" she said, bracing herself.

"On the Mount Roberts tram. Someone in the other gondola saw it as they were heading back down, when the two cars passed each other."

She clapped a hand to her mouth. "Oh my God. What about the passengers?"

"They're okay; they all got off the tram safely. The bomb is sitting on top. Not sure if it's on a timer or if someone plans to use a remote detonator."

"How could they plant that and not be seen?"

"I don't know, but the tramway people are frantic. If it goes off, it'll take down the whole structure on the mountain. We've cleared the area."

"You have a chopper taking the bomb squad up?" With the tram shut down, it was a steep, eighteen-hundred-foot hike; they'd never make it in time on foot.

"Right," he said. "It'll have to land further up in one of the clearings, so it'll take them a few minutes to hustle down to the tram once they're on the mountain."

It would be a miracle if they made it. "Can you send another chopper to the airport to pick us up?" The airport was only a few minutes' drive from the glacier, especially at maximum speed.

"I'll have it there in a few minutes."

She beckoned Nick and two Alaska State Troopers, filling them in on the bomb. "Nick and I are heading to the airport to jump on a chopper. I need you guys at the tram station. Lights and sirens, full speed. Let's go."

The trio of cars roared off.

"Whoever's doing this knows the schedule, Nick," said Regan, her hands gripping the wheel. "They know where and when the summit people will be touring."

"Think someone on the inside is feeding it to them?"

"Someone has to be. The first two were just warnings – deliberately planted where no one would get hurt. But the tram is one of Juneau's most popular tours. Its terminal sits right next to the cruise ship docks. Since it's June, that thing is packed with riders all day long."

Nick read her mind. "They're escalating."

Chapter Thirteen

FOUR BLOCKS from the tram station, outside the Baranof, the protestors spotted the bus inching its way up Franklin, sandwiched between a pair of police cars. As it crawled past the front of the hotel on the narrow street, the crowd chanted, "No nuclear waste! No nuclear waste!"

Part of the crowd broke off and followed the bus to the rear of the hotel, hoping to get closer to the passengers as they departed the bus. Herschel kept to the back of the running throng.

Police officers formed a human fence at the edge of the parking lot, blocking the protestors from coming any further. Herschel saw the uneasiness in the officers' eyes, knew they never could've imagined a standoff with their friends and neighbors over a policy issue, their job dictating which side they were on.

Would they stand firm, even use force if the crowd pushed them back? Or would they yield, let the protestors storm the bus?

There was no need for that. Secretary Vargas, along with her colleagues, saw that the crowd was growing, becoming more vocal. Saw that Alaskans and their environmentalist friends from all over the country would insist their voices be heard.

If Vargas truly was the populist she claimed she was, she would get the message.

The people had spoken.

≈

IT HAD begun to drizzle by the time the helicopter deposited them on top of the mountain. Regan instructed the pilot to stand by, then she and Nick took off, heading for the tram.

Regan had a sense of déjà vu as she raced through the woods at full clip, hopping over exposed tree roots that traversed the trail like distended veins. Mixed with the anxiety was a youthful exhilaration she hadn't felt in a long time.

They passed the Raptor Center and were almost to the tram when Regan froze. The man's back was to her, but she'd recognize him anywhere. Shiny black hair and caramel skin that revealed his Tlingit heritage; the trademark wide-legged stance, arms crossed.

Danny Brice seemed to sense she was there. He turned slowly, dark eyes meeting hers. "Regan," he said nonchalantly, as though he last saw her yesterday, not half a decade ago. As though they'd parted amicably, not with an ugly scene that left her shaken for months.

"Danny," she said in a voice so eerily flat that Nick shot her a quizzical look. Regan moved stiffly past the detective to go stand beside Chief Lamont, who had his focus riveted on a member of his bomb squad.

The officer was clad in a special reinforced suit that made him look like he was about to step on the moon. He moved gingerly onto the gondola, which had been lowered to make the top even with the platform. Dangling from the cable, no longer locked into the steel frame next to the landing platform, the car swayed slightly under his weight.

The suit prevented nimble movement. He crawled with painstaking care across the rain-slick metal surface to keep from taking a deadly plunge, but if he took too long getting to the bomb, he could vaporize before their eyes.

He leaned over the bomb, peering at it through the tiny rectangular window of his head gear. Slowly, he reached toward the explosive, clippers in his gloved hand. Regan's skin prickled; she heard the sharp intake of breath from all the officers witnessing the man's brave performance.

He cut the wire, then paused. Turning toward them, he pulled off his glove and held up a pointer finger, indicating one minute left on the timer, then gave them a thumbs up. Lamont and the others broke out in a cheer of relief.

The officer held the device aloft as he inched on his butt toward the platform. He paused at the edge of the gondola and waited for the swaying to subside before sliding the defused bomb onto the concrete.

Slowly he stood, about to step off when a gust of wind caught the gondola. His feet slipped out from under him and he fell, careening toward the edge.

Regan grabbed Nick's arm and held her breath.

The officer looped his arm through the metal piece that connected the car to the cable above, his body hanging off the side like a rag doll. The collective gasp was louder this time.

Two other members of the bomb squad standing nearby threw off their head gear and gloves, reaching for their fallen comrade as the gondola swung back toward them. They caught him by one leg and he dangled precariously, upside down, for what seemed like an eternity. Finally, the two men got enough of a grip to drag him to safety on the platform.

For a moment, the officer lay flat on his back, not moving. His two rescuers sat beside him, gasping for air.

"Thank God," Regan muttered under her breath.

The color had drained from Nick's face. "Give that man a medal."

She gave a jittery laugh, loosening the death grip on his arm. Her gaze happened to land on Danny, who watched them with a smoldering look.

Regan put her hands on her hips and glared until he turned away. *Don't even think about trying to pull that crap with me.* Beneath her mental cheekiness, her heart was beating fast, her hands shaking.

"That just aged me another ten years," said the chief, removing his glasses and rubbing his eyes.

"He's good," said Regan.

"He oughta be … you guys trained him," said the chief.

"Then you better give him a big fat raise or we'll steal him from you."

"Don't even think about it," he said, moving off toward the heroic officers.

Regan pulled out her cell phone to call McKee. "The bomb's defused," she reported, ready to get on with witness interviews.

"That's good news," said McKee. "But here's some that isn't: Ella Vargas insists on addressing the crowd of protestors."

"What? When?" She glanced at her watch: eight forty-five p.m.

"In fifteen minutes."

CHAPTER FOURTEEN

R EGAN FELT like a pinball, bouncing from crisis to crisis. This one, Vargas's decision to speak to a riled-up mob, made her furious. The secretary knew the security challenges of such a move – the toll it would take on the officers who were frantically defusing bombs and trying to nab whoever was planting them.

Was this about retribution for Regan's refusal to reduce the charges against Slade? If it was, it could come back to bite her in the butt.

Vargas was betting heavily on her reputed ability to get protestors to yield. Since the summiteers weren't bowing to her energy plan, defusing the protestors would give her the leverage she needed.

But it was an arrogant gamble. A local station was doing a live feed to CNN and MSNBC, even though it was one in the morning on the east coast. Hardly prime time, but a stumble could still be costly for the secretary if she found herself in a news loop that played over and over.

Protestors were screened as they entered the Baranof and ordered to place their picket signs on a growing pile near the door. They traipsed between two long rows of cops and assembled in the Treadwell Ballroom, where the large square had been replaced by rows of chairs. In front was a stage with a podium and a microphone. Reporters lined the first row; TV cameras dotted the back of the room. Regan marveled that they'd gotten there so quickly.

She went to where Vargas and Trevor waited in a vacant meeting room. "Madame Secretary, I wish you would reconsider," Regan pleaded. "Our manpower in the field is stretched dangerously thin in order to accommodate this … dialogue, as you call it."

"Well, Agent Manning, knowing what a professional you are – your ability to spot egregious behavior almost before it happens – you should be able to handle it just fine." Vargas gave her a thin smile; Trevor looked smug.

"Besides, this is my style – something I like to do whenever I have the chance. Talk directly to constituents, see what's on their minds."

"Then why didn't you do it yesterday, before the crowd doubled in size and turned up the volume?" Regan said tersely. The flood of adrenaline from the day's events, which began at three that morning, had left her exhausted and foul-tempered.

Vargas's eyes narrowed. "Do not question my decisions, Agent Manning. And do not speak to me in that tone of voice again or I'll see to it that your next assignment is somewhere in the Aleutians. Are we clear?"

Trevor broke into a grin as he watched the exchange. He moved over and touched Vargas's arm. "It's show time, Madame Secretary."

❧

HERSCHEL COULDN'T take the chance. He knew that little creep Trevor Wolf would blow the whistle if he set foot in the Baranof. He would watch Vargas's speech on TV in his room at the Driftwood Lodge.

Herschel was feeling good. The world looked brighter. Greener. Until today, he couldn't recall the last time he'd smiled. In a festive mood, he stopped at Foodland on the way back to the motel and bought himself a frozen banana cream pie, a treat he hadn't allowed himself in years.

Now it was almost thawed. He sat down at the table in his room and poked a fork into the dessert. A plastic tine popped off, making him jump. He had a hearty laugh as he grabbed a plastic spoon and dug in again.

Maybe things had finally reached the tipping point. Maybe this spirited group in Juneau would be the ones to spark change. Maybe —

A knock at the door interrupted his thoughts.

"Herschel Baker? It's Agent Jenesco with the FBI."

CHAPTER FIFTEEN

W HAT ABOUT Colorado?" said one protestor. "Why don't you put the nuclear waste dump there?"

Watching the show from the back of the room, Regan wanted to say, "Yes, Madame Secretary, why not build it in *your* back yard?"

"Well, as a matter of fact, sir, Colorado was considered," said Vargas. "However, for a number of reasons, Alaska was a better choice. Besides, with its positive fiscal impact on this state – and the jobs it will bring – the facility is a real opportunity, folks."

In her fifteen-minute opening pitch, she'd tried to make it sound like Alaska was The Chosen One. But the protestors weren't buying it. They started talking at once, outshouting each other with their arguments.

The secretary flicked a glance at the TV cameras, her face clouded with uncertainty. She shifted feet and looked down at the podium.

A woman near the front stood up, quieting the clamor. "Secretary Vargas, do you understand what's at risk? Alaska is unique. The ecosystem up here is delicately balanced. You will endanger wildlife and destroy our pristine landscape with this nuclear waste facility. Whatever the so-called fiscal impact is, it's not worth it."

The crowd roared in agreement. Vargas smiled indulgently.

A man yelled, "This is earthquake country. What happens if we have another massive tremor like we did in sixty-four?"

More shouting. "Yeah! Radioactive waste will spew everywhere!"

Vargas shook her head. "No, it won't. Please, ladies and gentlemen, let's try to keep the discussion calm. I invited you in here to engage in civil discourse, not shouting and accusations. This high-level nuclear waste storage repository has undergone a great deal of study to determine the safety features necessary to ensure it remains functional and intact in any event, including an earthquake. We will mine tunnels with deep holes for storage of the waste canisters, which will be suspended from flexible cables that prevent the type of jarring that would result in a rupture. The repository will be situated miles from any town with significant population, and it won't cause damage to the environment."

"Can you personally guarantee that?" yelled an audience member.

"Well, nothing is a hundred percent certain, of course, but —"

"What about the towns without significant population? Are they expendable?"

"Of course not. They will be —"

The crowd began chanting, drowning her out. "No nuclear waste! No nuclear waste!"

"Please, folks ..." Vargas put her hands up, attempting to quell the racket.

She met Regan's gaze. Regan made a slicing motion across her neck.

The secretary paused, appearing to consider whether there was any way to reverse the debacle and get a victory. Finally, she leaned toward the microphone. "Thank you, ladies and gentlemen," she yelled above the din. "I appreciate your input. Thank you for coming." Vargas stepped down from the stage and marched toward the door, she and her chief of staff shielded by a throng of agents.

I hope you're proud of yourself, Regan thought bitterly as she watched the secretary leave. *All you've done is add fuel to the fire.*

&

HERSCHEL HADN'T said much.

"He was pissed that I was there," said Nick. "Didn't want to talk. Kept glancing at the TV. Clearly, he wanted to listen to the secretary's speech, so I deliberately took my time. Asked him everything I could think of except whether he wears boxers or briefs. I think I was close to getting a pie in the face."

Regan yawned. "A what?"

"A pie. Herschel was eating a pie." Nick yawned.

"So he didn't admit to any involvement with Green Globe?"

"Nope. Claims he has no knowledge of any group setting up in Anchorage." He rubbed his eyes.

Regan sighed. Nothing was going to be easy. Why couldn't he just say, *Yeah, I'm Green Globe's new leader, we're building bombs, what are you going to do about it?*

"Did you give him a warning?" she said.

"I did," said Nick. "Told him to stay out of the Baranof."

"And he said, 'No problem,' right?"

"Close. Said we had no right. I said that since he saw fit to threaten Trevor, we would consider filing charges if he set foot on the premises again. He denied threatening Trevor; said he just – quote – 'talked to the little shit.'"

They thought about that a moment, then they both started giggling. The giggles erupted into a punch-drunk belly laugh.

"Hey, Nicky, let's go see if the hotel has any pie. We didn't get any dinner."

"I'm too tired," said Nick. "I'm heading to bed."

"C'mon. I bet Gail would love to have the chance to wait on you again."

"Then she's going to have to wait 'til tomorrow. I'm beat."

Regan had to admit her own fatigue. "You're right – time to call it a day. Hopefully it'll be a bomb-free night."

CHAPTER SIXTEEN

THE RINGING phone woke her.

No, Regan groaned. She peered at the clock with one eye. Five-thirty. *Ugh.*

"Manning."

"Regan?" A young woman's voice.

"Yes?"

"It's Kate."

Kate who? Then she remembered and came fully awake. "Kate! How are you doing?"

"Uh, I'm doing okay, I guess ... except for my face," she said with a self-conscious laugh.

"It'll heal soon, Kate. It hasn't even been a week yet. I just hope you've been able to make some progress on the other stuff – you know, the emotional part. Knowing you don't have to put up with abuse from anybody, including Congressman Slade."

Kate said, "Uh, that's why I'm calling. See, Regan, Paul didn't mean to go that far. It's just that – well, he can't take it when men flirt with me. But he didn't mean to hit me. He feels as bad as I do."

Oh no. No.

"Kate, I know you want to believe that. I know you think you love him. But Paul is an abuser. He's a narcissist. Not only is he cheating on his wife, he's beating you up because he's afraid you're cheating on *him*."

"You don't know what he's gone through to get where he is," Kate said defensively. "He came from nothing. Now he's one of the most powerful men in Congress. You don't see what he does for people every day, Regan."

70

Regan sighed. "No, I don't. And I don't have to. I watched him commit aggravated assault against you. He needs to pay for that, even if you don't think so. If he did this to you, he could do it to someone else. He has a major problem with anger, Kate. You need to come to terms with that."

"I want you to get the charges dropped." Kate tried to sound commanding, but her voice shook.

Did Vargas put Kate up to this?

"Has anyone threatened you?"

"No."

"Do you need protection? Are you in danger?"

"No. I'm fine. I just want the charges dropped," she said more forcefully.

"I'm sorry, Kate." Regan hung up.

॰

AFTER BREAKFAST, Regan stood at the front doors, staring out at the crowd that continued to mushroom, choking off traffic to North Franklin Street.

"JPD sure has its hands full," she said. Never in her four years on the force did they face anything like this.

"It could be worse," said Nick. "They could be throwing stuff. Looks to me like they're a pretty polite crowd."

"Uh huh. Maybe that's because they don't appear to have a leader with malicious intent. Like whoever it is planting the bombs."

"Well, if the bomber decides to get in front of this parade, the situation is going to get explosive – pardon the pun. We'll be seriously outmanned if they get it in their heads to storm the hotel."

Regan spotted Danny pushing his way through the crowd, heading for the Baranof. "Uh, let's go to the command post," she said hurriedly.

Nick looked confused at her sudden haste. "Right," he said. "Let's go to the command post."

"I was just getting ready to call you," McKee said as they walked in. "A lady who works in the gift shop at the top of the tram wants to talk to you about something she saw yesterday. Something to do with the bomb."

"Did you ask her what it was?" said Regan.

"She said she'll talk only to you," he said irritably. "I leaned on her hard, but she wouldn't budge."

Regan sighed. "Okay, I'll run up there. Nick, could you organize the security team for Perseverance? I'd like them up there within the hour."

Nick nodded. "Okay, listen up," he called to the officers in the room.

Regan stepped into the hallway and came face-to-face with Danny.

"Hi," she said guardedly.

"Hey. The chief is tied up – wanted me to check in with you, see what you need us to be doing."

What did I do to piss off the chief?

"I, uh, let's see …"

Focus, she barked at herself.

"How about … well, we could use you – I mean you and the other detectives – uh, here in the hotel. Just in case that crowd outside decides to come inside."

"Right." He wasn't accustomed to taking orders from her; it seemed to amuse him. Or maybe it was the stammering.

Get a grip, girl.

She breathed deeply. "So how have you been, Danny?"

"Great. You?"

"Great."

"Good."

"Okay then." She clasped her hands together and smiled. "I need to run." She started to move away.

"Not the first time I've heard that," he muttered under his breath.

Regan stopped. *"Excuse me?"*

"I said I'll get some of our people rounded up to help you Fibbies out."

"Right," she said crisply. "You do that."

CHAPTER SEVENTEEN

ONE LESS excursion, thanks to shoddy security. Truth be told, she didn't like heights anyway; not getting to ride the tram wasn't much of a disappointment. But she'd ripped that little hotshot agent to shreds like it was a stunning blow.

Vargas felt increasingly frantic as she convened the day's meeting. The summit wasn't going the way she planned at all. These people were supposed to make minor tweaks to the plan and approve it. Instead, they'd turned into a pack of vultures, picking it apart like it was a dead moose.

And the dialogue with protestors in front of a national TV audience failed miserably. She could only imagine what the president thought.

She promised him she could deliver; if she didn't, she would fail her first big test as energy secretary. Eli Sanford would discount her, possibly even find a way to get rid of her. Not only would she lose the bully pulpit to push for increased funding for wind and solar energy, her political career would be all but cooked.

Carney said, "Madame Secretary?" She prayed someone else would speak up so she could ignore him. No one did.

"Go ahead, Mr. Carney."

"I want to challenge the proposed timeline for reducing foreign oil imports," he said, glancing down at the papers in front of him. "I just don't believe it's realistic. People aren't yet ready to kiss their SUVs goodbye – not when oil is available."

"And what happens when oil *isn't* available anymore, Mr. Carney? You know as well as I do that the OPEC countries have been inflating their number of reserves in order to protect production quotas. If we're to believe their numbers, that means reserves are the same as they were a decade ago. Personally, I don't believe it."

The reporters in the room scribbled frantically.

Damn. That was not the sound bite she wanted coming out of the summit.

Carney's smile was smug.

Alaska's congressman, a member of the committee she formerly chaired, came to her rescue. "I think what you're saying, Madame Secretary, is that no one – not even the OPEC countries themselves – are completely certain how large the reserves are, isn't that right? The numbers are estimates."

"Yes, that's what I meant." She flashed him a smile of gratitude.

Carney spoke up again. "With our enhanced recovery tool, we'll be able to get to oil that's been largely inaccessible, both on domestic and foreign soil. From a political standpoint as well as a practical one, that approach has a lot more merit than some of these others in the plan."

"Are you referring to the rotary steerable device that isn't finished yet? Until it is, Mr. Carney, that tool is just a concept."

Carney glared at her.

Mostly silent the previous two days, Dr. Prince spoke up. "I agree with Mr. Carney. From an economic standpoint, it makes sense to continue to tap known sources of energy for the time being. I don't disagree that we should step up exploration of alternative sources – but not to financially favor them over oil until we have a better sense of their cost-benefit ratio and their sustainability. We're not there yet."

Several others, including the governor, chimed in with similar opinions. The environmentalists yelped in protest.

Vargas watched the skirmish, regretting that she'd ever pushed for this useless summit. "Being able to *reach* more oil doesn't *produce* more oil," she said in a raised voice, trying to take back the reins. "It just depletes it faster."

"Right!" one environmentalist chimed.

"But there could be undiscovered basins," said Carney. "Rather than put all of our eggs in the alternative energy basket, we need to commit additional funding for systematic exploration and testing, especially in countries not situated in the Persian Gulf."

Seismic surveys and other technology revealed that the chances of finding promising new basins were slim, but Carney stubbornly clung to the notion that it was simply because of insufficient funding. *Cling to the old, refuse to explore the new.* It was the beating heart of their mutual loathing.

Prince said, "Let me say that I believe building more nuclear power plants is a must. I support the president's position on that. They are one of the most economical forms of energy production, and if they're done right – using a Breeder Reactor – they can provide cheap electricity for generations." He paused, but his expression showed that he wasn't finished.

He looked at Vargas, eyes flashing. "But under no circumstances does it make sense to build a nuclear waste storage facility in Alaska. We have an eight-hundred-mile-long pipeline traversing this state, transporting crude for the nation's oil supply. We will not be on the receiving end of the nation's radioactive waste.

"You say there's no danger, but Alaskans have been sold that bill of goods before," the professor continued. "If you've done your homework, Madame Secretary, you know that the agency that pre-dates yours, the Atomic Energy Commission, planned a thermonuclear explosion on the northwest coast of Alaska in the fifties – with total disregard for the effects of radiation on Eskimo populations living nearby. The Inupiats led a grassroots protest and got it stopped. You could even say they started the environmental movement. Without the Internet or cell phones, I might add."

The youngest member of the summit team, a woman in her thirties, wore a look that said, *You've gotta be kidding me.*

Prince continued. "If you think that protest was something, just wait 'til you see the one that will take place if plans for this facility go forward. Now we *do* have the benefit of technology, which means those people outside are just the tip of the iceberg."

Several around the table applauded, the lawmakers most vigorously.

My God, this is a nightmare.

Governor Larson spoke up. "I, too, oppose a nuclear waste facility in Alaska, but perhaps it would be more useful to discuss alternate solutions for nuclear waste disposal rather than just express our opposition," he said, looking around the table. "After all, Secretary Vargas is only doing what the president asked her to do – so let's be part of the solution, not part of the problem."

"Thank you, Governor," she said. "But let me just assure all of you that the proposed nuclear waste facility has been studied in excruciating detail. I guarantee that it is safe. Beyond that, the fuel sources under consideration in this energy plan are not mutually exclusive. As I said at the beginning, the key word is balance. With a little bit of compromise, a little bit of willingness to explore new options, we all win." She made eye contact with every person around the table except Carney. "Most importantly, the country wins."

Carney said, "I appreciate what the governor is saying, but I think Dr. Prince makes an outstanding point with regard to the nuclear storage facility. As we've all seen, Alaskans don't want it. Can we just take that out of the plan for now?"

This was classic Carney, exploiting any possible weak spot he could find. And it didn't take a genius to assume she'd made a promise to the president.

What he didn't know was how she'd boasted a little, saying that holding the summit up here and being able to talk directly to Alaskans would get them on board. *It's as good as done,* she'd said.

Suddenly it occurred to her that maybe he *did* know – if the president shared her boast with Landry Ness. She got a sick feeling in the pit of her stomach.

"Where do you suggest we store nuclear waste, Mr. Carney, on the moon? Let's be practical, folks. Every state we target for the facility will fight it because they're bowing to public pressure. I believe it is important for this administration to educate them about innovative new methods used for the disposal of spent fuel rods because, though we may all agree on the benefits of nuclear power, it is irresponsible to move forward on building new plants until we have identified a site where waste can be safely stored. It's as simple as that."

"But can we take Alaska off the table?" Carney persisted.

Vargas felt herself losing the reins, both on the summit and her temper. She gave the oil man a rigid stare and hissed, "I'll agree to that, Mr. Carney, when you agree to reduce the proposed timeline on foreign oil imports by half."

CHAPTER EIGHTEEN

THE SIX-MINUTE tram ride to the top of Mount Roberts gave Regan a chance to clear her head. The clouds had departed, and the morning sun glittered on the water. Fishing boats headed outbound toward Stephens Passage, dwarfed by a giant cruise ship inching its way up the narrow channel. Floatplanes buzzed around like flies at a barbecue, adding a colorful splash to the Juneau summer.

The scene captivated her. Was it the familiarity, or simply the idyllic setting? Whatever it was, she relished the moment of tranquility.

She spotted the chocolate-brown clapboard house where it sat just across the channel, off Douglas Highway. The house where, as far as she knew, the stuffed animals, sports awards, and teen memorabilia still resided in the peach-colored bedroom, frozen in time.

Regan felt a sensation in her chest, a jumble of emotions struggling to get out. She was adept at keeping them locked up like prisoners, but it came at a cost. An exceptional career, period.

Her occasional dates were token attempts at convincing herself she could be in a relationship if she really wanted to be – that men still found her desirable, if a little career-centric. She even dated one of those men, an agent on the Evidence Response Team, for several months, until he made a fatal mistake: he proclaimed his love for her. He was also a sloppy cop. She could never love a man who bungled evidence.

But she longed for the intimacy of a loving relationship. Instinctively she knew it was time to make some changes – to have the courage to open herself up, to let people in.

For starters, she needed to make peace with her hometown and the people in it. Enough with the guilt already. And back in Washington, she needed to stop shunning every man who showed a little interest.

As the tram locked into the steel frame at the top, Regan felt lighter already. She smiled at giddy tourists as she moved along the wide walkway. The crowd was more sparse than usual for this time of year; word of yesterday's bomb scare had to be making the rounds.

She stepped inside the gift shop, glancing around at glass cases filled with ivory carvings, Eskimo baskets, and other Alaskan trinkets.

"Regan the Rocket!"

A voice she'd recognize anywhere. Her former teammate bolted out from behind a case and gave Regan a high-five.

"Allie Oop! They lettin' you run this place?"

"Yeah – like that's some big deal," she said with a shrug. "I made better money as a waitress. And this is only a summer gig. But hey, I get to boss people around, so it's all good, right?"

"Allison?" interrupted a young clerk. "This doesn't have a price on it."

"Make one up, Mandy. I need to meet with this lady, so don't bother me unless we're being robbed." She turned to Regan and smiled. "See what I mean? C'mon, let's go to my office."

Regan followed her to the tiny office. She moved stuff off a wooden chair opposite Allie's desk and sat down.

"Sorry for all the shit in here," said Allie. "That's the problem with having an office the size of a bathroom stall. So, how the hell have you been, Regan? Geez, what's it like being in the FBI? That's so cool."

Regan laughed. For the first time since she'd arrived, she felt her shoulders relax. "It's great, actually. I love my job."

"You married? Living with someone?" Allie was never one to hold back, on or off the court.

"No and no. Haven't had the time or the inclination." She noticed she said it with a little less conviction than usual, though. "Hey, Allie, Agent McKee said you saw something that might be related to the bomb on the tram. Can you tell me about that?"

"Yeah. There's a guy working for us this year that seems a little off. Gives me the creeps. Anyway, he was working yesterday when the bomb was found. He was loading the tram cars on this end."

Regan pulled a small notepad and pen from her pocket. "What's his name?"

"John Aldridge. He's from somewhere down south – Seattle or Portland or someplace like that. This is his first summer – and I hope it's his last."

"Can you describe him?"

"Longish brown hair, frizzy, full beard. Tall and lanky."

"How old?"

"Late twenties, early thirties."

"Was he acting suspicious or doing anything you thought was strange?"

"He's always acting strange," said Allie. "The only thing I thought was weirder than usual was that he was wearing a bulky vest."

To conceal a bomb?

"If you remember, Regan, it was about seventy degrees yesterday – hotter than hell. That is until the clouds moved in again in the evening. Anyway, I was thinking he had to be absolutely baking in that insulated vest."

"Is he up here today?"

Allie shook her head. "It's his day off."

"Do you have an address for him?"

"No, but I can get it for you. Hang on." Allie picked up her phone and made a call. She fished through the piles on her desk to find a blank piece of paper, settling for the back of a candy bar wrapper.

"Here you go." She handed the wrapper to Regan.

"Thanks. We'll see what Johnny's up to."

"Great. Make him go back to wherever he came from if you can. And when you get all those bigwigs out of town, let's go play some b-ball. Relive the glory days."

MCKEE CALLED to complain. "Do you realize how short-handed we are? Nick moved everybody up to Perseverance. Only four of us to cover things at the Baranof besides the officers guarding the top three floors. With that mob outside, we're extremely vulnerable."

"I talked to JPD, and they'll have some detectives there to help out shortly. Assign them wherever you need to, McKee."

"Okay, but I have to tell you, Regan, I'm uncomfortable. The crowd is definitely getting bolder. Louder. Other guests are complaining, and hotel staff is scared they're gonna bust in."

Regan was scared about that, too. "I'm heading down on the tram in a few minutes," she said. "I have a stop to make first, then I'll be back there."

She stepped outside and moved to a viewing platform perched on the mountain's edge. The vista was breathtaking, but she didn't have time to enjoy it. She leaned over the railing and scanned the terrain, looking for trails. It was a sheer drop to the forest below.

All at once, she felt hands on her back.

CHAPTER NINETEEN

SOMETHING WAS up. Mac had talked to both Carney and Trevor that morning, and they gave very different accounts of the summit. What should he report to his boss?

He paused at the secretary's desk. "Is he free?" he asked.

"Yes, go on in, Mac."

Mac gave two sharp raps on the door before he opened it.

"There you are," said Ness. "What have we heard from Alaska?"

"It's hard to say, sir. Bob thinks he has the support to derail Vargas's plan. Trevor reports the secretary is confident she can keep it intact and get the group to sign off."

The vice president furrowed his brow. "Somebody's delusional. If I had to guess, I'd say it's your pal Trevor."

Reluctantly, Mac had to agree.

He and Trevor had been buddies since law school. In the ten years since they landed in D.C. together, Trevor had been disgruntled, bouncing from one congressional office to another. Mac joined the staff of then-Senator Landry Ness and had been with him ever since.

Mac used his clout to get his friend the job with Vargas, and Trevor seemed happier, more settled. Complaining less, but not exactly effusive about his boss, either.

That's why Mac was puzzled. This morning, Trevor had painted a far-too-rosy picture of the summit, odd given that everyone saw Vargas bomb with her little press stunt.

"Well, the summit wraps up tomorrow, so I guess we'll find out," said Mac. "If Bob's right, Vargas might find herself in the hot seat."

Ness smiled. "We can always hope."

⌒

HERSCHEL WATCHED Wayne work the crowd. He'd met the short, pudgy activist before, when Wayne came to see him about joining the Alaska Separatist Party. Herschel politely declined, but he did leave the door open to some collaboration.

He made his way over to him. "How's it going, Wayne?"

"Herschel!" he blurted. Then he lowered his voice a little. "Isn't this something? Man oh man. Bill can't believe it either." Wayne glanced down at the device in his hand; Herschel figured it was some kind of souped-up cell phone.

Herschel didn't even own one. Who would need to reach him?

"Dr. Prince is sending text messages to me from inside the meeting room. We're keeping each other apprised. He says Vargas isn't backing off the nuclear waste dump. Thinks it may be time to storm the fort, get her attention."

Herschel felt a jolt of alarm. "*Storm the fort?* Why in the world would we do that?"

"Shut the summit down. Run those people out of town. Send a clear message that Alaskans won't stand for a toxic waste dump in our state."

Herschel shook his head in dismay. "We don't need a riot, Wayne, we just need a conversation with Vargas."

"She tried that, remember? Big flop."

"I don't mean her addressing the crowd. I mean a couple of us sitting down with her to explain Alaska's environmental concerns. Share our knowledge with her in a calm manner, not by shouting."

Wayne laughed. "You sure don't look as prissy as you sound, Baker. I hate to break it to you, but I think the time for calm sharing has passed. Prince agrees."

Herschel tried to think. How could he talk some sense into them?

"Wayne, would you send Prince a message for me? Tell him I need to meet with him – ASAP." Since Professor Prince wasn't likely to come out, Herschel would have to find a way to get in.

"Okay, sure ... but I don't think you're going to change his mind, Herschel. He's as excited about this as I am."

CHAPTER TWENTY

G ET YOUR hands off me!" Regan shrieked.

"Okay, okay, I was just playing around," said Danny, holding his hands up. "Don't get your knickers in a knot."

Regan's heart beat wildly; she was too furious to speak.

"You should see your face," he said, chuckling. "You look like you're ready to shoot somebody."

In the blink of an eye, the years were swept away. They were back in those final, tortured weeks of their affair, when the good-natured Danny, the man she loved, morphed into a monster. The change had apparently stuck.

"Seems like you would be more focused on catching terrorists in your town than playing childish games. And why are you even up here? I asked you to help out at the Baranof."

Danny's face colored; the smile disappeared. "I wanted to talk to you."

A rush of memories flooded her brain like a worn-out video: Danny's plan to leave his wife for her … the junior detective who leaked their affair … Danny's fury over her decision to join the FBI. His threats. How she had taken the brunt of the scorn from people. Most of all, the look of disappointment in Chief Lamont's eyes.

For five years, she'd carried the guilt like a bag of wet sand. Now, pent-up rage bubbled inside her, killing the tranquility she felt an hour before.

She crossed her arms in front of her, quelling the emotion so she wouldn't go too far and say something she'd later regret. Finally, she met his gaze. "There's nothing to talk about, Danny. Our relationship was a mistake. We paid the price. Let it go."

She saw a flicker of pain before he clenched his jaw, his dark eyes turning to stone. "Don't flatter yourself. I wasn't asking you out on a damn date, I just wanted to know how you were."

"Couldn't be better. I'll see you back at the Baranof."

☞

REGAN FOUND herself in front of a fifties-vintage clapboard house just off Calhoun Street. The green paint was faded and chipped; one white shutter was missing, giving the house a lopsided look, like a woman who had lost one of her false eyelashes.

Regan knocked. An elderly woman came to the door, her shoulders so stooped that she had to crane her neck to see Regan. "Yes?"

"Hello – I'm looking for John Aldridge. Does he live here?"

"He rents my basement apartment." She pointed to the worn steps at the side of the house and shut the door.

"Thank you," Regan said to the wood pane in front of her. It needed paint, too.

She descended the soggy wooden steps and knocked on John's door. No answer. She knocked again. "Mr. Aldridge? FBI."

Still no answer. She leaned over and peeked in the window. The curtains were parted just enough for her to see a sliver of the living room. Just enough to catch a glimpse of a man's foot and lower leg lying prone on the floor.

She ran back up to get a key from the landlady. "Now what?" the woman said grumpily. "I'm trying to watch my program."

"My name is Regan Manning," she said hurriedly. "I'm with the FBI. I think Mr. Aldridge might need some help. Could you open his door for me?"

"FBI? Why is the FBI checking on John?" She paused. "Say, are you Devlin Manning's girl?" She seemed to forget all about John.

"Please, ma'am, hurry. The key."

The woman toddled over to a maple hutch in the dining room and dug a key out of a soup tureen. She handed it to Regan. "Here. And don't forget to bring it back."

Regan charged back down the stairs and let herself in. The man on the floor looked just the way Allie had described him – except he was no longer acting strange. He was no longer acting at all.

⇛

"WHO IS he?" said Nick.

"His name is John Aldridge. He worked at the Mount Roberts tram." Regan recounted Allie's story.

Nick shook his head. "I wonder what he got himself mixed up in … what would piss somebody off enough to stab him to death." He inspected the knife wounds on Aldridge's back.

"Good question. Whoever it was, they attacked him when his back was turned, so he might not have even seen it coming."

They pulled on latex gloves and began a search of the apartment while they waited for the coroner and Chief Lamont to show up.

The landlady, Ruby Little, hadn't been much help. She didn't know much about her tenant, except that he was from somewhere else and only here for the summer. And he paid his rent in cash.

Nick fished a Blackberry from the man's pocket. "Let's see what this little gem tells us."

Regan wandered into the bedroom. Taped on the wall was a poster of LaMarcus Aldridge, forward for the Portland Trail Blazers. Probably John's favorite athlete because they had the same last name. She was a fan of Aldridge's, too; not only a good basketball player, a pianist to boot.

She struggled with the closet's folding doors. The ones in her apartment in Alexandria acted up like this, too.

She tried the lift-slide motion she used at home and finally got the doors open. A skimpy collection of clothes hung there, including the insulated vest Allie mentioned. She pulled it out and began examining it for traces of gun powder used in the pipe bombs.

"Regan," Nick called from the living room.

She poked her head around the corner. "Yeah?"

"Take a look at this email that came to his Blackberry." He held the device out to Regan. "From our pal Randy Strathman."

Get out of there before the FBI figures things out.
This is not your fight, Cory. Don't go down for it.

"*Cory?* John Aldridge is Cory Winslow?" In the picture Lindsay circulated, Cory wore a buzz cut like Strathman's. He looked completely different with long hair and a beard.

Regan glanced back at the poster on the wall. The dead guy on the floor didn't *share* a last name with Portland's Aldridge.

He'd borrowed it.

CHAPTER TWENTY-ONE

THE POLICE were doing their best, but they couldn't keep the mob confined to the sidewalks.

Driving up the street to the hotel was like trying to drive through a dense forest. Regan flipped on the Suburban's flashing grill lights and set the siren to the piercer tone.

The protestors scooted over just enough to let her pass, shouting and shaking their picket signs at her. She shivered.

McKee was right. They were getting bolder.

Regan spotted some faces she recognized in the crowd. They looked at her accusingly as she drove by – as though *she'd* brought this battle to their front steps.

She stopped next to a young cop and rolled down her window, flashing her ID. "How's it going, Officer?"

He leaned close, his voice low. "It's a miracle they haven't overtaken us. We're way outnumbered." His face was pale, his eyes round with fear.

"I know," said Regan. "I'm going to try to get you some backup. We're spread pretty thin, though."

"What do we do if they challenge us? What if they try to invade the hotel?"

"First of all, Officer —" She glanced at his nametag. "Officer Tillis, get that look off your face. I know this is overwhelming, but it won't help if you look like you're about to faint."

He took a deep breath and did his best to change his expression. The effect was almost comical.

"That's better," said Regan. "I'll get you some help."

She pulled around to the parking lot and entered the back of the hotel. Truth was, she was as scared as poor Officer Tillis. She was just more practiced at faking it.

Regan walked into the command post, startled to see Trevor Wolf hovering over Lindsay where she sat in front of a computer screen.

"Mr. Wolf, can I help you with something?" said Regan.

The smile on his face faded. "No, I was just asking for an update from Agent Pryor. She graciously supplied it."

Lindsay wasn't authorized to be giving updates. And Trevor wasn't supposed to be inside the command post. "Please come with me, Mr. Wolf."

Trevor gave Lindsay a little wave and followed Regan into the hallway. She gave him a harsh look. "First of all, only law enforcement personnel are allowed in the Douglas Room. It is necessary in order for us to maintain a high level of security. Secondly, Mr. Wolf, if you have questions about this operation, you bring them to me."

He gave a derisive laugh. "Forgive my transgression, Agent Manning. It's just that I don't have much faith in your ability to effectively lead this mission. Not after a terrorist waltzed right past your so-called high level of security."

Regan leaned forward, close enough to count the freckles on his pug nose. "Like it or not, I'm team leader on this mission. You want information, you talk to me. Got it?"

Trevor backed up and gave her a salute. He turned around and entered the summit meeting across the hall.

Herschel was right – he is a little shit.

Lindsay looked contrite when Regan stepped back into the room. "Sorry, Regan," she said quickly. "I didn't tell him anything except what he already knew – that we're monitoring the premises. But I know I should've chased him out of here."

Behind her, the computer monitor's split screen showed four live camera feeds: the top two floors of the hotel, where the VIPs were housed; the entrance and front desk; and the lobby and hallway leading to the Treadwell Ballroom.

"That's okay, Lindsay, but let's be sure not to let non-law-enforcement people in here again."

Especially that creep.

"I won't. I don't think Trevor really wanted information anyway – I think he just came in to talk to me. I've had a couple conversations with him in the lobby, and he acts all goofy around me. This morning he said, 'You ever think about getting transferred to D.C.?' He was talking in this smarmy voice, like he was trying to sound sexy or something. Yuck."

Regan laughed. "Uh oh, crush alert."

"I know, right? Like *that's* gonna happen." She turned back around to face the monitor. "Hey … is that Herschel?" She pointed to the screen.

Regan rushed over to look. "Where?"

"Up the stairs to the left of the elevators."

Regan charged out the door. She spotted McKee talking to Danny and two other JPD detectives in the lobby. Danny stood in his typical stance, arms crossed, listening with an aloof expression. None of them was watching the front door.

"Herschel Baker just went up the stairs," Regan panted. The officers took off running.

She rushed back to the command post, pondering how Herschel could've gotten past the screening officer at the front door. "Was he wearing some kind of disguise, Lindsay?"

"He was wearing a fishing hat and glasses. But I recognized his walk. I've conducted surveillance on his protests in Anchorage more times than I can count."

"Can you rewind the video?"

Lindsay replayed the footage of Herschel's entrance.

Regan studied the man as he moved away from the door, past the front desk and elevator bank, keeping a brisk pace as he headed for the stairs off to the left. He wore khakis and a navy sweatshirt with ALASKA stenciled across the chest; a feather-like lure was stuck in the brim of his fishing hat. A camera hung from his neck.

Herschel had taken pains to look like a friendly fisherman from the lower forty-eight. Not a rabid treehugger from up north.

"Hmm," said Regan. "I wonder what Herschel's fishing for in the Baranof."

೮

"THAT WAS Herschel Baker?" The screening officer was incredulous. "I didn't recognize him from the picture. I apologize, Agent Manning. I should have paid closer attention."

"It's not your fault, Officer. There should be at least two of you up here anyway. I'll get a JPD detective to help you out. I just wondered, though, if you noticed anything unusual in the items Herschel emptied from his pockets into the bowl. A knife, maybe?"

"Nothing I recall. No, no knives."

"What about a hotel key card?"

"No, I don't think so."

Some people were entering the hotel. "Okay. I'll let you get back to work."

She was headed for the stairs when her phone beeped. "Manning."

"Hi, honey. It's Dad."

His voice stopped her dead in her tracks.

"Hi," she said tentatively, a flood of emotions swirling through her – joy, hope … suspicion. Dread.

"I need to talk to you. Can you come to my office?"

Exasperation. "No, I can't, Dad. I'm working."

He gave an audible sigh. "Then I guess we'll just have to talk now. Regan, I'm getting complaints from every direction. Townspeople are upset over the bombs, the police can't handle all the protestors arriving from God-knows-where, the tour companies are losing business because people aren't getting off the ships – it's a mess…"

And he doesn't even know about the dead body yet.

"… and it's my job as mayor to straighten it out."

"I know, Dad, but things should get back to normal in a couple days."

"Do you have any idea how much money those tourists bring in every day? You need to shut it down *now*. Get the secretary and the rest of those people out of here. I'm nervous, Regan. Things are damn close to the boiling point."

Maybe he was right; maybe the best thing to do was pull the plug before someone else ended up like Cory Winslow.

But this summit was sanctioned by the highest levels of government. Regan thought of AR, of his faith in her ability to complete the mission and keep dignitaries out of harm's way. It wasn't the Bureau's practice to step in and shut things down unless the danger level was off the charts.

They weren't to that point. "I can't, Dad. Sorry."

His voice became more terse. "Why, because it's me asking you to do it?"

"Of course not. Don't be ridiculous."

Not everything's about you, Dad.

"Regan, are you willing to shoulder the blame if someone gets hurt? Or killed?"

She bristled, matching his tone. "We have forty-eight more hours to get through. And we *will* get through them."

"I hope for your sake you're right. Otherwise, you might be forced to turn tail and run again." He hung up.

CHAPTER TWENTY-TWO

W E CAN'T find him," said McKee. He was out of breath from running up and down stairs. "He isn't in the stairwell, and he isn't in the hallway on any of the five floors that don't have security cameras. Or the basement."

"Then he has to be in a guest room," said Regan. "Which suggests he's connected to someone staying here. Let's get an officer on each floor, positioned between the stairs and the elevator so they can keep an eye on both."

"Do we have enough personnel still on the premises?" He made no effort to mask the judgmental tone.

Regan ignored it. "We do, but it leaves us pretty thin here on the first floor. Since Perseverance is secured, I'll get a few members of my team to come back and help us out."

She opened her phone to call when it beeped in her hand. "Hi, Al."

"There's been an oil tanker explosion in the Strait of Hormuz," Rinehart said without preamble. "Ship belongs to an American company."

"Okay," said Regan, unsure how the news pertained to the mission. "What happened?"

"Hit a floating mine."

"Who does the tanker belong to?"

"Stratum Shipping."

"Doesn't ring a bell."

"Stratum is a subsidiary of Axis Oil."

"*Axis?* Oh my gosh, Al ... I don't think Robert Carney knows. I saw him leaving the restroom to go back into the meeting room ten or fifteen minutes ago."

"You better go tell him," said AR. "I expect he'll want to head back to Houston."

～

HERSCHEL SAT facing Prince in Wayne's room on the third floor. "I don't think you understand, Bill. People could get hurt. Is that what you want?"

"Of course not, but this movement will change Alaska forever. If there's some pain involved, it is in service to the greater good," said Prince.

Herschel stared at the professor in disbelief. And people thought *he* was an extremist.

"The way I see it," Prince continued, "this is our chance to run Vargas out of here. Get rid of that vile energy plan once and for all and send the message that Alaskans are not to be trifled with. Believe me, when that crowd starts stampeding through the front doors and confronts Vargas and the rest of the conference people, the FBI won't waste any time shutting this little party down."

"A stampede? I don't think that's wise ..."

The professor's eyes hardened. "What's the deal, Herschel? I thought you agreed to support ASP on this. You said you'd help us get that energy plan killed."

"The *plan*, not the people, Bill. I want to try to talk to Vargas, give her a way to back off the nuclear waste facility and still save face."

"Oh, really? You think we haven't been trying to do that the last three days? She's resolute when it comes to that part of the plan – even more so when Bob Carney tries to push her to take it off the table."

Herschel perked up. "That's what I mean! She won't yield in front of the whole group. You and I can talk to her in private, provide her with a sound argument that she can take back to the president. That way, we win and she doesn't lose."

"Listen to me, Baker. We couldn't have scripted the situation better. Nobody in ASP could've *ever* imagined this number of protestors. There's at least a thousand people out there, and Wayne is getting them mobilized. Each one of his text messages is more ecstatic than the last. We're *united*, Herschel. We have the power of the people. Let's use it."

Herschel looked at the professor, at the determination glowing in his eyes, and felt the full weight of his dilemma. Isn't this what he'd spent twenty years fighting for? People to stand up for Alaska's delicate environment before it was too late?

Not like this. Not by risking human life for the sake of nature.

"Are you with us, Herschel? Wayne's waiting. He's watching his cell for the word *Go*, then he leads the charge. That's all it takes and this thing's over."

Herschel gave Prince one last, desolate look before he got up and left the room.

CHAPTER TWENTY-THREE

WITH PRINCE out, maybe she could get some traction with the others before he returned. She was just sorry Carney hadn't left, too.

"Ladies and gentlemen, it's clear we have work to do in assuring Alaskans of the minimal risk to this state with the nuclear storage facility. It's important that —"

"Madame Secretary," said the congressman who served on the committee Vargas formerly chaired, cutting her off. "With all due respect, I don't believe *any* amount of work we do will change their minds. Or ours. Even though the proposed facility is state-of-the-art, we can't know for sure there won't be radioactive pollution in the event of, say, a major tremor."

His comment threw her. For more than a decade, he was a key ally; he was the last one in this group she expected to oppose her.

"Congressman, that type of event has been accounted for in the design of the facility. It has a unique suspension feature that will —"

"Secretary Vargas, have you ever witnessed the destruction caused by a massive earthquake?" His voice held a conviction she'd never heard before.

"Not firsthand, no," Vargas said. Her tone was guarded.

"Well I have. I was in elementary school when the Good Friday earthquake hit Anchorage in sixty-four. I will never forget the sight of that devastation as long as I live. It's beyond anything you can imagine. It is absurd to think those radioactive canisters would remain intact in an event of that magnitude. I'm sorry, I cannot and will not support the construction of a nuclear waste facility in Alaska. Not under *any* circumstances."

No one else spoke; all eyes were on Vargas. She'd begun to construct a response in her head when she heard the door open.

Damn ... Prince is back.

But it wasn't Prince. It was Regan Manning.

"Sorry for the interruption, Secretary Vargas, but I need a word with Robert Carney."

Carney had a quizzical expression as he got up from his chair and headed for the door.

To Vargas, it was a gift from heaven. A chance to nudge the environmentalists to speak up without getting beaten down by Prince or Carney.

As soon as the door closed behind the oil man, she said, "Okay, folks, for now let's shift our focus to wind and solar energy."

&

"EXPLODED? DO you know if anyone was killed?" His astonishment seemed exaggerated, like he was playing the part of a concerned CEO rather than actually being one.

"We don't have a lot of details yet, Mr. Carney," Regan replied. "I'm sorry, has someone already notified you? You don't seem particularly surprised."

Carney shrugged, losing the act. "Why would I be? It's the Strait of Hormuz. It's a dangerous area." Carney pulled out his phone and checked his messages. "I have a couple voicemails, so I'm sure my people have tried to reach me." He flashed a toothy smile and moved away from her toward the lobby, phone to his ear.

Trevor rushed out of the meeting room, skidding to a halt when he saw Regan standing ten feet away.

"Can I help you, Trevor?"

"Uh ... no, I was just checking to see if something was wrong."

"Nothing you need to concern yourself with."

He narrowed his eyes and appeared to debate a moment before he turned around and disappeared back into the meeting room.

She caught movement out of the corner of her eye; she glanced up and saw Danny marching toward her, a handcuffed Herschel Baker in tow.

She met them halfway. "So there you are, Mr. Baker. I'm Regan Manning, FBI."

"Agent Manning, those people outside —" He seemed agitated.

"Yes, what about them?"

He started to answer when his words were drowned out by a deafening crash, followed by a mass of shouting protestors invading the hotel like a tsunami.

CHAPTER TWENTY-FOUR

MAC HAD left two messages for Trevor, but he hadn't heard back. He made his way to the vice president' office. "Heard from Bob yet?" he asked Ness in a casual voice.

"No. Grace tried to get him on the phone, but he didn't answer. Hasn't returned my call." Ness got up and began to wander around the office, pausing to inspect paintings as though he'd never noticed them before.

"Maybe he's on his way back to Houston," Mac offered.

He turned to face Mac. "Maybe, but why hasn't he called from the plane? He always calls from the plane."

"I don't know, sir. Maybe they're out of cell phone range when they're in flight up there."

"Then why not use the other phone thing?" Ness gave a flutter of his hand.

"The satellite phone? Don't know, sir."

And it didn't explain why he hadn't heard from Trevor.

"Let's try the hotel." Mac moved over to the phone on Ness's desk and put it on speaker before asking Grace to get the Baranof on the line.

After a couple minutes, Grace said, "I'm sorry, Mac. There's no answer."

&

"STOP RIGHT there!" Regan screamed.

She and Danny faced the crowd, weapons drawn; McKee, who had just come up the basement stairs, positioned himself nearby, Glock pointed at the invaders.

The storming protestors stopped and flung their hands in the air. "Don't shoot!" someone squealed. They began bunching themselves together like spooked cattle.

All except one. A short, stocky man with gray peach fuzz on his head stood slightly apart. His wide smile curved right up to his shiny red cheeks, giving him a cherubic look. The grin crumbled when he spotted Herschel in handcuffs.

"Back up, people," Regan shouted. "Turn around and leave the hotel now or you will be placed under arrest."

Peach Fuzz said, "We want to talk to Secretary Vargas. She needs to see for herself what she's up against if she goes ahead with that toxic waste dump."

The crowd starting cheering.

Regan glanced toward the Treadwell Ballroom to make sure none of the VIPs had slipped out to see what the fuss was about. Only Trevor stood there, glued to the wall, eyes as big as snowballs.

Regan glanced at Danny, communicating with her eyes and a tiny twitch of the head that he should move closer to the ballroom, guarding it and Herschel at the same time.

Danny backed up slowly.

They'd always been good at that – the unspoken communication. Until they got the brilliant idea to take things beyond police work.

Lindsay witnessed the scene on the computer monitor and scrambled into the hallway, weapon drawn. Regan kept her eyes on the crowd as she asked Lindsay in a low voice, "Did you alert the other officers on site?"

"I did. They're positioned between the elevators and the coffee shop."

Regan shouted, "Secretary Vargas has seen and heard you. She is well aware of your opposition to the nuclear waste facility. Please leave the premises *now*."

Protestors looked at each other, uncertain what to do; they stared at Peach Fuzz, waiting for his cue.

"We want her to tell us face-to-face that Alaska is no longer a viable site," he said. "Then we'll go."

Regan kept both her gaze and her aim steady. "Not gonna happen."

Not that it wasn't tempting to drag the secretary out to face the music.

Peach Fuzz ran a hand over his, well, peach fuzz, a scowl on his face. Everything grew still, as though someone had hit a giant pause button. The only sound was the hotel switchboard ringing unanswered.

Finally, the pudgy man turned and waved the crowd back. The general signaling retreat.

When the lobby cleared, one man remained, wearing an expression that was hard to read.

Dr. William Prince.

CHAPTER TWENTY-FIVE

"YOU'LL NEVER guess what Lamont and I found." Nick could hardly contain his excitement.

Regan, tense enough to crack if someone bumped her, had one hand on the door of the Treadwell Ballroom. She didn't have time for guessing games. "What, Nick?" she said impatiently.

"The source of the pipe bombs. All the components, and one bomb that was assembled except for the timer."

"*Where?*"

"Tool shed next to the house John Aldridge – I mean Cory Winslow – was renting. Mrs. Little let him use her husband's old workbench to – quote – 'tinker around.'"

"So Cory *was* our bomb builder."

"Yep."

Who was he working for? Not his half-brother, at least not anymore; Strathman warned him to get out of town. Said it *wasn't his fight.*

Whose was it?

Was the Green Globe Defense League back in operation or was that just a ploy to divert the FBI's attention?

Regan's mind raced: Carney's phony reaction to the explosion of his tanker, Herschel disguising himself to get past hotel security, Dr. Prince in the lobby, wearing a look of ... *elation.*

How did the pieces fit together?

She told Nick about the protestors' invasion, how they knocked over the metal detector at the front door. "The screening officer was injured in the stampede."

"How bad?" said Nick.

"He's pretty banged up, but he'll be okay. The desk clerk said he put up his hands and tried to stop them. He got knocked down and managed to crawl underneath the screening belt. Probably saved his life." Regan felt a stab of self-recrimination; would two officers stationed there have been able to stop the initial surge?

Probably not. No, of *course* not.

"What about the VIPs? How are they taking it?"

"I was just on my way to talk to them," she said. "I suspect Dr. Prince has already clued them in, though; he was standing near the elevators when the crowd cleared out."

"You think he's involved in this?"

"Yes, Nick, I do. I just have to figure out how."

∾

"THIS JUST keeps getting better and better," Vargas said with a shake of her head.

"Ma'am?" said Regan.

"The security for this summit – or rather the lack of it."

Her words stung. "Madame Secretary, I —"

"Save it. I'm sure the director will be interested to know that his person in charge up here can't even keep a band of picketers from marching right through the front door. Thank goodness they're a fairly docile bunch."

The other meeting officials watched in silence.

Vargas's charge blew the lid off Regan's temper. She stepped closer to the secretary, her voice an angry growl. "Maybe security for this summit would be tighter if you weren't doing everything you could to undermine it. You added excursions to the schedule at the last minute, you invited that 'band of picketers' in for an impromptu meeting without clearing it with us first, you complained bitterly when we canceled your excursion on the Mount Roberts tram out of concern for the safety of you and your colleagues. All of *that* in addition to the fact that ever since we stepped off the plane, we've been dealing with bombs – one of which destroyed a natural landmark that is the very *essence* of this town, and another that could have ripped one of Juneau's most popular tourist attractions right off the side of the mountain and killed innocent people in the process. How *dare* you think —"

Regan caught herself. Only through sheer will did she keep from clapping a hand over her mouth, horrified at her outburst.

She glanced at the faces around the table. She was stunned to see the nods, the looks of support.

All at once, she understood.

Ella Vargas was scared. Her life had been in peril, yes, but that was more abstract than the imminent threat to her career. The secretary simply didn't have the support of the group. Her back was to the wall.

"I apologize, Madame Secretary," Regan stammered. "We are doing everything humanly possible to ensure your safety for the rest of this summit."

Vargas gaped at her, mouth open, no sound coming out.

Regan decided to depart before the secretary found her voice. Turning, she saw Trevor Wolf standing near the door. He wore a look of unbridled glee.

CHAPTER TWENTY-SIX

THEY PULLED into the parking lot at the police station.
"Think Herschel will spill his guts?" said Nick.

"I hope so," said Regan. "He could be key to helping us figure this thing out."

Chief Lamont met them as they entered. His clothes looked rumpled, the bags under his eyes and the lines in his face pronounced. "So far, our boy's not talking."

"We'll give it a shot," said Regan. She turned to face the chief straight on and said quietly, "You okay, Pat?"

He nodded. "Yeah, kiddo, I'm okay. It's just that bombs and dead bodies aren't part of a typical day at JPD. That's *your* scene."

"I think we'll all be glad when the summit wraps up tomorrow and those people get out of here. But JPD has done an amazing job. Every single officer has stepped up." Regan thought of the bomb squad guy hanging off the tram. "Big time."

"They're probably glad to have a little excitement," Lamont said. "C'mon, interview room is this way."

Regan looked at him and smiled.

The chief said, "Right. You know where the interview room is."

Regan walked up to the one-way glass. Herschel sat at the metal table, completely still; whiskered and gloomy, he looked like a shadow.

Danny stood near one wall. Neither man spoke.

Regan took a deep breath. "Okay, Nick, let's go."

They knocked and entered the room.

"Hello again, Mr. Baker," Regan said cheerily as she and Nick took their seats opposite him.

Only his eyes moved as he glanced at them both. He didn't speak.

"Let's start with today's visit to the Baranof. Nice disguise, by the way. I like your fishing hat, especially the orange feather lure. Nice touch." The hat sat between them on the table like a holiday centerpiece.

Herschel stared at Regan; she could see the intelligence in his eyes, the aversion to playing games. She decided to tone down the pseudo-friendly BS.

"Why were you in the hotel, Mr. Baker?"

Herschel didn't answer.

"Did you meet with someone there?"

"Am I under arrest?"

"No, you're not. You're being detained for questioning because of the earlier incident with Mr. Wolf. If you recall, you were asked not to return to the Baranof."

Herschel appeared to struggle with himself over whether to cooperate.

Regan pressed on. "The FBI office in Anchorage has reason to believe you may be involved with a group known as the Green Globe Defense League."

Herschel looked insulted. "They're eco-terrorists."

Regan raised her eyebrows. "Some people think that's what you are, Herschel."

"Because I believe we should protect the environment? Because I care enough to get in politicians' faces? That makes me a *terrorist*?" His face was flushed, eyes blazing.

"Are you acquainted with a man named Cory Winslow?"

"No," he barked.

"What about John Aldridge?"

"Don't know either of them."

He didn't blink, didn't hesitate. He was telling the truth.

She decided to try another tack, see if she could shake anything loose. "Last fall, there was some logging equipment damaged by tree spiking in the Chugach Forest near Anchorage," said Regan. "An arrest was never made, but there were some fingers pointed in your direction. Did you spike those trees, Mr. Baker?"

Herschel shook his head, a mournful look in his eyes. "No, I did not. I am against logging in the Chugach, but not enough to do something like that, Agent Manning." He paused a moment. "Just because a citizen of this country exercises his right to speak out, you people label all of us as extremists and start surveilling us. You dig through our trash, searching for bomb ingredients. You probably bug our phones. But let me make myself perfectly clear: *I am not an eco-terrorist.* I am an environmentalist. There's a distinct difference."

"I appreciate the clarification," said Regan. "So tell us what you were doing in the Baranof."

Herschel sighed. "Attempting to head off an invasion."

⌘

CARNEY WAS glad to be out of there. He could hardly stand to look at Ella Vargas another minute.

As the Learjet reached cruising altitude, he dialed the vice president's office. Ness was in a meeting, so he asked for Mac.

"Hey, Bob. We were getting worried. Where are you?"

"On my way back to Houston."

"We tried to reach you. We called the hotel, but for some reason there was no answer. What's going on up there?"

"Oh, some protestors tried to storm the hotel," Carney said casually. "You must've called during that time."

"*Storm the hotel?*"

"That's right. They wanted Vargas to tell them face-to-face that the nuclear waste facility proposal was off the table." He laughed.

"Did she?"

"No, the FBI chased them away," said Carney. "The whole thing was pretty uneventful, actually. Have you gotten any details on the tanker explosion?"

"Not yet," said Mac. "The CIA is looking into it. What about your people? What have they heard?"

108

"Not a lot. Just that nobody was killed, thank God. They don't have any idea who placed the floating mines."

Mac said something to someone in the background. "Hey, Bob, I need to run. What's your ETA in Houston?"

Carney looked at his watch. "About five hours from now. Have Landry call me when he's free."

After he hung up, Carney had the on-board hostess pour him a Glenlivet. He stared at the scenery below and sipped his drink.

Things had gone quite nicely in Juneau. Vargas got creamed by the locals *and* the summiteers; the last place on earth a nuclear waste facility would land was in Alaska. She would have to scramble to find an alternative or risk losing her job.

As for the timeline limiting foreign oil, Bill Prince would never go along with it – and he had the sway to make sure others didn't, either.

Beautiful.

Vargas would have no choice but to go back to the drawing board on the whole energy plan, which would tie her up for months. That bought him some much-needed time to sort things out in the Caspian and get the rotary steerable device through production.

And just in case the summit didn't conclude precisely that way, he had his man on the inside looking out for him.

Trevor Wolf.

CHAPTER TWENTY-SEVEN

W HY THE change of heart, Herschel?" said Regan. At the police station earlier, getting him to talk had been an exercise in futility. Why was he suddenly overcome with a sense of civic duty?

There had to be a motive.

He sat on the bed in the motel room, an unsealed envelope in his hands. Regan noticed he kept his little home away from home tidy – wardrobe, toiletries, and books all arranged in neat rows, table clear of debris. If he had a weapon, it was tucked somewhere out of sight.

"I'd like you to deliver a letter to Secretary Vargas," he said. "Since she didn't have time to see me, you know, she told me to write to her."

"You planning to make some kind of veiled threat?" said Nick. "Oh, wait, that's right – you're just a friendly treehugger, not an extremist."

Regan gave Nick a look that said *dial it down, partner.* She wanted to know why they were here. It wasn't because of the letter.

"Here – read it." Herschel held it out to her.

Regan took the letter from the envelope and began to read. His handwriting was small and precise; it filled four sheets of hotel stationery, both sides. A mini-treatise on Alaska's delicate ecosystem and the damaging effects of overzealous exploitation of the state's natural resources. And why a nuclear waste facility in Alaska's interior would be lethal.

Regan marveled at his writing ability, at the presentation of his argument in a clear, convincing manner. Not a single threat, veiled

110

or otherwise, but she saw his passion. Saw why it mattered that his voice and those of other environmentalists be heard.

"This is good, Herschel. Why didn't you just do this from the beginning?" She handed the letter to Nick.

Herschel shrugged. "I thought it would be better to talk to her face-to-face, answer any questions she might have. I see now that that may not have been the best route."

"I'd have to agree," said Regan. "After all, Vargas does have other environmentalists and experts to call upon at the summit."

"Like Professor Prince." His tone was less than admiring.

"Right. What do you know about him?"

Herschel didn't answer.

"If you want us to deliver this letter, Herschel, you'll need to give us something in return."

"I expected as much." The environmentalist looked at his hands, gathering his thoughts. "Prince is unstable."

Regan flicked a glance at Nick that said *here we go, now we're getting somewhere.*

She sat down at the table. "How so?"

"He's so busy running the show with the Alaska Separatist Party that it's a wonder he's had time to make enough of a name for himself as an expert on resource economics to be invited to the summit. Let alone *teach*, which is what he's paid to do."

"He's running ASP?" Regan hadn't seen that coming.

"Pretty much. He keeps his name off the ASP website and their other materials, but he's the one who developed their platform and wrote their positions on issues. Prince's biggest thing is that he's pushing for complete repatriation of all public lands in Alaska."

"Meaning he wants the state to be independent?"

Herschel nodded. "And control all of the state's resources, especially oil and gas. Prince has gone to great lengths to establish his position in the party so that if independence happens, he'll play a major leadership role."

Regan leaned forward. "What great lengths?"

Herschel paused, then appeared to decide he'd gone too far to turn back. "A man named Stewart Gentry was ASP's party chair.

He and Prince didn't get along. Prince told me himself that Gentry didn't know his ass from a hole in the ground and that the party didn't have a prayer of advancing under his leadership."

"Did he oust Gentry from the party?"

"In a manner of speaking. A year ago, Gentry died suddenly. His brakes failed and he slid off the road and hit a tree. He might have survived, but it was wintertime in Fairbanks – thirty or forty below at the time – and he froze to death before anyone discovered the so-called accident."

"What makes you think it *wasn't* an accident?" said Nick.

"It was a brand-new pickup. Gentry had just bought it in the fall."

"Did anyone suspect foul play?" said Regan.

"The Fairbanks police questioned people, but nobody knew anything. They let it drop."

"What about Prince? Was he questioned?"

Herschel shook his head. "No."

"So why do you think he had anything to do with it?"

"Just something in his manner," said Herschel. "He called me not too long after Gentry's death and tried to encourage me to join the party. Said ASP was going to be playing a much larger role in Alaska politics now that Stewart was gone, and I should get on the bandwagon."

"Why you, Herschel? Are you a big supporter of their platform?"

"Actually, there's very little we agree on. But Prince said he wanted someone knowledgeable about Alaska's environmental concerns who could articulate them effectively."

"So he loves you for your mind," said Nick.

Herschel looked at Nick like the agent was a mosquito he wanted to slap. "The one thing we *did* agree on was the need to shoot down Secretary Vargas's proposed energy plan," he said. "Especially that toxic waste dump. Through peaceful protests."

"And when Prince decided to ramp things up, go beyond the peaceful protests, you tried to stop him," said Regan.

Herschel nodded.

She was right; the letter to Vargas was a ruse to get them here. Despite his ambivalence, Herschel wanted to confess what he knew about Prince, get it off his chest.

She searched his whiskered face, his pewter gray eyes, but there were no signs of vindication. Only resignation.

"Thanks for telling us this, Herschel. The Bureau will want to take a closer look at Dr. Prince, and we'd like your cooperation. I'll need your contact information so someone from the Anchorage Field Office can get in touch with you." She'd let McKee take it from here.

Herschel nodded and reached for a notepad and pen on the bedside table. He jotted down his address and phone number and handed the paper to Regan.

She stood. "I'll make sure Vargas gets your letter. If she wants to talk to you, she can reach you here?"

"Only for a couple more hours. I'm flying back to Anchorage tonight."

"Maybe you should stick around another day."

"I can't. Harry's home alone and might be low on food. I have to go."

"You have a relative who lives with you?"

"No – no family. Harry's my cat."

Regan felt a stab of pity for Herschel. A lonely man, isolated not only by intellect but also by circumstance.

CHAPTER TWENTY-EIGHT

A DEAD body?"

Vargas folded her arms tightly across her abdomen, so upset that, for the moment anyway, she forgot to be angry at Regan for her outburst earlier. "Do you have any idea why this Cory person was planting the pipe bombs?"

"Here's what we know, Madame Secretary," said Regan. She explained Cory's relationship to Randall Strathman, and Strathman's involvement in the Green Globe Defense League. "What we don't know is whether Green Globe is trying to make a comeback, or if this is an isolated set of events aimed at you and the Alaska Energy Summit. Whoever Cory was working with wants to get your attention."

"I see," said Vargas. She moved to the window, staring at the street below. "Some of the protestors have gone home," she noted, mostly to herself.

Trevor sat in a chair nearby, his face a stony mask.

"We're checking the numbers on his Blackberry to see who he's been talking to," Regan said. "And of course we'll put the squeeze on Strathman."

Trevor shifted in his seat.

"Keep me informed," said Vargas.

"One other thing," said Regan. "Herschel Baker, the environmentalist who requested the meeting with you earlier, wrote you a letter." Regan took it from her pocket and held it out to her.

Vargas looked at it like Regan was attempting to hand her a snake.

"Remember you told him to write to you?"

Vargas nodded.

"Well, he did. I've personally checked it out; it isn't tainted with anything and it doesn't contain threats of any kind."

Vargas took the envelope and set it on the coffee table. "Fine."

Regan sighed. "Madame Secretary, I think you should read it. Mr. Baker is extremely knowledgeable about Alaska's environmental issues."

"He's an eco-terrorist," Trevor declared.

"No, Mr. Wolf, he isn't. There is nothing in his background to support that. If you're simply saying that because he frightened you, you're off-base." Regan kept her voice even, careful not to use a strident tone.

"I'd bet money he's the one who killed that bomber."

His statement stunned her. "Why would you say that?"

"Because he's probably the one that hired the guy in the first place. Wanted to run us out of here. Something probably went wrong – maybe they got into an argument – so he killed him. Or maybe he planned all along to get rid of him after he didn't need him to plant any more bombs."

Vargas gaped at Trevor. "Do you think so? It makes sense. You have to admit, Agent Manning, it makes sense."

"No, Madame Secretary, it *doesn't* make sense to accuse someone of murder simply because he is protesting a nuclear waste facility. That logic would implicate at least a thousand people. Baker wasn't even among them when they stormed the hotel."

Trevor said sharply, "Didn't you cuff him?"

"We took him in for questioning only because he was on the premises when we asked him not to be. But he wasn't part of the invading crowd." Regan wasn't going to supply additional details.

"And you just let him go?"

"Yes, we let him go."

Trevor looked at Vargas and made a gesture that said *See how incompetent these people are?*

Regan bristled. "And now it's your turn, Mr. Wolf. I'd like to ask you a few questions. Please come with me."

CHAPTER TWENTY-NINE

MAC BREATHED a sigh of relief. "Hey, man, I was starting to worry about you. Thought maybe Alaska broke off and sank into the Bering Sea."

Trevor said, "No, things have just been a little nuts lately … you know, with the summit and all. Sorry I didn't call you back yesterday."

"That's okay. Hey, I hear some protestors invaded the Baranof."

Trevor gave a snort. "Tried to crash the summit meeting, demanded that the secretary remove the nuclear waste facility from the energy plan. Like *that's* going to happen."

"Really? The word we're getting from Bob Carney is that Vargas needs to start looking for an alternative site."

"Oh – uh, well, he may be right. I mean, there *has* been a lot of opposition to the secretary's plan in its current form. She knows there will have to be some major revisions before it'll pass."

What the hell is going on?

In a story in the *Washington Post* that morning, Secretary Vargas was quoted as saying she remained confident that the energy plan she proposed would be adopted by Congress and sent to the president.

His flip-flopping puzzled Mac. "Hey, Trev? Are you really okay?"

"Sure," Trevor said quickly. "Why wouldn't I be?"

"I don't know. You don't sound like yourself."

"No, I'm good. More than good. I met a girl."

Met a girl? Trevor hadn't dated anyone since Mac and his girlfriend, Sara, had set him up with one of Sara's friends more than a year ago. It had been a disaster; Sara's friend still wasn't speaking to her.

"Yeah? You gonna stay up there and settle down?"

"Nah," said Trevor. "She's an FBI agent. I told her she should transfer to D.C."

Smooth. "Hey, that's great, Trev."

"Her name's Lindsay. She's really ... hot." He giggled like an eighth grader.

"Okay, well tell Lindsay your buddy Mac says hi. So what do you think ... is Vargas facing serious opposition to her plan? You think a September launch is still possible or are we looking at a delay?"

"Uh, it's hard to say. Someone said Axis isn't quite ready with that new extraction tool, so maybe September isn't realistic anymore."

"Someone like Vargas?" The only other someone who knew that was Carney.

"Yeah, I think so. She said we may be looking at a delay."

An uneasy feeling bloomed in Mac's chest. Vargas would never in a million years cave to the oil man.

"Hey, Trev, did you get a chance to talk to Bob before he left there?"

"A little here and there. Why?"

"No reason. Just wondered if he said anything about the tanker explosion."

"No, not really. Just that it could be the IRG that planted the floating mines."

His words landed like a physical blow. Carney didn't know about the suspected involvement of the Iranian Revolutionary Guard until *after* he left Alaska. Mac was sure of that because he was the one who told him.

Which meant there was no way for Trevor to know. Unless he talked to Carney.

CHAPTER THIRTY

IT WAS the last day. Vargas was running out of time.

There's not a snowball's chance in hell, she thought gloomily. *These people won't budge.*

She dressed and applied makeup by rote, her thoughts consumed with what she would say to the president. Was there *any* way to paint this that didn't make her look bad?

On the phone an hour ago, her husband tried to reassure her that things would work out, even if she was forced to step down. "I'm a doctor. You're a lawyer. We won't starve, Ella."

"I know, Peter," she said. "But I have no desire to practice law. And the kids are in high school. If I was suddenly a stay-at-home mom after all these years, they'd freak."

Peter laughed. "Honey, I think you're jumping the gun. Maybe Sanford won't look at it that you oversold the Alaska nuclear waste site. Maybe that's just *your* assessment."

"Believe me, he'll look at it that way. You don't know how eager he is to get that facility built so we can get on with putting up more nuclear power plants."

"Ella, you'll land on your feet like you always do."

Peter the friendly pediatrician, the eternal optimist. It's what she loved about him, but this morning his exuberance made her want to reach through the phone and choke him.

Her cell phone rang again. Did he want to give her one more dose of annoying cheer?

But it wasn't Peter. It was a former aide named Eric whom she'd helped to land a plum job as head of marketing at Hanston Oil.

After some friendly chitchat, Eric got down to the reason for his call. "I heard something that I think could make your day," he said.

"Good, because my day isn't looking so good. What'd you hear?"

"Bob Carney might be trying to bribe government officials in the Caspian region."

Vargas's heart started to thump. "How credible is your information, Eric?"

"Very," he said. "One of those officials contacted our CEO – through a third party, of course – and more or less invited him to make a counter-offer."

"Did the official name Carney?"

"No, he referred to him as 'one of your competitors.' All the oil companies are exploring non-Gulf regions, but only Axis is aggressively ramping up operations in the Caspian right now. Has to be Carney."

Vargas had to restrain herself from shouting *YES!* into the phone and scaring poor Eric half to death.

"And there's more," he said.

Vargas felt giddy. "What?"

"That rotary steerable device that Axis is developing? Carney fired the engineer who designed it as soon as the schematics were complete because the guy had the nerve to expect the promotion he was promised. Guess where he works now?"

"Hanston?"

"You got it."

If Hanston gets its act together, it can steal the lead out from under Axis.

"You're right, Eric. You did make my day."

❧

REGAN AND Nick hadn't been able to squeeze much out of Trevor. She pressed him on his relationship with Robert Carney; he flatly denied anything more than simply knowing the man, acknowledged that Carney and his boss weren't the best of friends. But by the end of the interrogation, the smirk had disappeared at least. Victory.

Now it was time to deliver some bad news to Strathman.

"I'm sorry to have to tell you this, Randall, but your brother Cory is dead."

Silence on the other end.

"Randall?"

"I'm here."

"We saw the email you sent him. The one where you told him to get out of town. Said it wasn't his fight. Whose fight is it?"

"I don't know." His voice was strained with grief.

"I think you do. And I think it's in your best interest to tell me." More silence.

"C'mon, Randall, talk to me."

"You can't prove I had anything to do with it," he said quietly.

"Oh, I'm pretty sure I can, but that's beside the point. I'm more interested in Cory's involvement. If you fill me in on that, I'll consider not telling Monroe officials about your outside activities."

Strathman was silent for so long she thought maybe he'd hung up.

"Randall?"

"Yeah?"

"Do we have a deal?"

"I'll get back to you."

CHAPTER THIRTY-ONE

CARNEY WAS temporarily speechless.

"Bob? Are you there?"

"Yes, I'm here."

"Good. And just so we're clear, I believe that what you're attempting to do is a violation of the Foreign Corrupt Practices Act. I'd sure hate to see you have to trade mansion living for a jail cell, my friend."

Vargas hadn't felt so pumped since Sanford named her to the cabinet.

"I don't know who your sources are, Ella, but they're feeding you a line of bull." She noticed he spoke without much fervor, and his voice held a slight tremor.

She had him by the balls.

"Well, then, I guess we'll just have to play it out and see where it leads us. Goodbye, Bob."

"Wait."

❧

HOW MUCH did Vargas really know? And who told her?

"I'm not admitting to this ridiculous charge, Ella, but I don't want the hassle of an investigation, either. What do you want?"

He already knew.

"Support for the energy plan."

He hated this woman.

"The timeline for reducing foreign oil imports is unrealistic, maybe even dangerous," he said.

"Then they can talk about that in committee. Let members of Congress weigh in, see if anyone agrees with you."

Carney knew most of them would be tempted to bow to pressure from their constituents to step up alternative energy, but he would dump enough cash into a lobbying effort to make sure they didn't vote that way.

"Fine," he said. "I'll support the plan."

"Excellent. I look forward to working with you on its passage, Bob."

❧

"CAN YOU talk?"

"Yeah, I stepped out of the meeting. What's up, Bob?"

"We have a problem," said Carney. "Vargas found out about the Caspian deal."

"Who told her?" Trevor spoke in a frantic whisper.

"That's what I want to know." Carney's tone held a veiled accusation.

"Wait, you don't think *I* told her, do you?

"Don't know, Trevor. Someone did."

"Not me, Bob. I'm not suicidal."

"Well, we're going to need to do something about this."

"What?" The frantic whisper again.

"I think you know."

"Now wait, Bob —"

"It's not like you haven't solved problems before, Trevor."

"Yeah, well, I didn't plan for it to go that way. Cory said he wanted out, said he was leaving Juneau. He was all shook up. I had no choice."

"I assume you're still interested in the position here at Axis, correct?"

"Yes, of course. It's just that —"

"Well I have some good news, Trevor. You just got a promotion. How do you like that? A promotion before you're even officially on board." Carney chuckled. "I think you'll like it … you're going to be my chief assistant."

"Your chief assistant?"

"That's right, Trevor. And it comes with a hefty pay raise over your *old* job as the assistant to Axis's R & D director." He laughed.

"Okay," Trevor said with a sigh. "Consider the problem solved."

CHAPTER THIRTY-TWO

THE WEATHER gods pulled out all the stops for the summiteers' last night in Juneau. After three straight days of drizzle, the sun was a treasure.

Regan had forgotten how delectable fresh-caught Alaska salmon was, even more so accompanied by the smell of the campfire and the fragrance of the trees that crowded around the group at Perseverance.

Spirits were high, especially Ella Vargas's; somehow she'd managed to pull off a victory and get the group to go along with the energy plan. The only exception was the nuclear waste facility in Alaska, which she promised to subject to further scrutiny along with other potential sites. For now, that was enough to satisfy its detractors.

The group, sated with good food and Alaskan ale, settled in to listen to forest ranger Jack Landis give a talk on the Tongass National Forest. After that, he would lead a group hike for those who were interested.

Regan's team and the Anchorage agents had arranged themselves in a perimeter around the summiteers. Nick kept peering at the woods behind him.

"Son," Regan whispered, "bears are a fact of life up here. Don't worry; I'll punch their lights out if they try to eat you." Her impersonation of McKee was dead on.

Nick chuckled. "No worries; I can run like a bunny rabbit, remember? Hey, where is the fearless McKee, anyway?"

"He stayed at the Baranof to man the command post. I suggested he have one of the less senior agents do it, but he insisted."

"What a strange duck."

Regan nodded. "I think he's a little socially awkward."

"You're very astute."

"Thank you." Regan turned her attention to Jack Landis. The man was certainly easy on the eye.

She'd introduced herself to Jack before dinner, chatted with him while the others filled their plates. He had a quality that drew her – a placidness that was absent in the men she was typically around. But then again, they were agents and cops. Placidness could get them killed.

The fervor in Jack's eyes as he spoke to the group revealed that, for him, forestry wasn't just a job. It was a calling. Like law enforcement was for her.

She spotted Vargas and Trevor off to one side engaged in deep conversation, the chief of staff nodding while his boss spoke. Vargas pointed to a trail nearby, and they moved toward it.

Regan jumped up and rushed over to them. "Are you two going for a hike?"

"Yes, we are," Vargas said curtly. "We have a confidential matter to discuss."

"It might be better if you go with the group. You could hang at the back where no one can hear your conversation."

"Thanks for your concern, Agent Manning, but we'll be fine." Vargas's voice was firm. "We're just going to walk up to the falls that the ranger talked about."

"Ebner Falls. And I'm coming with you. I'll stay out of earshot."

"No, Agent Manning, you are *not* coming with us."

"Madame Secretary, my primary duty is to ensure your safety. I can't do that if I let you out of my sight in an open area like this. Please, I'd like your cooperation."

C'mon, lady, give me a break.

"There's no real danger. The bomber is dead, the summit is over. We won't go far."

Vargas was not going to yield. Regan decided not to argue the point further; she would simply follow them, stay out of sight.

She made a gesture that said, *Fine, go ahead.*

They moved off, Vargas's cherry-colored shirt soon swallowed by the trees.

CHAPTER THIRTY-THREE

TREVOR SEEMED as floored by the news as she had been. "So you still keep in touch with your former aides, huh?"

"Not all of them, but Eric was different," said Vargas. "We were on the same wavelength from day one." Suddenly aware of Trevor's feelings, she said, "But you're better at some things than he was." Even though she couldn't think of anything right off hand.

"Sounds like he's still loyal to you," Trevor said quietly.

"I think he feels indebted because I pulled strings to get him his job at Hanston. But he had also watched Carney and I square off over and over again. He knew I'd want to know about Carney's little back-room deal."

"Pretty good timing."

"Unbelievable. Now without Carney pushing back on the timeline for foreign oil imports, the other oil execs will follow his lead since he's been carrying their water for the past decade." She turned to her chief of staff. "Trevor, our little energy plan is back on skates."

"But what about the nuclear waste facility?"

She gave him a sly grin. "Further study will show that the interior of Alaska is still the best place. We'll have an easier time getting it approved away from here. I hate to admit it, Trevor, but these Alaskans are harder nuts to crack than I expected."

As they neared Ebner Falls, the trail sloped downward at a precipitous angle on their right. Vargas stopped to catch her breath, perching on a fallen log. She grew still, letting the scents and the sounds of the forest invade her senses.

"I've missed the woods," she told Trevor. "I'll be glad to get back to Colorado when I've finished my work in Washington." The Rockies beckoned her, but she wanted to return on her own terms, not because she was forced out of her post.

"The woods feel oppressive to me," said Trevor, glancing around. He seemed out of sorts.

Vargas laughed. "Not surprising for a Kansas boy. You're used to those wide open spaces."

He turned and looked at her, searching her face.

"What is it, Trevor?"

"Nothing. Why don't we keep going?"

"Yep, let's keep going." She popped up, glancing at the sky. The sun didn't show any signs of going down. It was summer solstice, when the days were at their longest point; the daylight would stick around for at least three more hours.

"I wonder how Alaskans fall asleep at night with all this sunlight," she mused. As she walked, she tilted toward the left to keep her distance from the steep slope on the other side.

Trevor didn't answer. Her mind had just registered that he was awfully close to her when she felt his hands on her shoulders. A split second later, she was tumbling downward, sharp branches poking at her like a mob of angry protestors.

She flailed her arms, attempting to grab something to break her fall. After what seemed like forever, her body plowed into a tree, knocking the wind out of her. Dazed, she lay gasping for breath.

A limb had torn a gash in her left shoulder, but she hardly felt it. The shock of Trevor's betrayal had left her numb.

What is he doing? Why is he trying to hurt me?

Quaking with fear, she peered up, trying to see if he was still there. She couldn't see him through the dense brush.

She gingerly pushed herself up and tried to assess the damage. Apart from the blood trickling down her arm, she was in pretty good shape. If she'd landed three feet to the left, a huge boulder would have broken her fall – and likely every bone in her body.

Would Trevor come after her, try again? She cursed her choice of the red shirt; she couldn't be easier to spot if she carried a flashing neon sign.

Vargas crawled behind the huge rock. She knew he had to be coming for her.

She cursed herself for not letting Agent Manning follow at a discreet distance. She had acted petty – but she hadn't expected her chief of staff to toss her off a cliff.

She left her cell phone in her room. If she screamed for help, would anyone besides Trevor hear her? She remembered that the FBI cleared the area of other hikers for the evening, so it wasn't likely.

Where can I hide?

She spotted a mine entrance a couple hundred yards away. Could she make it without Trevor seeing her?

She popped her head up from behind the rock and did a quick scan. She heard the gentle rustle of leaves, heard water running in a creek nearby. Didn't hear footsteps.

Vargas pulled herself up on shaky legs and began running, tentatively at first, then picking up speed as she pushed through the heavy underbrush.

And then the rustle of leaves above her turned to thrashing. She looked up and back to the left; Trevor had spotted her, and he was closing in.

≈

REGAN HAD lost sight of the cherry-red shirt. She stopped to listen, didn't hear their voices anymore.

She started to sprint. If she caught up to them and pissed off the secretary, so be it; she had a job to do.

The trail turned narrow and steep on one side; she looked down, wondering if they could've slipped. "Secretary Vargas?" Her voice echoed through the trees.

No reply.

Regan began running again, scanning the area as she went. Where could they be?

She tried to remember what Vargas had said. Something about a confidential topic. But all evening she'd seemed euphoric, even neglecting the dirty looks. Had she and Trevor planned something to take place on Perseverance Trail?

Regan couldn't fathom what it would be – or why.

She tried calling their names again, but there was still no reply. She pulled out her phone. "I need your help, Nick – I can't find Vargas and Wolf."

"Okay, where are you?"

"Remember the trail they took, that I followed them on?"

"Yep."

"Just stay on it. Bring four or five of our people with you – and Jack Landis."

CHAPTER THIRTY-FOUR

REGAN STARED at the gaping mouth of the mine and shivered. Just inside the entrance sat a row of supplies, including lanterns. She peered into the darkness but saw no light emanating from anywhere.

Why would they come in here? Abandoned mines were perilous places to be. She learned that lesson the hard way.

"Let's go back," her best friend Samantha had said. "This place freaks me out." The rest of the group watched Regan, waiting for her cue. Waiting to see if they should be scared, too.

Maybe it was the beer that made her so daring. But if they were caught drinking, her dad's friend, Chief Lamont, might lock them up. She'd be kicked off the basketball team because she'd signed a pledge to adhere to the zero-tolerance policy.

Still, it felt good to be reckless for a change, to tempt fate. "C'mon, Sam, don't be a weenie. Let's keep going."

She shivered as she stepped back into the sunlight to call the chief.

Lamont sighed loudly. "Damn ... I thought we were home free. The summit's over, they're about to get out of here. And now this."

"I'm not planning to let that jet leave town without them tomorrow, Chief. Could you get a chopper over here to search? Tell them the secretary's wearing a red shirt so she should be easy to spot."

"Will do. Let me know if you need additional backup."

A few minutes later, Nick and the others showed up.

"Okay, people, let's divide up and search the area. We'll have chopper assistance shortly. Nick and Jack, I'd like you two to stay here." After getting their assigned areas, the rest of the officers took off at a fast clip.

She turned to Jack. "How familiar are you with this mine?"

He made a wavering motion with his hand. "Somewhat – I went in it with Joe Percy a couple summers ago. He's the mine manager."

"How far in?"

"Quite a ways, but not all the way to the other end that comes out just off Thane Road."

"This mine connects to *that* one?" Good thing she hadn't known that when the teenagers got the idea to go exploring that summer night. She might've coaxed them into hiking all the way to the other end, just to see if they could make it.

Maybe she'd have ended up with a worse injury than the cut above her left elbow that required almost seventy stitches. She'd been lucky it wasn't her shooting arm.

It was the first time Regan saw her dad so furious he couldn't speak.

"Yeah, this section here is the Alaska Gastineau, also called Perseverance Mine, and it connects with the old AJ – Alaska Juneau – mine."

"The mine ruins that used to sit on the side of Mount Roberts … what was that structure?"

"The part that was imploded? That was AJ's mill operation."

"Hmm," she said. All she knew was that the ruins on the mountainside inexplicably drew her – and somehow she talked her friends into going along. She'd always been something of a leader, but it was her first inkling of the power she wielded. It took a few more years to fully comprehend the responsibility that came with it.

Now, she would never deliberately lead people into harm's way. Unless there was simply no other choice.

"Okay, I think we better get Joe Percy here to help us out. I'll have Detective Brice go get him."

As she talked to Danny, she observed Jack poking around nearby, surveying the scene with the ease of someone who was entirely in his element.

He intrigued her. The man had an air that contrasted sharply with the energy of law enforcement types. His wavy light brown hair was streaked with gold from all the time spent outdoors; he wore it longer than the close-cropped style worn by most of her colleagues. His brown eyes were warm, inviting, not expecting trouble around every corner. And he looked *really* good in that ranger shirt and jeans.

When she hung up, Regan told Nick, "Danny will get the mine manager here shortly. I hope we won't need him, but at least he'll be on standby."

She paused a moment, looking down.

"What is it, Reegs?"

"I shouldn't have let Vargas go off without me. This shouldn't have happened."

"If you recall, she didn't give you a choice."

"Doesn't matter, Nick. It's my responsibility to protect her, and I *didn't*."

Nick put his hands on her arms. "Stop blaming yourself. She's a high-ranking government official, and she gave you a direct order. Besides, we're going to find her."

Regan searched his eyes, saw the faith there, drew strength from it. She nodded.

Jack made his way back over to them.

Regan said, "How far into this end of the mine can someone go before things get pretty hazardous?" She and her friends had entered on the other end.

"Here, I'll show you. There's a mine map just inside the entrance." Jack led them to it, pointing as he explained. "The mine has thirteen levels and lots of areas of decay. Without a lantern, they'd flat-out be risking their lives. Even *with* one, it's dicey."

Why would they come in here? What possible reason could they have?

An image niggled at the back of her brain: the look on Trevor's face when Regan pulled Carney out of the meeting to tell him about the tanker explosion. Was he tied up with Carney?

If he was, it put a whole different spin on things. Maybe Vargas had gone from being Trevor's boss to being his hostage.

She heard the chopper overhead and crossed her fingers. Her phone vibrated on her belt; a number she didn't recognize. "Manning."

It was Randall Strathman. "I'll take the deal."

CHAPTER THIRTY-FIVE

VARGAS'S BODY shook from head to toe. She was terrified of the mine, even more terrified of her chief of staff.

"Why, Trevor? I don't understand." Her voice echoed in the cavern.

In the lantern light, his pale face reminded her of someone who'd come back from the dead. "Be quiet," he growled.

She'd been crazy to run in here, to think she could hide from him. It had taken him less than five minutes to find her cowering in an indentation only steps from the entrance. But she hadn't dared to go further into the creepy darkness without a lamp.

Now, they picked their way alongside the old track that once transported rail cars filled with gold ore. The rails were rotted in places, the ground uneven. Vargas watched her step, trying not to stumble.

"Trevor, please. I'll give you anything you want. Whoever's paying you to do this, I'll double their offer."

He stopped and stared at her. "Always controlling things, aren't you?" His voice was filled with contempt.

"Is it Carney? Did he hire you to ... do this?" She couldn't bring herself to say *get rid of me*.

"I said to be quiet." He started moving faster, pulling her along beside him.

They lurched along in silence for twenty minutes or more, Trevor holding the lantern aloft every so often as though he were looking for something. Maybe a way to escape. Maybe a way to finish the job he started before.

The gash in her shoulder ached. She peered through the slice in her shirt to see how deep it was; she couldn't tell, but it still oozed blood.

"Can we rest a minute, Trevor? My shoulder really hurts."

Trevor stopped, holding the lamp up, his haunted face revealing the inner turmoil he felt. "Sit over there." He pointed to a hollowed-out spot.

Vargas sat against the rock wall and closed her eyes. What if she never saw Peter and the kids again? She thought of thirteen-year-old Maria, bubbly and sociable like her dad; handsome Gabe, at sixteen already a debate champion and tennis standout at his school. Good kids. Loving husband.

What if I never hear their sweet voices again?

She put her face in her hands and wept.

"This isn't about you," Trevor said in a low voice. He sat ten feet away, arms perched on his bent knees.

Vargas looked up. She wiped her eyes and waited for him to go on.

"I'm just tired of always being at the bottom of the heap."

"Trevor, I've never treated you that way. I've never —"

"I finally have a chance to be somebody, and I'm not going to pass it up."

"I told you," she pleaded, "I'll sweeten any deal you've been given. Please, Trevor. I want to go home to Peter and the kids."

"Must be nice," he muttered.

Was he softening? Did she dare nudge him further?

No, get him talking about something else.

"Tell me about your family in Kansas. Do you get to see them very often?" It occurred to her that she'd never asked about them before.

"No. Dad and my two brothers do just fine without me. He always said I wasn't a natural farmer like they were." His face was etched with bitterness.

"And they don't have a brilliant legal mind like you do."

"I've never practiced a day of law in my life. Too busy following politicians like you around." The note of contempt crept back in.

Keep him calm.

"Politicians like me are worthless without people like you, Trevor. I've always said that it's the legislative staff members who are really running things in Washington." She'd actually never said that, but there was a kernel of truth to it. "You guys are the ones who keep us all on track."

"And yet *you* guys are the ones who make the big bucks, get all the glory."

"Then become one of us, Trevor. Run for office. You'd be great."

He made a scoffing sound. "You don't get it, do you?"

"What?"

"I've never won any popularity contests. I probably couldn't even get my own family to vote for me."

His remark struck a sad chord; she'd never focused on the man enough to really understand him. He'd simply been someone there to serve her needs.

"I'm sorry I haven't taken the time to know you better, Trevor. I truly am. And I promise to change that. From now on, I'll give you a much broader role in my office. I'll give you the authority you've earned."

He stared at his feet, quiet.

Please let him believe me.

Trevor reached up and pulled the back of his hand across his eyes. He jumped to his feet. "C'mon, let's keep going."

"Where? It's too dangerous in here. Please … can't we go back?"

He reached down and grabbed her injured arm, jerking her up. "As I said, I have a chance that I'm not going to pass up."

CHAPTER THIRTY-SIX

I'LL DO my best to keep this from coming back on you, Randall," said Regan. "Now tell me what you know."

He hesitated a moment before answering. "Trevor Wolf came to see me. Said he was looking for names of some old Green Globe members who could do a little work for him. Cory needed money really bad – he was living on the street in Portland. So I gave his name to Wolf."

"You offered up your own brother?"

"Half-brother. It's not like we shared bunk beds growing up. I didn't even meet him until we were in high school. But still, I didn't expect him to be in danger. He was only supposed to spend the summer in Juneau, get a job, plant a couple bombs. Nobody was supposed to get hurt."

Regan said, "Was he Green Globe's bombmaker?"

"Sort of —" He coughed.

"Sort of a bombmaker? Either he was or he wasn't."

"Okay," he sighed loudly, "he was."

"Who was Wolf working for?"

"He didn't tell me that. And I wasn't dumb enough to ask."

"No, you were just dumb enough to get your brother killed."

"Don't you think I know that? I have to live with that the rest of my life." She could hear the desolation in his voice.

"I'll be in touch, Randall." Regan hung up.

So Trevor hired Cory. Maybe Trevor killed Cory, too.

And that meant that Ella Vargas was in deep trouble.

❧

BY THE time Joe Percy arrived with Danny, the officers scouring the designated area, along with the chopper pilots, had reported in. No sign of the secretary. The mine was the only choice left.

I'd rather eat bugs than go in there, Regan thought miserably.

"City maintenance crew started doing some work in here today," said Joe. "Otherwise this stuff wouldn't be sitting here." He pointed to the lanterns, hard hats, and other supplies near the entrance. "And your visitors would be stumbling around in a space where you can't see your hand two inches in front of you."

"How far is it to the other end?" said Regan.

"Four-and-a-half miles."

"How hazardous?"

"Very. There are a series of tunnels you have to move through to get to the other end, and many of them have obstacles – rusty old mining equipment, large pieces of rock, stuff like that. There are also holes in the floor that the miners used to move between levels. Many of the ladders are rotten."

"Don't you conduct tours in the mine?"

"Down on the other end, and we don't go too far in. It's all staged and tightly controlled. We bore some holes into rock and demonstrate the ore-crushing process the miners used to use. The tourists aren't allowed to wander off on their own."

"What about those who enter here like Vargas and Wolf did?"

"We can't control that. It's no different than the trails or the glacier or anyplace else that has potentially dangerous features. The area's loaded with them."

"So it's enter at your own risk," said Nick.

"Right, and most people don't have to get very far in to see that the risk is substantial," said Joe. "They usually turn back."

Unless you're too pig-headed and full of yourself.

"I'm going to give the bullhorn a try, see if I can get them to respond," she said to no one in particular. It was a last-ditch effort.

She reached for the bullhorn Nick had brought along. "Secretary Vargas, are you in here?" Regan's voice ricocheted through the cavern. She waited a moment, then said, "Trevor Wolf, if you can hear me, please respond."

C'mon, Trevor. Do me a freakin' favor and come out.

"Secretary Vargas, can you hear me?"

No answer. *Damn.*

"Okay," she sighed, "I guess we're going to have to go in."

"I'll come with you," said Jack.

"Me, too," said Joe.

"That won't be necessary," Danny said quickly. "We need to keep it to law enforcement."

Regan turned to look at him. "At this point, we don't have any reason to think Trevor is armed, Danny. And Joe and Jack have a much better knowledge of this mine than any of us. If they're willing, I'm grateful for their help."

Danny gave her a look of annoyance. He never liked her to argue with him, which made her do it every chance she got.

"Okay, Joe," she said, "why don't you tell us what to do?"

The mine manager grabbed hard hats with lamps from the pile of supplies nearby and began handing them out. "For starters, let's get these on."

CHAPTER THIRTY-SEVEN

TREVOR WAS growing increasingly agitated. The secretary kept glancing at him out of the corner of her eye, just in case he tried to push her again.

Suddenly he stepped into a hole and stumbled sideways, catching himself but dropping the lantern. Vargas snatched it up, debated plunking him in the head and shoving him into oblivion.

Two problems: using the lantern as a weapon might cause it to break; there was no way she could get out of here alive without it. And she wasn't a murderer.

"Give it to me," he growled when he got to his feet.

She handed him the lantern, sorry she hadn't shoved him while he was off-balance. She'd been afraid he'd grab her arm and take her with him.

So it really wasn't about murder at all. After all, he was probably planning to do the same thing to her.

What was stopping him?

"Trevor, I know I should've paid more attention to you – I see that now," she said through chattering teeth. "I mean, an intelligent man like you with tons of talent should be playing a much more prominent role in the Energy Department."

And who knows, maybe you will when you get out of prison.

She saw a glimmer of hope in his eyes, saw that he wanted to believe they could walk out of here and return to Washington as though nothing had happened.

"Secretary Vargas, are you in here?" Regan's voice echoed way off in the distance. "Trevor Wolf, if you can hear me, please respond."

Agent Manning was her new best friend.

Trevor stopped, his shoulders stiffening. The tiny sliver of hope in his eyes vanished, replaced by the frantic look of a trapped animal.

"Trevor," Vargas said quickly, "I'll tell them we wanted to explore the mine and got lost. I won't tell them about you pushing me. I *promise*."

"Like they'll buy that."

"Why wouldn't they? They've never seen any discord between us." *She* hadn't even seen any discord between them, which is why Trevor's actions shocked her.

For several moments, Trevor was silent. Then he turned and looked at her, his face a mask of resignation. "Okay."

᷿

MAC PUT in a call to Carney. "What's going on with the oil import timeline? Did you back off?"

"Yeah," said Carney, his voice a little too casual. "We were spinning our wheels, so I decided to go along with Vargas for now. I'll get it stopped when Congress gets hold of the plan."

"I see," said Mac. He'd never known the oil man to back off a fight, especially with Ella Vargas. "Have you talked to Trevor?"

"Trevor? No, why would I talk to Trevor?"

"He mentioned the Revolutionary Guard having something to do with the tanker explosion. I just wondered how he knew that since I didn't tell him."

"Don't know," Carney said, his usual Texas drawl strangely absent. "You'll have to ask him."

"I would if he'd answer his phone." Mac gave a forced laugh, trying to soften the veiled accusation he'd just made.

"I think they're supposed to be at a place called Perseverance tonight. Salmon bake. Maybe Trevor went off on a hike."

"Maybe so," said Mac. "So unless a bear got him, I'm sure he'll call me back."

"I'm sure he will."

The conversation left Mac more convinced than ever that Trevor was mixed up with Carney. As soon as his friend got back to Washington, Mac was going to set him straight.

It was true, Trevor had a king-sized chip on his shoulder. But Carney was the *last* one who should knock it off.

CHAPTER THIRTY-EIGHT

THE FLASHLIGHTS and head lamps cast a wide glow and helped them circumvent the hazards, but Regan was still on edge. Had it been this suffocating, this *treacherous,* all those years ago when she insisted they keep going?

Insane.

She peered at the craggy walls and hard-packed earthen floors as they picked their way along. How did miners do it?

"Kinda creepy, isn't it?" Jack had moved up beside her.

"Totally," she said. "Miners must feel like moles, burrowing underground all the time. Can you imagine what it'd be like in the winter? You'd never see the sun."

Jack smiled. "I'd go crazy. I've gotta be outdoors."

"Me, too." The vast difference between Jack's outdoors and hers struck her. The forest versus city streets.

"How long have you lived in Juneau, Jack?" she asked.

"Almost five years."

So he'd arrived shortly after she left.

"Like it?"

"Love it. I was a Navy brat with no roots until I got here. First time I set foot in this town, I knew I was home."

Regan started to reply, but she heard a sound. She held up her hand and everyone stopped. "Secretary Vargas? Trevor?"

No reply, but they heard definite movement coming from a tunnel off to their right. She drew her weapon and signaled for the others to follow her.

"Ooph," said Danny as he tripped over a rock and fell. "Shit."

"You okay?" said Regan. She and Nick both reached to help him up, but he waved them off.

He jumped up and stomped ahead. Regan and Nick exchanged a smile.

Off in the distance, she saw a tiny fragment of light. "Secretary Vargas?"

"We're okay," Trevor yelled back.

Thank God ... she's alive.

She'd been more fearful about Vargas's fate than she'd admitted to herself. Beyond the obvious relief for the secretary's sake, Regan simply couldn't afford to blow this mission.

Without her career, she was nothing.

The group picked up speed through the narrow tunnel, skirting the debris in their path. "Keep moving toward us," she called.

Soon they could make out two dark silhouettes coming toward them, the shape of a man and a woman illuminated by a single lantern.

స

THE CLOSER they came, the more nervous Trevor got. It looked like an army advancing toward them. How many were there?

He knew Vargas too well, knew she would never let him go unpunished. She was lying to him to save herself.

He should have stabbed her instead of shoving her off that cliff, but he couldn't bring himself to do it. She hadn't been cruel to him, just dismissive; he lacked the vengeance to thrust a knife into her back. Pushing her meant that any injuries she sustained, fatal or otherwise, weren't directly administered by him. And that helped him justify what he had to do.

Regan led the pack as it moved closer.

They know I killed Cory. I'm going to be arrested.

As Trevor slid his hand into his pocket, he recalled the old line: *Never bring a knife to a gunfight.* But any weapon was better than none, even if it was just an Alaskan souvenir that was never intended to be a murder weapon.

"Secretary Vargas, are you all right?" said Regan.

"I'm okay," she said, her voice quivering as she reached up and cupped a hand over her shoulder wound. "We got lost, and I took a nasty spill."

Trevor watched her face to make sure she wasn't giving off distress signals. He clutched the ivory-handled knife and considered his options.

Shove the knife between her ribs, eliminate Carney's problem. Feel the bullets rip through me, eliminate mine.

"Trevor?" said Regan. "Are you okay?"

She hadn't reholstered her gun. She knew.

I will not go to prison. The visit with Strathman at Monroe had nearly suffocated him.

Trevor moved fast, flinging an arm around Vargas, knife blade at her neck. "Take one more step and she dies."

"Trevor, no ..." The secretary's voice was pierced with anguish.

In less than a heartbeat, a row of guns was pointed at his head.

"Drop the knife, Trevor." Regan's voice was low and lethal.

He flipped off the lantern and kept his head behind Vargas's, her body shielding him as he inched backward into the inky darkness.

CHAPTER THIRTY-NINE

THEY PICKED their way along the narrow tunnel, keeping Trevor and Vargas in their sights. The smell, a mixture of earth and rust, transported Regan back to her teenage trek. Just like before, the unceasing darkness gave her the sense that something sinister lurked in the shadows, but this time she had no desire to find out what it was.

She began breathing deeply, sucking air into her lungs. "Looks like we're about to get some field experience in hostage negotiation," she said, trying to distract herself.

"Like I said before, you talk, I'll aim," replied Nick.

"I hope talking is all it will take." The words of former FBI hostage negotiator Clint Van Zandt slithered through her brain: *We can always kill 'em tomorrow.*

Regan had ordered the team to establish a perimeter around both ends of the mine to cut off any means of escape for Trevor. Now she ran through her mental checklist before initiating formal contact with the chief-of-staff-turned-hostage-taker.

Too bad Trevor hates me. It put her behind the eight ball starting out – meant she'd have to work harder to establish a connection with him.

She tried to push back the self-doubt that had plagued her throughout the mission, tried to get her head into that space where, until now, FBI operations always took her: calm confidence, the certainty that she would do everything humanly possible to get a positive result. No lives lost.

The irony of the situation wasn't lost on her. Throughout the summit, both she and Ella Vargas had been fighting for their professional lives. She understood the secretary's refusal to admit defeat, fully comprehended the cost of failure.

They were after the same thing. Both wanted a win.

But right now it was their personal lives that mattered. Vargas needed to go home to her family; Regan needed to mend fences with hers.

It's make-or-break-it time, kiddo.

She saw flashes of moments when the game was on the line, her team down, clock running out, ball clutched between her hands. *Make the shot and go home a hero, miss it and you're a loser.*

She relished that scenario, loved the laser-sharp focus and single-minded purpose it sparked in her. She never missed the shot.

Regan felt a surge of adrenaline. "Okay, Nick, let's get this done."

〜

TREVOR KNEW he could end it in an instant if he just had enough courage.

There's no way out. Stab her and get it over with.

"Trevor, nothing's changed." Vargas's voice was nasally; he could tell she was crying. "I give you my word – *I will not tell them.*"

He nudged her along in front of him, glancing over his shoulder every few seconds. They were still back there, keeping their distance. If they shot him, the bullets would hit her, too.

Trevor saw that the tunnel widened up ahead. In the lantern light, he could make out an old ore cart sitting off to one side, along with a pile of rusted rails.

When they reached it, he shoved her down, told her to sit against the cart. He set the lantern on the ground, out of her reach, and held the knife out to his side, pointed at her, as he peeked around to see where their pursuers were.

"Trevor!" called Regan, her voice reverberating off the walls. "Tell me what it will take to resolve this peacefully."

Peaceful for you means prison for me. No way.

"I know you don't want to hurt the secretary. I've seen the way she relies on you, how much she trusts you."

Trevor looked at Vargas. She stared at him, her eyes riddled with fear as she waited to see what he would do.

The knife felt slippery in his sweaty palm.

Stab her and get it over with. Do one thing right before you die.

He switched the knife to his left hand and wiped his right hand on his pants. As he switched it back, he said, "I'm sorry, Madame Secretary. It's not about you. I made a promise to Carney."

As he leaned in, Vargas's face contorted with shock.

Chapter Forty

MARK MCKEE is nothing if not steadfast," the chief reported as he passed out bottles of water to the group. "He has things under control at the Baranof and plans to maintain his vigil until every last VIP is safely on a plane out of here."

"Good," said Regan. The other VIPs probably weren't in any danger now, but it helped to know McKee was on top of things just in case.

"It's like a helicopter air show out there," said the chief. "News crews, medevac, state troopers. Hope they manage to stay out of each other's way. How's it going in here?"

Regan looked toward the ore cart and shook her head. "Can't get him to talk to me. I don't think he really wants to hurt Vargas; I think he's just scared and doesn't know how to bring this to an end." She kept her eyes averted from the rusted rails; the last time she saw one, it had her blood all over it.

Lamont looked around. "Jesus, this place gives me the creeps." He gave an exaggerated shiver.

"How close to the AJ Mine entrance are we, Joe?" said Regan.

"I'd guess about a mile," said the mine manager. "Closer to that end than the Perseverance end for sure. Just a ways beyond where they're sitting behind that cart, there's a chamber that housed winches used for hoisting the mine's elevator."

"What's in there now?" said Nick.

"Big chunks of concrete with rebar poking up out of them. There's also a big hole where the elevator shaft used to be. You can look down to the levels below."

"So we need to keep them from moving in that direction," said Regan.

"Right," said Joe. "Otherwise they may not see the hole until it's too late."

"Trevor?" Regan called. "Talk to me. Is the secretary okay? We have some water here. Would you like some water?"

For a few seconds, there was no response. Then Trevor said, "Yes, we need water."

"Okay, I'll give you the water if you let Secretary Vargas talk to me, tell me she's okay."

Silence.

"Trevor?"

"She's okay."

"I need *her* to tell me that."

Another silence, this time stretching at least a full minute. A burning ball of fear gathered in the pit of Regan's stomach. *Oh no, did he* —

"I'm okay," the secretary said in a trembling voice.

Regan expelled her breath. "Good. I'll bring you the water. I'm not armed, Trevor." She slowly moved toward the cart.

About ten feet away, Trevor blurted, "Stop. Toss it the rest of the way."

Regan could see half of Trevor's face as he watched her approach. She stopped and pitched the bottles of water. "Trevor, let's end this. I know both of you are cold and tired and —"

"Get back!" he shouted.

Regan retreated to her former spot. "Okay, tell me what you want, Trevor. What's it going to take to get us all out of here?"

No response.

"Let's go back to the hotel and get some sleep. It's been a long day; we're all tired. What do you say, Trevor?"

Regan wished she could see him so she could gauge how he was feeling, what he might be about to do.

"Get us some blankets," he said.

Regan glanced at the others, her shoulders slumping. "Looks like we're spending the night."

CHAPTER FORTY-ONE

S HE TRIED to pull the blanket up and realized it was a fleece jacket. Jack's.

Regan sat up and turned to see Jack sitting beside her, leaning against the wall. He opened his eyes. "Morning," he said with a smile.

"Is it?" She stretched, her body one big aching mass from sleeping on the hard dirt surface.

Jack nodded and pressed the backlight on his watch. "Almost five o'clock."

The chief had left last night, promising to bring food and coffee first thing this morning if nothing happened before then. Joe Percy had left with him, planning to return along with the food.

Nick was still asleep. Danny leaned against the opposite wall, staring at them.

"You okay, Danny?"

"Fine," he said. His eyes were black and cold.

"Get any sleep?"

"Some."

Nick woke and sat up. "Man, I've slept in some questionable places before, but this one takes the cake." He cocked his head to one side and then the other, trying to pop the kinks out of his neck. "Remind me not to sleep in a mine again."

Regan smiled at him. She craved the fresh air, the morning sun. *Anything* but more of this dank, shadowy mine.

But to get outside, even for a moment or two, meant navigating back through roughly three-and-a-half miles of perilous tunnels.

Or moving past Trevor and his hostage to get out the other end. Neither was an option.

It was time to bring the standoff to an end. "It's morning, Trevor. I'm ready to get out of here. Are you ready to get out of here?"

Regan ran her fingers through her hair, fixing her ponytail even though Trevor couldn't see her in the dim light. They'd been trained that the negotiator should try to look fresh, not beaten down.

"Are you hungry, Trevor? Chief Lamont is bringing us some food."

Regan maintained the one-way conversation for nearly an hour until the food arrived. She'd never been so grateful for a cup of coffee in her life.

"I'm not getting anywhere," she said, sighing in frustration. "Nick, maybe it's time you took over."

Nick shook his head. "I couldn't do any better than you. Not even as good as you."

"He doesn't like me, Nick. I'm having trouble making a connection with him, and it's preventing us from moving toward a peaceful resolution. We're stalled."

Nick said, "I don't know if I —"

Regan had a sudden flash. "Wait – what about Lindsay? Trevor has a crush on Lindsay."

"She's outside the mine on the Perseverance end," said the chief. "She's camped out there with your team."

"Let's get her in here," Regan said excitedly.

"I'll go bring her in," said Joe. "I can probably move faster through here than anybody else."

"Thanks, Joe."

"There's someone else out there, too, Regan," said the chief.

She turned to look at him. "Who?"

"Your dad. I told him no civilians besides Joe and Jack were allowed up here, but he insisted."

He's here to chastise me for letting them get in here in the first place. He'll tell me this is all my fault. She turned away from the chief, forcing her focus back to the man on the other side of the ore cart.

"Trevor? I have some food and coffee for you and the secretary."

ঌ

VARGAS HADN'T slept. She didn't dare close her eyes, just in case Trevor came toward her with the knife again. She may not be able to coax him out of using it a second time.

"Trevor? It's Lindsay."

Trevor bolted upright from his slumped position against the cart. He crept to the side and peeked around.

"Hi, Lindsay," he said. "What are you doing here?"

"I came to talk to you."

Vargas was stunned at the transformation in Trevor's face. Whoever thought of using Lindsay to negotiate was brilliant.

"Oh," he said. "What about?"

"About this ... situation. About how I know you really don't want to be in it."

Trevor's eyes filled with tears. "No, I ... I didn't mean for it to turn out like this, Lindsay. Things just got out of hand. You have to believe me."

"I *do* believe you, Trevor. Why don't you come out so we can talk about it?"

Vargas saw conflicting emotions play across his face.

Was he dating anyone in Washington? She had no idea. Right now, there was no one in the world but Lindsay.

It gave Vargas renewed hope. "Lindsay wants to see you," she whispered. "I swear I'll tell them you never meant to hurt me."

He appeared to run the scenario through his mind, his expression turning grim. "No, it won't make sense."

"What won't?"

"If I never meant to hurt you, if I wasn't guilty of anything, why would I be holding you hostage?"

"Nobody knows you made a deal with Carney," said Vargas, a chill running through her at the mention of her nemesis. "Nobody's *going* to know."

"Trevor?" said Lindsay. "Will you talk to me?"

154

His head dropped to his chest, a pathetic sob escaping from him. *"Why?"* he whispered mournfully. "I could've had a chance with her. Why did I agree to do this?" He slid to the ground, his back against the cart, hands over his eyes.

Vargas raised up slightly, looking for the knife. She couldn't see it; had he put it back in his pocket?

No time to waste. Move.

She leaped to her feet and started to run, but Trevor caught hold of her ankle. She wrenched herself free, scampering away from him. Away from where Lindsay and Regan and the others waited beyond the cart.

Toward the winch chamber.

CHAPTER FORTY-TWO

THE SECRETARY had disappeared into the darkness, running blind. Trevor bolted after her.

"Ella, *stop!*" Regan screamed, dropping the political decorum.

The officers drew their weapons and took off at a full clip, trying to head off the pair before they reached the winch chamber.

Nick shot past them like they were standing still. The beam of his flashlight caught Trevor making a sudden leap over a lump of concrete. He must've spotted the giant hole and the debris surrounding it; he skidded to a stop and reversed course, away from the chamber and into an adjacent tunnel. Nick went after him.

"Ella, don't move!" Regan shouted again as they neared the chamber. The officers' flashlights lit up the space and showed Vargas running wildly, her arms outstretched to keep from slamming into a wall.

"The hole … watch the hole …"

Vargas was only inches from the yawning cavern where the elevator had once been. She stopped suddenly, jerkily backing away from it as she watched for Trevor to spring from the shadows and grab her again.

Regan saw what was about to happen. She dove for Vargas, but it was too late. The secretary tripped over a chunk of concrete, then lurched sideways when her back came into contact with the spokes of rebar jutting out of it like rusty spears. The sudden move shifted her balance toward the hole. Flailing, she reached for the rebar, grabbing nothing but air.

At the last second, just before she disappeared over the side, the secretary's face slackened, the horror replaced with a look of sad resignation.

☙

"HE CLIMBED in there," Nick said breathlessly, pointing to an opening that led into a shaft. "I'm going after him."

"No, Nick," said Regan. "Joe said a lot of those ladders are rotten."

"So what do we do?"

"Let me try talking him out."

The quaking in her limbs had begun to subside, but the scene she'd just witnessed was seared into her brain. Especially that look on the secretary's face in the moment before she fell to her death.

Regan leaned into the shaft, shining her flashlight beam on Trevor. He had climbed upward about twenty feet, perching himself between two of the mine's levels. "It's over, Trevor. Give it up."

His eyes looked ravaged, his body rigid as he clung to the ladder. "I don't want to go to prison," he said in a whiny voice.

She felt repulsed by this sorry excuse of a man. "Yeah, well, Ella Vargas is dead, Trevor." She couldn't keep the bitterness out of her voice.

His eyes widened even more. *"Dead?* No! I didn't … I didn't …"
His sobs echoed eerily in the shaft.

"Come down now."

Come down or I'll shoot you down, you bastard.

Trevor's hands clutched the side rails so tightly that they looked translucent. His head rested against one of the rungs.

"Trevor?"

"No …"

"Please come down now. I know you didn't mean to hurt the secretary." Regan spoke through gritted teeth, the hand on her gun itching to pull the trigger and end everyone's misery.

"No …"

Regan backed out of the opening and turned to Nick. "He's not moving."

Lindsay had just come to see if she could help. "Want me to try?"

Regan nodded, aware that her own manner reeked of disgust.

Lindsay leaned into the shaft. "Trevor? It's me, Lindsay. Why don't you come down here so we can talk?"

Trevor made a moaning sound.

"Hey, Trev?" said Lindsay. "C'mon, we'll get it figured out."

He continued to moan. Lindsay turned to Regan and shrugged.

"Okay, I'm going to get him," said Regan.

"Wait a minute," said Nick. "If it's not safe for me, it's not safe for you, either."

"But we can't just leave him there. He made it up the ladder, and I weigh less than he does."

"Let me do it, Regan."

"No," she said, scowling at her partner. Regan couldn't begin to explain to Nick the gut-wrenching guilt she felt. She let the secretary intimidate her out of doing her job and now Vargas was dead because of it. "Keep your flashlights pointed in the shaft so I can see what I'm doing."

She climbed through the opening and stepped onto the ladder. Trevor was still lodged there, unmoving, emitting a mournful wail.

"I'm coming to help you down," said Regan. She reached for the side rails to pull herself up, planting her foot tentatively on the next rung to make sure it would hold her weight.

She glanced below but couldn't see the base of the ladder in the darkness. She had no idea how far down it went and didn't intend to find out.

She started to take another step but the next rung was missing; she was forced to get a foothold on rock and use the side rails to boost herself up.

A stream of water coursed down the right side of the shaft, creating tiny waterfalls from the crossbeams.

No wonder the ladder is half-rotten.

"Trevor, could you meet me halfway? I'm going to get you out of here."

Trevor lifted his head off the ladder, pausing a moment before shifting his gaze downward toward Regan. He wore a wild-eyed, crazed look; suddenly, he reached out his right arm and began pulling himself upward, away from Regan.

"Trevor, no – stay there!"

But he didn't listen, too determined to get away.

Regan started moving faster up the ladder.

"Regan, wait," Nick yelled. "We'll grab him up on the next level."

"You can't get there in time," she gasped, doing her best to close the gap between her and Trevor. "Trevor, stop or I swear I'll shoot!" Except that she wouldn't dare turn loose of the side rail to grab her gun.

Trevor fished in his pocket. He pulled the knife out and pitched it at Regan's head.

"You little shit," she muttered under her breath as the knife bounced off her shoulder and careened downward. She listened for a thud but didn't hear one.

Suddenly her limbs felt like lead. The shaft felt stifling, airless, making her lightheaded. She *had* to get out of this awful place and into the light.

Keep going. It's almost over. She drew a deep breath and stepped up to the next rung.

An ominous creak. The wood beneath her feet felt damp and mushy.

Nick said, "Regan, are you —" just as the rung gave way, toppling her downward into the void.

CHAPTER FORTY-THREE

THE SUN blinded Jack as he stepped out of the mine. He and Joe had escorted the paramedics to Vargas's body; now, back outside, he moved out of the way to let the stretcher carrying the sheet-draped corpse pass by.

After the stillness of the mine, the cacophony of helicopters overhead was almost deafening. He watched two news choppers jockey for position, each wanting to be first with the footage of whatever was going down. If they weren't careful, it might be the news choppers themselves.

Chief Lamont stood near the ambulance, his face grim as the paramedics loaded the secretary's body into the back. He glanced uneasily at the sky.

Jack walked over to him. "Any word yet on Trevor Wolf's arrest?"

The chief shook his head. "Apparently he climbed into a shaft and headed up the ladder. Regan went after him."

Jack felt his chest tighten. "I hope she's okay ... those ladders aren't in very good shape."

"She'll be fine," said the chief. "Regan's as scrappy as they come. She'll drag him out of there by his hair if she has to." He gave a faint chuckle, but Jack could see the concern in Lamont's eyes.

A beefy, red-haired man hurried over. "Any word yet, Pat?" He emanated anxiety like a drunk giving off the smell of booze.

The chief introduced Jack to Mayor Manning. "I was just telling Jack not to worry about Regan. You know how scrappy she is."

"Scrappy or not, that's a hell of a dangerous place," said Manning. "Ever since she was a little kid, I warned her to stay out of those mines, but she didn't listen. She had to defy me and ended up almost getting herself killed."

"But she's not a little kid anymore, Dev. She's a skilled FBI agent, for cryin' out loud."

"What, you think that makes her indestructible?"

"Of course not, but —"

Jack was about to interrupt when the chief's radio crackled. "Chief?"

"Go ahead, Danny."

"Regan —" His voice broke.

Jack froze.

The chief said, "Regan *what*?"

" —fell."

≈

MAC COULD only hope Trevor was on his way back to Washington. The hotel hadn't told him much, even when he said it was the vice president's office calling.

He considered calling the FBI director's office, but what could he say without revealing his concerns that Trevor Wolf was mixed up in something he shouldn't be?

He did call the secretary's office; they confirmed her schedule, indicated she was due back in Washington at seven p.m., but they hadn't spoken with her today.

Mac felt frantic, as though his sixth sense picked up on something his brain didn't fully comprehend. All he knew was that he had a very, *very* bad feeling.

Should he confront Carney? Should he reveal his suspicions to the vice president?

Mac glanced down at the tiny pile of paper clips he'd pulled into useless strands of crooked wire. He stood, shoving his hands into his pockets, and headed for Ness's office.

CHAPTER FORTY-FOUR

REGAN SLAMMED into the ledge and struggled to remain conscious. Sleep beckoned like a Siren, but a voice in her brain warned her to stay awake.

She lay there, wedged between two crossbeams and sprawled against a rock protrusion. Her hardhat fell to the bottom, bonging and clanging all the way down.

Regan heard Nick screaming her name, frantic. She saw flashlight beams veering back and forth like a pair of spotlights in the night sky.

She tried to yell, "I'm okay," but all that came out was a squeak that was barely audible.

Her head felt wet; she touched the wall to see if one of the mini-waterfalls was dripping on her. She pressed her hand against her wet hair; just as she pulled it back, a flashlight beam found her. Her hand was covered in blood.

"Regan?" shouted Nick, his voice bouncing off the walls of the shaft.

Since her voice seemed unwilling to cooperate, she lifted her arm and waved.

"Okay, stay there, I'm coming to get you."

Stay there?

Gently probing with her fingers, she discovered the gash was deep. It tingled as the blood poured from her head. She felt pain in her midsection.

She reached for her radio, but it had fallen, too. She tried to sit up; a wave of dizziness forced her back down.

Regan saw a shape on the ladder above her. Nick coming to rescue her.

"Can you hear me, Regan?"

"I can hear you," she said softly.

"Jesus, how badly are you hurt?"

"I have a cut on my head that's bleeding pretty good. I'm having some trouble getting upright."

"Okay, stay still."

She heard a creak.

"Nick, *stop*. Get off that rung."

"I'm trying to, but the one below it is missing ... hang on."

Regan kept drifting off. She couldn't see Nick; had he climbed back up, away from her?

"Nick?" She realized she was whispering. *Stay awake, Regan.*

She drifted in and out of dreams.

The rusted rail protruded at an odd angle, catching her off guard, slicing into her arm. Excruciating pain, numbing guilt. It took forever to hike out, to summon help. Fear, remorse. At least they got rid of the beer before the paramedics arrived.

"I won't let you go," Danny was saying.

He'd said that over and over. But she'd had no choice. She had to leave so he could go back to his wife. So she could get on with her career.

"I won't let you go," he said again.

He was here beside her. In the mine shaft. Lifting her.

"Danny?" she said, confused. "How did you —"

"I climbed up from the level below. Can you put your arms around my neck?" He had removed his outer shirt and was pressing it against her head.

She reached up, one arm around his neck and the other hand taking hold of the blood-soaked shirt, while he lifted her from the ledge. Pain shot through her abdomen.

"I've got her, Nick," Danny yelled. "Go get Wolf ... I'm taking Regan back down the way I came."

"Tell him to be careful, Danny," said Regan. "The rungs are really bad up there."

"He knows. He watched you fall. Okay, we have to try to balance our weight. Do you think you can stand up?"

"I'll try," she said in a shaky voice.

"Go slow. I'll hold on to you."

She stood on the nearest rung until the wooziness passed, then began moving with painstaking care, inching slowly downward while Danny gripped her arm.

Regan fought waves of dizziness as she tackled each step. She glanced up; the images above her were blurred. She could hear Lindsay coaxing Trevor.

"Hey, Regan? I want you to know how sorry I am," Danny said quietly. "Just in case I don't get a chance to tell you later."

She turned her head sideways so she could see him out of the corner of her eye. The glare from his head lamp blinded her, casting his face into shadows.

"Wh — what?"

"For the way I treated you back then. Five years ago."

"Danny, please … it's … it's in the past …"

"Losing you nearly killed me. It was like the sun went down and never came back up."

"Danny … it's …" She struggled to form words, fought the blackness closing in around her brain.

"I've wanted to tell you that for a long time." His voice sounded a million miles away.

At some point, she was vaguely aware they were no longer in the shaft. The last thing she remembered was being draped in Danny's arms as he stood in his wide-legged stance, tears on his face, gasping for breath.

CHAPTER FORTY-FIVE

J ACK WATCHED as Lindsay emerged from the mine, Trevor in handcuffs beside her. Danny had just radioed the chief that Regan was injured but alive; the paramedics would be bringing her out momentarily.

Jack wanted to see her, to assure himself that she was okay. His distress, he knew, went beyond simple concern for a law enforcement officer injured in the line of duty. He wasn't sure why, but from the moment they met, he felt enormously drawn to Regan Manning.

The chief summoned the medevac chopper and waited in a nearby clearing. Regan's dad stood just inside the mine entrance, anxiously watching for his daughter to come into view. He clutched a cell phone, ready to call Regan's mother the minute he knew what to report.

Jack heard the approaching chopper, waited for it to touch down in the clearing behind him. His gaze was on Lindsay and Trevor as she steered him toward the waiting police car.

They were about ten feet from the car when there was a sharp pop that echoed through the trees. Trevor suddenly crumpled to the ground, a crimson spot sprouting on his back. Jack glanced up at the chopper overhead as it shot upward and veered away, circling toward the channel.

The chief saw Trevor go down and ran over. Lindsay felt Trevor's neck for a pulse; she looked at the chief with horror-stricken eyes and shook her head. They pulled out their guns, ready in case the chopper came back around.

The *clip-clip-clip* echoed loudly as the metal bird got closer. By now, a dozen officers had drawn their weapons, waiting for the helicopter to reappear.

Jack sprinted for the mine, out of the line of fire. He turned back around and saw the blue medevac chopper hovering overhead, the two pilots' faces frozen with fear. The one in the passenger seat had his hands up.

"Hold your fire!" the chief shouted. He waved the chopper toward the clearing.

A moment later, Jack saw the stretcher coming out of the mine, Nick and Danny following behind it stoically. Regan's eyes were closed; dried blood coated her forehead and matted her hair. Her face was deathly pale.

Amid the horror over what just happened, there was one detail that gave him a tiny shred of comfort: the sheet was tucked around Regan, not *over* her.

⁂

"IRAN DENIES any involvement," said Mac.

Carney's phone was on speaker; he wished he had one of those video phones his assistant was always harping about. He wanted a better gauge on Mac.

"Landry," he said guardedly, "do you have any idea what could be behind the attack on our tanker?" The vice president and his chief of staff had Carney on speaker, too.

"Not a clue," said Ness. "The president and I have made some headway with Hossein Monshizadeh. That's why this is especially puzzling. He's assured Sanford that Iran played no part whatsoever."

"Well, *somebody* blew it up. And I want to know why." He made his voice sound gruff and determined.

"Of course, Bob," said Ness. "We'll use every means at our disposal to identify those responsible."

Carney's cell phone vibrated on his desk. He looked at the caller ID. "Can you guys hang on one second?" He muted the speaker phone and picked up the cell.

"Carney."
"The Wolf hunt was successful."

CHAPTER FORTY-SIX

YOU SHOULDN'T have gone into that mine," said her dad. All her life, he'd been there to point out what she did wrong. He picked everything apart, including her performance on the basketball court. Even when they'd won. Even when she scored thirty points.

And she always responded with noisy indignation. But today the defensiveness was absent; today she was painfully aware of all the things she'd done wrong on this mission.

She should've listened when he told her to shut the summit down. If she had, Vargas and her chief of staff would still be alive.

"We should go now, Devlin," said her mother. "Let her get some rest. Sweetheart, we'll come back again tonight."

Regan nodded and closed her eyes. She wanted to sleep for a couple years.

"Reegs?"

Her eyes popped back open. Nick stood beside her bed, watching her with a tentative expression.

"Hey, Nicky."

"How ya feelin'?"

You don't want to know. "I'm okay," she said.

Nick picked up her hand in his and stroked it. "I know you, partner. So I know you're beating yourself up over Vargas. But it's not your fault. None of this is your fault. It's Trevor's."

"I messed up the mission, didn't keep a tight rein on it. I should've handed it off to you, Nick. I was too distracted by personal stuff."

"Listen, Regan. I'm a guy, and that means I have a fragile ego, so I'm only going to say this once. You on your *worst* day are a better team leader than I am on my *best* day. I know there were things here distracting you, but few of us have your instincts to begin with – so none of us could've responded to the escalating conditions any better than you did. Give yourself some credit."

Regan would've cried if her emotions weren't in shock. That would come later, she knew, when she squarely faced everything that had happened.

But she did know that if her career was in jeopardy, if she and Nick never worked together again, she'd been damn lucky to have had him for a partner. She squeezed his hand. "When do you guys head back to Quantico?"

"Tomorrow. First we're going to take in a little of the Juneau night life." He winked at her. "We're tourists, you know, so the first stop is the Red Dog Saloon."

Regan smiled and closed her eyes. "Have fun."

She was nearly asleep when she sensed someone in the room again. She opened her eyes to see McKee standing next to her.

"Just wanted to stop by for a minute," he said, looking slightly embarrassed.

"I appreciate it, Mark. Thanks."

"How are you doing?"

"Oh, you know, I've been better ... but it could've been worse." She gave him a feeble smile. "Get all those VIPs safely on their way home?"

McKee nodded. "Yes. They're finally gone. And I'm out of here, too, in a couple hours."

"You did a good job, McKee."

"Nothing compared to you." His expression was genuine, all traces of machismo gone. "You're really something, you know that?"

Regan said, "Something, but I'm not sure what ..."

"A courageous leader, that's what."

༚

169

SHE SLEPT for hours. When she woke up, Jack was sitting next to the bed reading a book. "Hi," she said groggily.

"Hi," said Jack. "I hope you don't mind that I'm here."

She wasn't sure why he was, but she didn't mind at all. "No, it's good of you to sit with me. I know you probably have work to do," she said.

He leaned forward. "It can wait. Do you need anything? I can go get you whatever —"

"Thanks, Jack, I'm fine."

The doctor came in, chasing Jack out while she examined her patient. After she was gone, Jack came back in and sat down.

Regan fixed her gaze on his eyes—gentle brown eyes that soothed her, made her feel less bruised. "So, Ranger Jack, tell me about yourself."

"Okay, Agent Regan, what would you like to know?"

"Tell me about being a forest ranger."

He talked about that, and about growing up the son of a Navy commander, the places he'd lived, how close he was to his sister, Kelly.

"She and her husband and kids are coming up in August," he said. "Can't wait to take them out on my boat."

"You have a boat?" Regan loved the water so much she suspected she was a mermaid in a past life.

"Yeah, and if you hurry up and get well, I'll take you out for a spin."

"Now *that's* some incentive," she said, smiling. She could think of nothing that sounded more appealing.

But right now, the fatigue was setting in again.

"You're tired," said Jack. "I'll go."

"Wait. Tell me one more thing, Jack. Did you see Trevor get shot?"

He nodded. "I heard the chopper, thought it was the medevac coming for you. It came in close and I saw Trevor fall. Saw the blood on his back." He looked down at his hands.

"What color was the helicopter?"

"Black and silver. Looked newer and more sleek than the ones usually flying tourists around up here."

A sniper in a sleek new helicopter. One owned by a corporation perhaps.

Maybe an oil company.

CHAPTER FORTY-SEVEN

MAC COULDN'T wrap his brain around it. Vargas and Trevor both *dead*?

Mingled with the disbelief was the nagging sense that he should have intervened – should've revealed his suspicions that Trevor and Carney might be up to something.

But to whom? Mac didn't trust the vice president not to run right to Carney. Ness's instinct would be to do whatever it took to help the oil man.

Just the way Mac wanted to help *his* friend.

First, he would call Trevor's parents. They needed to know that their son was a dedicated public servant, a skilled lawyer, a loyal friend. Mac would fly out to Russell, Kansas, for the burial.

It was the least he could do.

෧

"I'LL HAVE him picked up," said Al.

"Please – let's wait," said Regan. "We don't know enough yet, and Carney will deny any connection with Trevor."

From her vantage point on her parents' couch, Regan idly watched boats chug by on the channel as she talked to her boss. Paco, the family dog, curled himself on top of her feet, one eye partially open to be sure she didn't try to escape. On the floor nearby was an assortment of toys, slippers, and other goodies that the Jack Russell had rounded up for her.

Regan felt torn; she wanted to be on the next flight to Houston, but her body could barely make it to the next room. Thanks to a nasty concussion, standing for more than a minute was next to impossible.

172

"I can send Nick to Houston to investigate," Al said. "Who do you think I should pair him with?"

"Me," Regan said emphatically. She sat up, broken ribs protesting. "Ow."

"Now?"

"No, I said ... never mind. I want to do it, Al. I should be ready to go in a few days." She closed one eye; double vision made it look like some of the boats were sailing through the trees on Mount Roberts.

"No, Regan, I can't let you do that. For one thing, you're on medical leave for at least two weeks – maybe longer if your doctor doesn't report major progress. And after that, OPR will keep you tied up for awhile."

The Office of Professional Responsibility. The Bureau's internal affairs division that investigated potential violations of the law and breaches of FBI policy.

"How long do you think that's gonna take?" said Regan.

"As long as it takes for them to satisfy themselves you acted appropriately."

Regan slid back down to a reclining position.

"Believe me, Regan, I'm as eager to have you back as you are to be here. You're my best agent. But you need to take time to get well. You're no use to me injured."

Good old touchy-feely Al.

"Right, boss. I'll do that."

CHAPTER FORTY-EIGHT

HERE, the guys want to talk to you," said Nick.

Regan laughed as members of the team took turns talking to her before they boarded their plane. Each of them wished her well on her recovery and urged her to hurry up and come back. The team wasn't complete without her.

All for one and one for all. They were more than a team; they were a family.

She glanced at her mother, who sat in her swivel chair in front of the picture window, flipping through a magazine. The woman she hardly knew anymore.

But had she *ever* really known her? Her mother had never revealed much of herself, instead behaving as though she were an extension of Devlin Manning.

Granted, he had a personality that overpowered anything within a two-mile radius.

Hanging up her cell phone, Regan said, "Whatcha reading, Mom?"

Paco popped his head up, shifting his gaze back and forth between them. The dog had a long history of nosiness.

"Oh, just one of my craft magazines. I was thinking about making Christmas ornaments for the relatives."

"Christmas ornaments? It's only June."

"I know, but that way I don't have to hurry."

Her mother was always making something. Last fall, she sent Regan two crocheted angels. She wasn't sure what she was supposed to do with one, let alone two.

Oh – maybe they were ornaments! Regardless, Regan had never put up a Christmas tree.

"Uh, are you going to make angels like you did last year?"

"What? Oh, no, the angels weren't ornaments. Those were just decorations. Year-round. For protection." She smiled.

"Right! That's what I thought." Decorations for an apartment she was rarely in, protection from the dangerous felons she pursued on the street.

"Mom?"

"What, honey?"

"Are you … doing okay?"

Her mother lowered the magazine to her lap and looked at her. "Of course. Why wouldn't I be?"

"I don't know. I just wondered if Dad … you know …"

"We get along fine, Regan. You don't need to worry about me."

Regan had spent her entire life worrying about her mother. "I don't?"

"No, you don't."

"Hmm."

"You know, Regan, a lot of your dad's bluster is for show. When there's nobody around but the two of us, he doesn't bother."

How nice. He doesn't abuse you without an audience.

"So you're saying he used to pick on you and Colin for my benefit?"

"I think so. He knew he could get a rise out of you."

"And you think I should've just ignored him. Let him pummel you and my brother senseless with his abusive crap." She was aware of the bitterness that had seeped into her tone, but she couldn't help it.

"I know you were just trying to protect us, Regan. But I always felt worse about what it did to *you* than what it did to me."

Regan gaped at her. "Why didn't you ever tell me that? I would've backed off, left things alone."

Her mother gave her a knowing smile.

"Okay, you're right," said Regan. "I wouldn't have kept my nose out of it. But still."

"I know, honey. It didn't exactly make for a peaceful household. But your dad … he's … well, he's a *star*. I still consider myself lucky he chose me."

"A star? Mom, he treats you terribly. He *cheated* on you, for godsakes. You don't deserve that."

Her mother looked irritated. "That's all in the past, Regan. And don't try again to talk me into leaving him." She set her jaw and gave Regan a hard stare.

"I wouldn't do that, Mom. I'm hardly in a position to criticize someone else for having an affair."

She and her mother had never talked about Danny before, but Regan knew she knew. It had been the talk of the town.

"Susan Brice seems to have moved past it," said her mother. "I see her in the grocery store sometimes, and she always speaks."

Regan felt a stab of pain that made her physical injuries seem mild by comparison. The tears were coming, along with the self-recrimination, the second-guessing, the regret.

Washing over her like a tidal wave.

CHAPTER FORTY-NINE

REGAN SAT on the sand, mesmerized by the waves rolling over themselves and fizzling into foam along the shore. Paco scooped up a soggy piece of wood and trotted over, dropping his new toy on the ground in front of her. He twittered with anticipation. Regan tossed the stick, giggling as Paco streaked after it.

It felt good to laugh, to wiggle her toes in the sand, to breathe some fresh air after a week spent cooped up inside. She glanced around, watching kids throw seaweed at each other, screeching as they dodged the stringy, smelly stuff. Sandy Beach was probably the epicenter of their childhood fun, just like it was for her. Maybe for them, too, it was a refuge – a place to escape the family dynamic.

Regan hugged her knees to her chest and sighed. She felt utterly drained.

What was next? Would OPR find she acted irresponsibly, take her career away from her?

She closed her eyes, perching her head against her arms.

No. I couldn't take that.

Regan thought back to the day she arrived at the academy for seventeen weeks of training, buzzing with excitement like Paco with a new toy. Unlike other newbies, she never feared washing out – even when one of her firearms instructors seemed to make it his personal goal. The Bureau was her calling, and that knowledge carried her through the worst of the training, led to her early successes in the field. Almost from day one, her career trajectory had been skyward – maybe all the way to the Hostage Rescue Team some day. The crème de la crème.

Would this one mission wash it all away? Would the return to her hometown undo everything she'd carefully built the last five years?

Paco began to bark. Regan looked up, saw the dog's eyes fixed on something behind her. She turned; there stood Danny.

"I stopped by your parents' house. Your mom told me I could find you here." He plopped down next to her on the sand. "How are you feeling?"

Regan shrugged. "Lots to process."

"I mean physically ... how's your head? What about your ribs?"

"Getting better. At least I don't feel like I'm going to pass out every time I stand up. Ribs are still pretty sore."

He leaned forward and peered at her forehead. "Looks like the cut on your forehead's almost healed."

At the hospital the day after the rescue, she gushed over his heroic rescue. Pretended she didn't remember what he told her in the mine.

It was time to deal. "What are you doing here, Danny?"

He said defensively, "I just wanted to see how you —" He stopped. In a gentler tone, he said, "No, that's not true. I mean, yeah, I wanted to see how you were doing. You had some pretty serious injuries. But mainly I wanted to talk to you."

She waited.

He gave a loud sigh. "I can't ... I can't seem to get over you." He kept his gaze on the channel in front of them.

She reached over and squeezed his arm. For a minute or two, neither of them spoke.

"I had a talk with my mom the other day," Regan said finally. "I asked her why she put up with the way my dad treats her, why she stayed with him after he cheated on her. You know what she said?"

"What?"

"That even after all these years she can't believe how lucky she is. Despite Dad's imperfections, she loves him completely. Always has, always will. I thought she was too weak to leave him; turns out she was strong enough not to let him get to her."

Danny continued staring at the channel.

"She said she sees your wife in the grocery store sometimes. Said that Susan seems to have gotten past our affair. I think that's because, like my mom, she still loves the man she married. Despite a few imperfections."

He turned to her. "You call loving another woman a little imperfection? No, I don't think Susan stays because of her feelings for me. I think she doesn't want the boys to grow up in a broken home like she did."

"And why do *you* stay?"

"I – well, I guess I don't want that, either."

"You're saying you don't love Susan?"

Danny shrugged. "I don't know. All I know is that I don't have the feelings for her that I have for you."

"I see you've forgotten the way we bickered constantly – the way we were always competing with each other. It never would've lasted, Danny."

He smiled. "But it was exciting as hell, wasn't it? Even though I wanted to strangle you sometimes. Susan is ... I don't know ... too *nice*."

"It's a good thing, because I imagine she wants to strangle *you* sometimes. She's probably holding out hope the old Danny will return someday."

"The old Danny?"

"The sweet man you were when you married her."

The man you were before we royally screwed things up.

They watched Paco drag a rubbery bulb of sea kelp over and try to entice one of them into playing fetch. The dog eventually gave up and sat down; he glanced from one to the other, like he was hoping to see some fireworks. They both chuckled, then fell silent again, their gazes fixed on the channel.

"You're not ever coming back, are you?"

She knew he wasn't talking about Juneau. "No. I'm not. I did love you once, but I had no right to. You're a part of my past, Danny, not a part of my future."

He nodded. After a moment, he leaned over and planted a kiss on her cheek. "Goodbye, Regan."

.

CHAPTER FIFTY

ROBERT CARNEY didn't think there was any way they could tie Trevor back to him. Unless he had confided in Mac. But if he had, wouldn't Mac have told Ness by now? Trevor was his best buddy; Mac would probably be looking for some kind of revenge.

As the saying went, no news was good news.

Still, Carney needed to see for himself, just to make sure. He buzzed his assistant. "Get the Learjet fueled up. I'm going to Washington."

෴

THE DOCTOR unwrapped the bandage from Regan's midriff. "Go ahead and lie back," she said.

Regan stretched out on the examination table, peering down at her bruised body. "I think it looks better – the purple isn't as dark, is it?"

The doctor smiled. "No, you've got more of a lavender-and-yellow thing going on. How do the ribs feel?"

"Pretty good," Regan lied. They hurt like hell.

The doctor gently pressed on Regan's rib cage; it took sheer will to keep from flinching. But she had to have a positive report before she could go back to work.

"The cut on your head looks good. I'm going to remove the stitches."

"Okay," said Regan. "Then can you go ahead and clear me?"

The doctor looked thoughtful. "We may be pushing it a little bit, Regan. Your ribs are coming along, but they're certainly not healed yet. It'll take a month or two. And you've suffered a significant injury to your brain – which means your reflexes, balance and coordination, even your judgment may be impaired for awhile."

"I understand, Doctor. But I really need to get back to work. If I promise to keep my ribs bandaged and not tackle anybody, will you clear me? My boss won't let me come back until you do."

The longer Carney was out there without her breathing down his neck, the longer he had to cover his tracks.

The doctor hesitated. "I will, but you really do need to take it easy. I'm serious, Regan. If you don't let your body heal completely, you're going to cause yourself problems down the road."

"Got it," said Regan. She'd be on a Houston-bound plane tomorrow morning.

On her way out of the clinic, her cell phone beeped. "Ready for that boat ride?"

"Boy, I don't know, Jack. The mind is willing, but I'm not sure about the ribs."

"I promise not to hop over waves. We'll take it slow and easy."

A chance to be out on the water. The opportunity to spend time with Jack. She'd be out of her mind to pass up either one, let alone both.

"Okay," said Regan. "I'll see if I can persuade my mom to fix us a couple of her famous chicken-salad sandwiches."

"Perfect. I'll pick you up in an hour."

≈

WHILE SHE waited for Jack, Regan put in a call to FBI Headquarters. She asked for the intelligence analyst she usually brought in on cases.

"Hey, Jana, I need your help running down some information."

"Okay, go."

"See what you can dig up on Robert Carney, Axis Oil's CEO. Go the whole nine yards. And I need it today." She didn't have to tell her to keep it on the down low; that was Jana's modus operandi. Her discretion, along with her tendency to look beyond the obvious, made her Regan's go-to girl on intelligence.

"Will do, Regan. I'll get back to you."

Chapter Fifty-One

R EGAN, MEET Susie. Susie, this is Regan."
The Golden Retriever draped her head over the front seat, wagging her tail as Regan gingerly climbed into the Range Rover.

"Hi, Cutie Pie," said Regan.

Susie licked the agent's ear, causing Regan to scrunch up her shoulders. "Whoa, I think we should get to know each other first."

"Susie can't help herself," said Jack. "Being called Cutie Pie makes her go nuts."

Paco watched from the window as they backed out of the driveway. Jack stopped the car. "You want to bring your dog along? He looks kind of dejected."

"Oh no, Paco just thinks it's his job to monitor everything. He's about to go for his daily walk, which he adores, and besides, we'd spend all our time fishing him out of the water. He gathers anything that's loose."

Jack laughed as he pulled onto Douglas Highway. He felt giddy; he'd never looked forward to an outing on the boat with such anticipation.

"Boy, great day, huh?" said Regan. The sun gave her hair a coppery sheen; her sea-green eyes glowed.

The sight of her almost took his breath away.

"Umm," said Jack. "It's days like this that make up for all the rainy ones."

They crossed the Juneau-Douglas Bridge and turned left onto Egan Drive. When they drove past Aurora Harbor, heading toward the valley, Regan said, "Where's your boat?"

"Private dock near my house. Out on Fritz Cove Road."

"Well lucky you. It's beautiful out there."

"We like it, don't we, Sooz?"

Susie wagged in agreement.

"So, Regan, since I told you my life story the other day, probably more than you wanted to know, it's your turn. Tell me about you."

"Not much to tell really," said Regan. "Grew up in that house we just left – went to JDHS, then U Dub. Came back here and joined JPD; four years later, I joined the FBI."

Wow. She just boiled her whole life down to acronyms.

Jack wondered why she revealed so little of herself. His instincts told him to take it slow, get to know her bit by bit.

"You went to the University of Washington?" He'd already known that, of course; he watched her play basketball there. "Me, too."

"Really? When were you there?"

They compared college stories, discovered he was a senior when she was a freshman, learned that they both spent countless hours studying at a hole-in-the-wall diner just off The Ave while their friends opted for the popular coffeehouses.

"Best hash browns in Seattle," they said in unison, laughing.

Fifteen minutes later, they passed Auke Lake and Jack took a left on Fritz Cove Road. He drove a couple miles before turning again, this time onto a narrow dirt road that led to a house set back in a clearing.

"This is it ... home sweet home."

Regan looked around, her expression unreadable.

He wanted to say *Do you like it?* But that seemed a little, well, insecure. He hoped she did, was surprised that it mattered.

"Let's grab some bottles of water before we head down to the boat," said Jack.

Regan got out of the car and stood a moment, breathing in the woodsy scent. "What's that over there?" She pointed to a building with the same natural wood siding as the house.

"That's my shop."

"Hmm."

He watched her face expectantly.

She looked at him, a radiant smile slowly spreading across her face. "You have your very own slice of paradise here, don't you, Jack?"

She likes it!

"It's pretty great. C'mon, I'll show you the house."

Jack had always liked the masculine look of it; now he wondered if the coffee-brown leather furniture and chunky oak end tables looked *too* masculine.

Jeez, man, get a grip. He was acting like he'd never brought a woman home before.

But this woman was different. He wanted to impress her, yearned to spend as much time with her as he could while he had the chance.

Before she walked back out of his life and returned to hers.

CHAPTER FIFTY-TWO

REGAN STEPPED out on Jack's deck to take Jana's call. She watched seagulls in the cove swoop and dive as she listened to the analyst.

"Okay, here's what I have on Carney so far. He invests heavily in congressional campaigns, particularly the campaigns of those who formulate energy policy. He even has people on his own payroll who draft language for legislation regulating the oil industry. He testifies before Congress on a regular basis – more often than the other oil CEOs."

"Yes, our Mr. Carney does love the limelight," said Regan.

"He's on the A-list at Washington events. He's extremely popular – regarded by politicians as someone you want to have on your side."

"And funding your campaign."

"Right. His private jet makes frequent runs from Houston to Washington, D.C. I also looked at recent commercial flights, and I found that he's made three trips back and forth to Bahrain in the last six months, the most recent one a month ago."

"What do we know about Bahrain?" Regan pulled a notepad out of her purse and set it on the deck rail, scribbling notes as Jana talked.

"There's a U.S. naval base there at Juffair, which is about five miles north of Manama, Bahrain's capital. The U.S. signed an agreement with Bahrain in 1991 that gives U.S. forces access to Bahraini facilities. It also gives our military the right to pre-position material for a potential crisis. The Navy's Fifth Fleet is headquartered there, and it includes a battle carrier group and other naval assets. Other branches of the service also have personnel and equipment in the area conducting special ops and providing a forward presence.

"Bahrain served as the primary coalition naval base and the point of origin for coalition air operations against Iraqi targets during the Gulf War," Jana continued. "Before that, Juffair was just a tiny place with only a few people and not many buildings. Now, the place is thriving. Classy hotels and restaurants and a booming real estate market. The navy's presence grew from about a hundred sailors to more than twelve hundred."

"Is Carney involved in real estate over there?"

"Apparently he's trying to be. He owns a company called RBC Enterprises and he's been courting the naval commander, hoping to get a piece of the military pie. He's also putting up a hotel in Muharraq, which is the offshore island where Bahrain International Airport sits. A new causeway is being built to connect it to Juffair."

"Good work, Jana. Anything else?"

"I'm still digging. But there is one other interesting thing: Carney just split with his fourth wife, Resa."

༔

"CAN YOU meet me in Houston tomorrow?"

"What about your injuries?" said Nick. "It hasn't even been two weeks, Regan. And what about Al? Has he said you can return to the case?"

"My injuries are almost healed, but technically I'm still on medical leave until the end of the week. After that, OPR gets me for as long as they choose. That's why we need to go now."

"And you want me to be your partner in crime," said Nick. "Even though it might get me busted back to the complaint desk."

"You're right, Nick. I shouldn't ask you to do that. I'll just —"

"I'll see you in Houston. Let me know what time your flight arrives."

CHAPTER FIFTY-THREE

THE WATER lapped at the side of the boat as they drifted near Shelter Island. They'd finished their lunch; now they relaxed in silence, letting the sun wash over them.

Regan felt uncharacteristically tranquil around Jack. She liked how he was handsome in a North Face way rather than Brooks Brothers – or, for that matter, government-issue windbreaker with FBI plastered on the back. Not out to prove anything other than the fact that forests are sustainable with proper care.

Her thoughts slipped back to the mine, to that last look on Ella Vargas's face. Would Regan be that accepting of imminent death? No, probably not. She'd go out kicking and screaming.

Poor screwed-up Trevor. It had to be Carney who ordered the hit on him, and now Regan had to find a way to prove it.

"How do you feel about taking a little hike?" said Jack. "I'd like to get a closer look at some of the vegetation on Shelter."

She smiled, amused at the way neither of them ever quit thinking about their jobs – even when the attraction crackling between them was practically audible.

"Love to," she said.

Jack motored the boat slowly until it made contact with the pebbly shore, then killed the engine and dropped anchor. He pitched his sneakers onto the beach, then jumped off the bow. The water didn't quite come up to his khaki cargo shorts.

"Here," he said, "I'll carry you so you don't get your shoes wet."

Regan wasn't used to being taken care of; it made her feel a little funny. She almost rejected his offer – but then something told her not to.

As she climbed off the boat and into his arms, he held her gently, careful not to touch her ribs.

I think I could get used to this.

On the beach, he paused a moment longer than he needed to before setting her down. Regan wasn't sure if the color in his cheeks was a blush or a sunburn.

He busied himself wiping the sand off his feet until Susie, still on the boat, gave a yelp. She stood with her front paws on the starboard side, wagging her tail.

It made them both laugh, dispelling the moment of self-consciousness. "I'm not carrying you, you crazy mutt," Jack called to her. "C'mon." The dog plunged into the water and raced up to the beach, spraying them as she shook herself off.

The trio set off for the woods. As they moved along the mossy trail, bathed in a magical emerald glow, inhaling the rich scents of pine and spruce, Regan thought back to the day of her arrival – of the sudden image in her head that looked a lot like this.

Like it was a premonition.

Were she and Jack meant to be? She watched him study his surroundings with the eyes of an expert, fantasizing what it would be like to be in a relationship with him – to go for hikes and boat rides, to snuggle up with him on that fabulous leather couch. To know for sure that her heart was in good hands.

Maybe it wouldn't be the worst thing if OPR kicked me out of the FBI.

Who was she kidding? Today was a one-time deal. Better enjoy it.

Jack gave her a glimpse of his world, explaining how the constant maritime climate of the island differed with the more variable continental climate of his usual study area in the mountains above Juneau. She watched his whole being light up as he talked about tree mortality and vegetation layers and soil drainage.

Jack Landis, like her, was completely jazzed by his job. She sighed.

"I'm sorry," he said. "I'm sure this is boring you to tears."

"Not even a little bit, Jack. I love watching you talk about your work. I love seeing your *passion*."

He turned, gently pulling her into his arms, and gave her a long kiss. Afterwards they stood, foreheads touching, hearts beating, as though they were on a precipice, weighing whether or not to leap.

"Let's go back to my house," Jack whispered.

☙

REGAN HEARD her phone, but she couldn't make herself budge. She wanted to shut out the world, stay wrapped in Jack's arms forever.

When it beeped again ten minutes later, she sat up. "I better see who it is." She reached for her capris on the floor and pulled the phone out of her pocket. "Manning."

"Regan?" It was Chief Lamont. "I need to talk to you."

A cloud scuttled over her bliss. She pulled the sheet up to cover her nakedness. "What's wrong, Chief?"

"I just need to talk to you. Can you come by the station?"

"Now?" It was almost six.

"Uh huh, if you can."

"I'm ... wait just a second." She put her hand over the phone and turned to Jack. "Can you take me to the police station?"

"Of course."

She pulled the phone back to her face. "Okay, I'll be there in thirty minutes."

CHAPTER FIFTY-FOUR

I WANT you to listen with an open mind," said the chief.
Regan watched his face, confused. "Okay," she said tentatively.
"I've decided to retire at the end of August."

She hadn't expected that news, but it didn't really surprise her, either. She wasn't sure what it had to do with her.

"I want you to think about coming back and taking my place."

Whoa.

"Oh, I don't think my dad —"

"I told you to listen with an open mind, remember?"

" —would ever go for that —"

"Let me worry about your dad. You would be perfect, Regan. You have a range of experience that would serve Juneau well. And you're a hometown girl. A local celebrity."

"One with a tarnished reputation, as you well know. Besides, I'm only thirty-two, Chief. You were in your forties when you became chief."

"Some of us are just slow learners. I didn't have your expertise *or* your intelligence, Regan. And as for the tarnished reputation, that's hogwash – that exists only in your own mind. People remember you as an outstanding athlete and a good cop, not somebody's mistress."

"And how do you think that particular somebody would like working for me? I can't imagine he would be too thrilled. Danny would be a better choice for chief anyway ... unlike me, he's been on the job here the last five years."

"Danny's a great detective, but he doesn't have your skill as a leader. I saw it throughout the Vargas situation, Regan. You're the quintessential point guard, even when you're conducting a law enforcement operation. You learned young that your mind has to move in several directions at once – that you have to balance reaction with thought."

Right now, Regan struggled with that very balance.

I love the FBI ... I could be here with Jack ... I'd miss the action, the variety ... I could spend time with Mom and Dad ...

"I don't know, Chief. I'll have to think about it."

"Okay, but don't take too long. I'd like to know before I announce my retirement – before the city gets all hepped up on a search for my replacement."

"I'm leaving tomorrow," said Regan. "Heading to Houston."

"Houston? Aren't you on medical leave?"

Regan nodded. "But three people are dead because of Robert Carney. And I'm going to prove it."

Lamont leaned forward on his desk. "See? That's my point. You don't rest until the bad guy is brought to justice."

Regan shrugged, nodding.

The chief smiled. "Go make your arrest – and then make your decision."

&

"SO YOU'RE going after Carney." Her dad reached for a toothpick as her mother began clearing the table.

Regan got up to help her.

"Sit," said her mom. "I'll get it."

"What makes you think he'll do anything to reveal his guilt? He's back on his own turf. You'll have a harder time with him there than you had here."

Regan felt herself tense. "I'm pretty good at what I do, Dad."

He widened his eyes, looking offended. "Did I say you weren't?"

She'd dodged an argument with him long enough. "Yes, as a matter of fact you did. Maybe not in so many words, but you criticize everything I do, every single chance you get. I'm tired of it." Her voice was terse with challenge.

"You're just overly sensitive," he muttered.

"No, I'm not overly sensitive. I'm overly fed up with your superiority." She kept her gaze fixed on him, but out of the corner of her eye she saw her mother scrubbing a pan in the sink like it was coated with tar.

He turned defensive. "I've always said you were good at *everything* – from basketball to police work to who-knows-what." He paused. "Better than anybody I've ever seen."

His words floored her. "Said that to *whom*? Not to me."

"Well, no, because I didn't want it to go to your head."

"You thought it would be better for *my head* if I was under constant criticism? If I was made to doubt myself?"

"It doesn't look to me like it's hurt you any."

Tears sprung to her eyes.

"He does say that, Regan," said her mother. "You should hear the way he brags on you."

"Stay out of it, Carol. We're not talking to you."

Regan bristled, ready to fly to her mother's defense. "She —"

"And I wasn't talking to *you*, Devlin, so you can keep your mouth shut."

Regan's jaw dropped. She'd never heard her mother use that tone with him before.

Her mom looked at her and winked.

"What is this, pick-on-Dad night?" To Regan's utter amazement, he looked more amused than angry.

"Yep," said Regan. "And we're just getting warmed up."

CHAPTER FIFTY-FIVE

NICK MET her in baggage claim. "How ya feeling, partner?"

"Well, I'm not supposed to leap tall buildings or take down anybody larger than a fourth grader," said Regan. "Other than that, I'm great." She beamed.

"You *look* great." He narrowed his eyes. "Don't tell me you got laid up there in Alaska ..."

"Don't be crude, Nicky," she mumbled. She bent down and busied herself with her suitcase so he couldn't see her cheeks redden.

"Sorry. What's the plan?"

"Let's grab a taxi and head to our motel. I'll fill you in when we get there."

During the ride, Nick brought her up-to-date on things at Quantico. She hadn't been there in nearly a month; it felt more like a year.

They checked into their rooms and headed for the Denny's next door. Over burgers, Regan told Nick about Jana's intel and what they needed to accomplish in Houston.

"We're going to contact Resa Carney, see if she feels like dishing," said Regan. "So be ready to turn on that boyish charm of yours."

"Whaddya mean, be ready? It's *always* on." Nick winked at her.

"Oh, right. I forgot." Regan rolled her eyes. "We also want to get in touch with that former aide of Vargas's – Eric Jamison."

"What about Carney? Are we paying him a visit?"

"Depends on how things go. Maybe we'll just do a little snooping around."

"In that case, aren't you glad your partner's a surveillance whiz?" Nick was the Critical Incident Response Group's undisputed king of surveillance, mostly because he was the only one who actually *liked* it.

"I am. Did you bring along some disguises?"

"Yep. You get to be a ravishing blonde."

"What about you?"

"I get to be an old guy with a shiny noggin."

"Hmm. Better lose the chin stubble."

"That's exactly what Lindsay said."

"Lindsay?"

Nick's face colored. "Yeah ... we've kept in touch since the Alaska operation."

Regan smiled. "Does Nicky have a little crush?"

"No, Nicky has a *big* crush."

Regan couldn't believe she and her partner shared the same dilemma: how to navigate a long-distance romance. "Seems we have something in common."

"You have a crush on Lindsay, too?"

"No, idiot. On Jack. Who also lives in Alaska, which you may have noticed is more than three thousand miles from where *we* live."

"Ahh, the hunky ranger! I *thought* you were acting a little scatty every time he was around."

"I'm surprised you even noticed since you were so busy making googly eyes at Miss Maine." She popped a ketchup-laden French fry into her mouth. "Listen to us. We've reverted to junior high."

"Do you think she likes me?" said Nick.

"I don't know ... maybe you could send McKee an email and ask him if she ever talks about you."

&

"WE'D LIKE to know more about your husband, Mrs. Carney," said Regan.

"Resa. We're friends, remember? And he's my soon-to-be *ex-*husband, the bastard." She splayed her hands and checked her fingers to be sure the diamonds hadn't disappeared along with her spouse. Like Regan, Resa was a redhead, though hers was a rust shade whipped up in some lab.

"Do you know anything about his current projects in Bahrain?" said Nick.

She smiled wickedly, her gaze lingering on Nick. "He's tried to keep that on the down low so I can't get my hands on any of it," she said in a Texas drawl. "He forgets that he's the one who taught me about paying people to keep you informed."

"So you're not part of RBC Enterprises?"

"Not officially, no. But Texas is a community property state, God bless 'em. About RBC, I know that Bob has big plans for developing properties in Bahrain. I know that the Navy runs the show there, and Landry Ness pulled some strings with the naval commander."

Regan's pulse quickened. "For pay or just out of friendship?"

"Oh, for pay, of course. It's true they're good friends, but it's because they're equally greedy. *Everything* revolves around money."

Regan and Nick made eye contact. They both knew what that meant: if they could prove it, Landry Ness might be up on corruption charges.

"And there's more," said Resa, eyeballing Nick again. "I know Bob arranged to have that old tanker of Stratum Shipping's blown up. I heard him talking to somebody about collecting the insurance on the *Seacat*. Laughing, actually. People don't know the real Bob – how calculating he is."

"Do you know any of the specifics of the arrangement?" asked Nick.

Resa shook her head. "Unfortunately, no. I wish I did. I'd like to see him charm his way out of that one."

"Would you be willing to testify against him if this goes to trial?" said Regan.

"You're damn right I would," she said, poofing a hairdo that was already big enough to house a family of sparrows. "Then maybe he won't be able to afford that bimbo he's with."

Regan kept a straight face. "Good," she said. "One other thing, Resa. Your life could be in danger. Do you have adequate protection?"

"I think so. Four big bodyguards, three Dobermans, and a nifty new sub-compact semi-automatic. I'm well aware of the danger, y'all. Remember, I *am* married to Bob Carney."

CHAPTER FIFTY-SIX

ERIC GRIEVED for his former boss. "I just can't comprehend it," he said, his long, narrow face creased with sorrow. "I can't believe *anyone* would want to hurt the secretary, but especially her own chief of staff." He shook his head. "I talked to Dr. Vargas ... the family's a wreck."

Regan felt a stab of pity for them, especially Vargas's daughter, Maria. Her world had just capsized at an age when life was already one teen trauma after another.

Eric's wife, Lisa, carried iced tea into the living room on a tray. She set it on the coffee table and scooted from the room like she was about to be cuffed.

The evening air felt muggy. Regan guzzled her tea while Eric talked.

"Ella Vargas loved people," he said.

Except FBI agents who get in the way of her political agenda, Regan thought wryly.

"She was easy to work for ... very appreciative of anything I did for her."

"Did you know Trevor?" asked Regan.

"No, never met the guy. I heard from some old Washington buddies of mine that his personality was a little ... well, different."

"Different how?" said Nick.

"I guess he came across as having a chip on his shoulder – know what I mean? Something to prove. He didn't really socialize with other staff members, either Vargas's or other congressional aides. Except for one guy ..." Eric stared at the floor, searching his memory.

Regan waited.

"Mac somebody ..." Eric snapped his fingers. "Macauley Holman. Chief of staff to the vice president. That's who got him the job with Vargas."

Regan scribbled Mac's name into her notepad. It could prove to be a valuable lead. "Hey Eric, can you tell us about the guy who invented the extraction tool for Axis?"

"His name is William Fisher. Everyone calls him Fish. Carney screwed him over big-time."

"How?"

"Fish is an MIT whiz kid. Really brilliant but a little weird, too. When he went to Carney with his idea for the rotary steerable device, Carney was ecstatic – told him that once the prototype was built, Fish would be looking at a promotion to head of R & D. Made a huge deal about telling other employees that Fish had the kind of ingenuity Axis was looking for."

"What happened?" said Nick.

"According to Fish, Carney suddenly went cold. Wanted to slow down development of the tool, told Fish to stop bugging him about the promotion. Fish got all crazy, tried to figure out what was going on, so all of a sudden Carney fires him. Hanston snapped him up before anybody else could get him."

Nick said, "What happened to his prototype?"

"Axis has the schematics, so they don't really need Fish. I guess they're still working on the tool but just not fast-tracking it like they were at first."

"I'd like to talk to Mr. Fisher," said Regan.

"Sure. Stop by Hanston Oil tomorrow and ask for me. I'll take you to meet The Fish."

CHAPTER FIFTY-SEVEN

THE OIL tycoon lounged on the couch in Mac's office, flipping through the *Wall Street Journal*. They were waiting for the vice president to get out of a meeting. "Damn shame about your buddy Trevor."

"Isn't it," Mac said, barely keeping his temper in check.

"Who do you think shot him?" Carney said casually.

"Don't know. Thought you might have some idea about that."

"Me? Why would *I* have any idea?"

"Because you're one of the last people who talked to him."

"Just in passing. Listen, Mac, I don't know where you're getting this absurd notion that I had something to do with Trevor's death – or his decision to kidnap Vargas, either." His voice turned to a growl as he pointed a manicured finger at Mac. "But you're out of line and I intend to tell Landry." He sprang from the couch, slamming the door on his way out.

Offense is the best defense, Mac thought. *He's guilty.*

FISH ATTEMPTED to explain the finer points of the rotary steerable device; Regan felt her head start to spin. "Does Axis have exclusive rights to the design?"

"Yes, because I was employed by them when I developed it," said Fish.

"And they kept your schematics," said Regan.

Fish shrugged, his head bobbing in what was not quite a nod. "But?"

"But I made a copy of them before I left Axis."

"Which means," said Regan, "if Hanston decided to build the device, it could fast-track the project since the plans already exist."

"Right," said Fish. "But Axis filed for a patent. My boss is afraid that if we steal the design, we might get sued."

"Why can't you just tweak it a little?" said Nick.

"We could, but that means new schematics would have to be developed. That takes time, which means there's no guarantee we could get to the finish line before Axis. With this deal, timing is everything."

"Because?" said Regan.

"Because the early bird gets the worm. It's a revolutionary device, you see, so the first one out of the gate gets all the marbles."

Too bad Fish couldn't have described the way the device worked in clichés. Those Regan understood.

"Tell us about your relationship with Robert Carney," she said. "How was it prior to the issues that led to your dismissal?"

"Non-existent," said Fish. "In fact, I had a hard time getting in to see him to explain the tool's concept. I was pretty persistent, though, so he finally agreed to see me. Once he saw the design, he went ape-shit." He gave Regan a quick glance. "Sorry. Anyway, he practically promised me the moon and the stars if I'd work overtime on the drawings. He wanted to get the tool into production as soon as possible."

"So you worked day and night to get them done," said Regan.

"Bingo. I was pumped, man. Running on pure adrenaline. Got those babies done in record time. He starts talking promotion to head of R & D, a big fat bonus, all that sh —" He glanced at Regan again. "Stuff. We ramp up production, then bam, everything stops. Just like that."

"Did he explain why?" said Nick.

"Just said something came up and we had to slow things down. He stopped taking my calls, wouldn't see me. I wanted that promotion he promised ... I worked my ass off for it."

"So you threatened him?" said Regan.

"I wouldn't call it a threat exactly," said Fish. "Just said if he didn't give me the promotion, I would make sure the device had, shall we say, a mysterious malfunction. I was only kidding."

"You're lucky he didn't file charges against you," said Regan.

"Yeah, but couldn't I have gotten him for making false promises or something like that?"

Regan smiled. "Believe me, Mr. Fisher, if people could be convicted for that, there aren't enough prisons in the world to lock up all the offenders."

Chapter Fifty-Eight

AXIS OIL'S headquarters were as showy as the man at the helm. The glass-and-steel structure sat gleaming in the sun, reminiscent of Carney's bleached-tooth smile.

"I'm sure this place is a fortress," said Regan. "Resa said her husband has enough security to guard a small country."

Trees surrounded the property, so the landing strip and hangars weren't visible from where their rental car was parked. Thanks to Google Earth, they knew the structures were there.

Nick peered through binoculars, trying to catch a glimpse of what was on the other side of the trees. "Wonder how we can get a closer look."

"Local field office would probably take us up in a chopper, but if they check in with Al for approval, we're screwed," said Regan. She wasn't even supposed to be here. Nick had talked their boss into letting him take a preliminary look at things, insisted he didn't need a partner for that.

"Too bad we don't know anybody in the HFO we can sweet-talk," said Nick.

"Wait," said Regan. "I have an idea."

❧

THE HANSTON Oil chopper traveled south along the west side of the city on its way toward Axis.

"I've been meaning to get up here anyway," said Eric. "We needed new shots for the website since we expanded our headquarters last fall." He attached a zoom lens to an expensive-

204

looking camera and peered through the viewfinder. "This new puppy oughta do the trick nicely."

"Well, we appreciate the favor," said Regan, glad the blue helicopter wasn't sporting a Hanston logo on the side. She'd explained that they just wanted to take a quick peek at things without getting the local FBI in a tizzy.

"Listen, if it helps you pin something on Carney, I'm all over it. I'd bet money he had something to do with the secretary's death. Those two *hated* each other."

Even though Vargas had fallen to her death, not been pushed, she wouldn't have been in that mine if Trevor hadn't forced her. Regan was sure Trevor wouldn't have been there, either, if it weren't for Carney.

Once again, she went back to that look on Trevor's face, his reaction when Regan pulled Carney out of the meeting to tell him about the tanker explosion. Too much concern – or nosiness – for an aide to Carney's chief rival. More like an aide to Carney himself.

She couldn't wait to get back to Washington and talk to Mac Holman, see if he could shed some light on things.

They were coming up on Axis. She doubted they'd be lucky enough to spot the chopper carrying the sniper that killed Trevor; for all she knew, it belonged to somebody Carney hired.

Eric whistled in awe. "They have an entire fleet." He was looking down at the airstrip and hangars; two small planes sat idle while one was taking off. A helicopter sat next to the hangar on the end – red, not black and silver.

Nick peered through the binoculars. "Can you get in any closer without attracting attention?"

The pilot said, "I'll try."

"Careful," said Eric. "Knowing Carney, they'll shoot us down."

"Okay, let's make one low pass and get out of here. Nick, be ready to scope it out – try to see what's inside those hangars."

The pilot circled back around and flew just above the treetops, cutting across to the other side of the landing strip just above the front of the structures. Regan saw one worker on the ground look up at them, shielding his eyes from the sun.

"Uh oh, let's get out of here," she said.

The chopper quickly retreated; within seconds, they were miles away from Axis.

"See anything?" she asked Nick.

"I think there was a chopper in that far building, but I couldn't make out the color."

"I got it," said Eric, handing the camera to Regan. "Looks like it's black and silver."

CHAPTER FIFTY-NINE

"TERMINATE MAC?" said Ness.

"He's cocky as hell, Landry," said Carney. "Always has been. Now he's acting like it's *my* fault that friend of his died in Alaska."

The vice president had a confused look on his face. "Why would he think that?"

"That's the whole point," Carney said irritably. "He has no reason to think that. Just because Vargas and I weren't exactly pals doesn't mean I wanted her dead – or Trevor Wolf, either."

"Don't worry about Mac. He's just upset, that's all."

Carney didn't need Mac snooping around. Who knew what he could dig up with the power of the VP's office at his disposal?

The mercenaries who carried out the tanker explosion – dubbed "Operation Hormuz" – would never point a finger in Carney's direction. There were too many layers of people in between.

He thought the plan was brilliant, capitalizing on an incident that happened two decades before where the U.S. attacked an Iranian oil platform in the Persian Gulf. In retaliation, the Islamic Revolutionary Guard Corps, a special-forces unit separate from Iran's navy that patrolled the borders, laid mines in the Gulf, hoping to blow up American ships. The Iranian navy scrambled to remove the mines to keep from sparking a U.S.-Iranian scuffle.

Who was to say there wasn't similar intent now? President Sanford, with less than six months under his belt, was working to improve relations with Iran. The tanker explosion would keep him from giving away the farm and help Carney get rid of an aging tanker at the same time. He loved the synchronicity.

But he'd protected Ness, made sure he knew nothing about it. He didn't want his buddy caught in the crossfire. All he'd done was ask Landry to use his position to grease the skids a little in Bahrain – a little favor between friends. Carney said he'd make it worth his while, and he did.

After all, Ness planned to retire after Sanford's first term. *One and done* – then he and the missus were off to their expensive new digs in Grand Cayman.

Between now and then, Carney planned to use the office of the vice president like it was his own.

෨

IT FELT good to be home.

Regan soaked in the tub, inspecting her slowly fading bruises while she tried to assimilate everything that had happened since she was here last. Candles flickered on the edge of the tub, giving the room a soothing glow. In the corner sat a crocheted angel; Regan looked at it and smiled.

The long talk with her dad changed everything, took away the unremitting ache that had lingered at the back of her consciousness for as long as she could remember. Tears filled her eyes as she recalled his words – how he could never quite believe that this beautiful, talented child was his. How, when he learned of her being in the mine, it took him back to the time, years before, when she had almost gotten herself killed in there. When he was so scared he could scarcely breathe, let alone speak.

She finally copped to drinking beer that night, which made him laugh.

He admitted that goading her mother and Colin had been a misguided attempt to get them to be more like her, to stand up to him the way she always did.

That's a little weird, Dad, she'd said. He agreed, said her mother didn't put up with much nonsense from him these days. He'd smiled sheepishly; she smiled back. Told him he needed to make amends with Colin, too.

She tried focusing on the details of the investigation, but her thoughts kept straying to Jack Landis. Finally, she closed her eyes and let herself be swept away by the memory of him.

What about her conversation with the chief? How *did* she feel about taking his place?

Mixed. Dead center.

Get Carney first, then think about it.

Regan attempted to concentrate on the oil man, about how she planned to expose him, but her thoughts floated all over the place like untethered balloons. She replayed the past month, thought of how it turned her life upside down. How it tested her to the limit. Made her question, for the first time, her skill as an agent.

A month ago, her FBI career was her whole identity. She couldn't imagine doing or being anything else.

Something had changed. The demons were gone; she could return to Alaska if she chose. Or not.

Her mind drifted back to Jack, to the house in the woods. A little slice of paradise.

CHAPTER SIXTY

MAC AGREED to meet her for coffee at a Starbuck's a few blocks from the White House. At first, he was uptight and guarded. But as Regan shifted to her best negotiator voice, he dropped his arms and began to relax a little.

"Trevor Wolf and I both grew up in Kansas, but we didn't meet until we were in law school at KU," he said. "Constitutional law – we were the only two in the class who actually liked it." He slowly twisted his cardboard cup in a circle as he talked.

Regan stayed quiet.

"We came here together, loaded with ambition. And I think we did okay – we both pretty much achieved what we were after. But I have to wonder if it was worth it."

Regan watched the cup turn.

"We're mired in our jobs – just ask my girlfriend, who I hardly ever see. We work ridiculous hours. Trevor and I didn't get together with each other that often, even though we were best friends."

For several moments, he kept his eyes fixed on his cup, which he had stopped turning. Regan could tell he was too choked up to speak.

Finally, he looked up and said quietly, "I want to know why Trevor was killed."

"So do we, Mr. Holman. He was a dedicated public servant, not to mention your friend, and he deserves that," Regan said soothingly. "And I think you can help us."

"How?" A wary look darted across his face. He compressed his lips into a thin line, the edges of his mouth turning downward.

It told Regan that Mac was highly distressed. He seemed to be waging an internal battle.

"Mac, I'm going to be completely honest with you. I believe your friend was killed because he was working for Robert Carney – and Carney feared that Trevor would expose him." She paused to gauge his reaction.

He scratched his head, then crossed his arms. Regan saw his jaw tighten. He said nothing.

"Here's what I think," said Regan. "I think Carney's involved in a scheme that reaches all the way from Alaska to the Middle East. And the vice president may have some involvement."

"It's *Carney*, not the vice president!" he whispered frantically. "Ness had nothing to do with that tanker explosion." He stopped and glanced around. He looked back at Regan, and she could see the heavy burden he'd been carrying. It was written all over his face – and in his now-teary eyes.

"What about Bahrain?"

The chief of staff looked confused. "Bahrain?"

"Your boss may have been instrumental in getting Carney's development deals going there."

"No, that can't be right. He wouldn't do that."

"Even for his best friend?"

"I can't believe he'd —" He stopped. "Carney's trying to get the vice president to fire me. I accused him of having something to do with Trevor's death. If Ness goes along with him, maybe I can convince him that Carney's coming after me because he's guilty."

"I think you need to disappear for awhile. Trevor was shot by a sniper, and you could be next."

His eyes bulged.

"We'll protect you, but we need your help, Mac. Help us get the man who killed your best friend."

๛

SHE HATED to have to call James, but he was the only CIA agent she knew well enough to ask a favor of. And surely he was over his feelings of rejection by now.

211

"Hey, James, it's Regan. How's it going?" she said in a cheery voice.

"Fine. What's up?" he replied grumpily.

"I'm working on a project and I could use your help."

"So you want me to dig into agency files for you?" As an analyst in the CIA's Directorate of Intelligence, he had high-security clearance.

"More or less," she said.

He paused. "Okay. On one condition."

"Shoot," said Regan.

"Dinner with me."

She rolled her eyes. "I'm really locked up right now. Time-sensitive case."

"You still have to eat. Dinner tonight?"

She desperately needed the information James had access to. "Okay, but it'll have to be a quick bite someplace."

"Deal," he said cheerfully.

"I'm on my way over," she said grumpily.

CHAPTER SIXTY-ONE

"WHAT ARE we looking for?" asked James.

"Information about the explosion of the oil tanker in the Strait of Hormuz. Specifically, evidence pertaining to the Islamic Revolutionary Guard Corps' involvement," said Regan.

James typed on his keyboard and a screen popped up that gave a detailed summary of recent activity in the Persian Gulf. "Let's see … it says here that the IRGC denies involvement, as does the Iranian government."

"What does the intel say?"

"There's nothing that contradicts those assertions," he said, reading the notations on the screen. He turned to Regan. "So if the Revolutionary Guard didn't lay the mines, then who did?"

"Precisely. That's the million-dollar question. Was the strait swept for mines after the tanker blew up?"

"Yes," said James. "It looks like the Navy's Fifth Fleet used a thermal imaging sensor system to detect the floating mines that remained. They found seven that hadn't been detonated."

"Aren't the tankers that pass through the Persian Gulf equipped with those sensors?" Regan said.

James deftly manipulated his mouse. "Apparently they are, but the captain of the *Seacat* claims the system malfunctioned."

Convenient.

"So how was the crew warned?" she said. "There was only one injury and no deaths. I'd say that's something of a miracle."

"Hmm," said James.

"I think there's a strong possibility that this was a work-for-hire operation, James. I need to know who did the hiring."

"And who did the working?"

"That, too."

James scratched his chin. "I play basketball with a guy in our National Clandestine Service. Let me see what I can find out."

"That'd be great, James. You can tell me at dinner."

He grinned wickedly. "Pick you up at eight."

⮞

THE VICE president wanted to see him. Any other day, that was business as usual. Today Mac felt his stomach knot as he made his way to his boss's office.

"Mac, Bob tells me you've been making some pretty wild accusations."

Mac remained silent, watching Ness. Could he really be involved in something illegal?

"Mac? Is that true?" Ness's face was creased in a frown.

Mac said, "I didn't accuse him outright. But he *is* one of the last people to speak to Trevor. Don't you find that a little odd?"

"Why would that be odd?"

"Well, sir, I don't know of any reason for Carney to be talking to him."

"Maybe Bob was trying to get hold of Vargas. Look at all the people who call you wanting to talk to me."

If that argument held water, Carney would have made that point already.

"I think that's different, sir."

"I agree with Bob, Mac – you're out of line. He wants me to fire you."

Alarm shot through him. If he wasn't here, there'd be no one to protect Ness from Carney. Mac couldn't bear the thought of his boss being lured into Carney's scandalous deals out of loyalty to his longtime friend.

"Please, Mr. Vice President. I don't want to lose my job. I promise to back off. I won't mention Trevor to Bob again." He gave Ness an earnest look and waited.

Ness paused, staring at his hands. "Okay, Mac. Get back to work and leave my friend alone."

൙

"I COULD eat sushi every day," James declared, plucking a salmon nigiri from the black lacquer plate.

"So were you able to learn anything from your friend?" Regan asked.

James nodded mysteriously.

"And?"

"And the mines were PF-17s."

"Which means?"

"They're American-made."

"Is there a black market for them?"

"As it turns out, there is," James said smugly, taking a sip of beer.

"I need a name," said Regan.

"Charlie Burke. Former CIA."

"Retired?"

"Against his will."

"So he's using his extensive network in nefarious ways," Regan said.

James nodded. "And highly profitable ones, too."

"Interesting."

"Want to come over to my place for a glass of wine?" James asked, a hopeful look on his face.

Not a chance, Jimmy.

"Sorry, but I can't. I've got leads to chase. I appreciate your help, though, James. Dinner's on me."

CHAPTER SIXTY-TWO

NICK WAS the eye; Regan sat in the passenger seat munching on a bag of Cheetos. They were parked down the street from Charlie Burke's townhouse in Georgetown.

"Swanky neighborhood," Nick said, his gaze never leaving Burke's front door.

"Yep, business must be good," Regan replied.

"So you think he might be involved in the tanker explosion?"

"I think it's possible that he supplied the mines and the men. I'm betting Burke has a bunch of old associates to call upon for special projects like that, and I doubt many others have those same kinds of connections."

"You mean he has his own little army of mercenaries?" said Nick.

"Right. Former Navy SEALs and other highly trained military personnel. Maybe some former feds, too. I doubt he has much trouble lining them up if the price is right."

"I'm guessing if Charlie Burke gets involved in an operation at all, it's *only* when the price is right."

"Which means his clientele is limited to the very powerful and the very rich," said Regan, licking orange powder off her fingers. "Like vice presidents and oil magnates."

"So how many layers do you suppose there are between Charlie and his clients?"

"That's what I'm hoping to find out. Want a Cheeto?"

"No, those things stink."

Regan closed the bag and set it on the floor. She sat back and sighed.

"What's your problem?" said Nick, his eyes still fixed on Burke's house.

"Surveillance bores the crap out of me."

Nick smiled, giving her a quick glance. "Maybe Burke is still wrapping things up on this operation and we'll get a name of one of his associates. Would that rouse you out of your boredom?"

"You bet, big boy."

They were quiet for several minutes, each lost in thought.

"So you meet with OPR tomorrow?" said Nick.

"Day after tomorrow." Regan's stomach churned.

"You'll be okay."

"Well, if not, I guess I can always move back to Alaska."

Nick turned to her, his mouth open. "You're seriously considering that?"

Regan pointed toward Burke's place. "Eyes on your subject, pal."

≈

CARNEY WAS livid. "No identifying marks on the chopper?"

"No," said his assistant. "He just said a blue helicopter flew in low and the passengers appeared to be scoping out the hangars."

Carney's mind raced. Was it the FBI looking for the chopper that had been in Alaska? Did the Bureau use unmarked aircraft?

"Okay, I'm on my way back – I'll be landing in a couple hours. Tell that worker I want to see him as soon as we land."

"Will do, sir."

He'd just disconnected when his phone rang. "Yes?"

"Bob, it's Mac."

Carney didn't reply.

"I, uh, just wanted to apologize. I didn't mean to accuse you of anything … I'm just upset over what happened to Trevor."

Carney hoped Mac wasn't trying to pull a fast one. "We're *all* upset, Mac. What happened to Trevor and to Ella – it's unfathomable. I plan to do whatever I can to help the FBI find Wolf's killer."

"Thank you, sir. That means a lot."

CHAPTER SIXTY-THREE

THE AGING brown van was parked across from Burke's townhouse. The driver and his passenger jumped out – one male, one female. He wore black slacks and a white shirt; she wore a long black skirt and a white blouse. He carried a canvas briefcase while she carried a stack of *Watchtower* magazines. They began their undercover operation, going door-to-door, while the two agents in the back of the van set up their equipment.

"What if somebody invites them in and really does want more information about their faith?" Regan asked.

"The female agent – Ruthie – grew up as a Jehovah's Witness, so she's got it covered."

"Wow … imagine her family's surprise when she announced she was joining the FBI instead of the mission."

Nick laughed. "I bet *that* made her the black sheep of the family."

Charlie Burke opened the door and came down his front steps, clutching a leash with a German shepherd on the other end of it. He reminded Regan of Sean Connery – the way the actor looked in *The Presidio* in the late eighties. She still loved to watch that movie on cable.

Burke glanced at the van across the street and then at the two undercover agents a half a block away. Apparently satisfied, he turned and began walking in Regan and Nick's direction on the opposite side of the street.

They both ducked. Burke was former CIA and undoubtedly suspicious of everything. Even more so in his current line of work.

"So that's good, right?" asked Regan. "That means they can get inside with the bug and get out before he gets back."

Nick turned and looked down the street. "Right. But if we see him coming back, they'll slow up – wait until he's inside, then ring the doorbell and hand him a magazine. The bug will be in it."

"Won't he see it?"

"It's extremely small and glued somewhere in the middle. Not likely that he'll sit down and read the *Watchtower*."

"What if he tosses it in the garbage?"

"Unless he immediately dumps his garbage in the Dumpster, we'll still be able to pick up his conversations. If it does get taken out, we'll just watch for him to leave again and go in. Burke lives alone."

"What if he doesn't take that dog with him?"

"They have a tranquilizer gun." He saw Regan's stricken face. "Don't worry; it only knocks the animal out for a short time."

Regan slumped in her seat and rested her head against the headrest. "So now we sit and wait some more?"

"You got it, sister."

"Ugh. Don't *you* ever get bored?"

"Out of my skull. We surveillance guys live for the fifteen minutes of adrenaline-pumping action that comes after the hours of sitting."

"Jeez," said Regan. "Give me a good shoot-out any day."

CHAPTER SIXTY-FOUR

THE *WATCHTOWER*-toting agents had gotten in and out before Burke and his dog returned. They also left a bug-infested magazine rolled up in the handle of his door, just for good measure.

Regan drove to Quantico. Even though she was still on medical leave until tomorrow, she wanted to work at her desk, where she had access to the FBI database.

She jumped in and didn't come up for air until almost eight o'clock. But she had found some interesting stuff.

Charles Burke was involved in a failed CIA op in Tangier a few years before. It appeared that Burke was playing both sides of the fence – for the U.S. government as well as Tangiers International, reputed to be the largest investigations firm in the world. Though he was implicated in the disappearance of more than five million dollars intended to be used in a weapons deal with Moroccan rebels, the money was never found. Despite his pleas of innocence, the CIA parted ways with him.

Nothing more dangerous than a highly skilled, pissed-off former fed. Especially one who very likely had five million stashed away in a numbered bank account.

She checked his vital statistics. Born in Baltimore, economics degree from the University of Maryland, married for thirteen years to Margie Sampson, divorced for the last ten. No children.

Margie was remarried, and since the divorce had occurred so long ago, she probably wasn't still bitter enough to tell Regan anything juicy. Who knows, maybe they even parted as buddies who had just drifted apart. If that were the case, Margie would make a risky interviewee.

Burke owned property in Tangier and spent winters there. Regan didn't relish the thought of a trip to Morocco, but she'd see where things led.

She decided to check in with Mac Holman. She wasn't surprised to find him still in his office, even at this hour. "Hey, Mac. How's it going?"

"Fine," he said guardedly.

"So, would you like to grab a bite to eat?"

"Uh, I can't. I've got work to do here."

"Okay. Can we get together and talk when you're finished up there?"

"It's going to be late."

"I can stay up late," said Regan.

"I don't know. I'll have to see," he said, eager to hang up.

"Mac, we need to talk."

"I've got to go."

"Well, you have my number. Call me."

He hung up.

Mac was still on the fence. And the longer he remained there, the more dangerous things became.

❧

AN HOUR later, engrossed in her research, the ringing phone made her jump. She hoped Mac had had a change of heart.

It was James. "Am I interrupting anything?"

"No, just doing a little work on the investigation. You still at the office?"

"Yes, and I found something you might find interesting. The PF-17s are manufactured in Pennsylvania. Company called Sampson Industries. They make mine detection equipment – and guess what, they even throw together a few explosive mines, too, just for fun."

"You said *Sampson* Industries?" Regan's pulse quickened.

"Right," said James.

"Burke's ex-wife's maiden name is Sampson. I bet Sampson Industries is owned by his former in-laws."

"Uh, let's see ... Martin Sampson is the owner."

"Excellent. Thanks, James." She hung up before he could ask her out for dinner.

She typed in a name on the keyboard. "Okay, Martin Sampson, let's see what we know about you."

Martin and Margie Sampson were fifty-three-year-old twins from York, Pennsylvania. Marty was an industrial engineer who worked twenty-five years at Imhoff-Greyson, a global defense and technology company. Five years ago, he left to start his own company.

Maybe Charlie Burke was a silent partner in his former brother-in-law's venture. In exchange for hefty sums of cash, Sampson no doubt supplied Burke with goodies to ply his trade.

But Burke was no dummy. Regan was pretty sure he didn't pull up to the loading dock himself and drive off with a truckload of mines.

She called Nick. He sounded subdued.

"Did I catch you napping?" Regan said.

"Sleeping with my eyes open. It's a special skill."

She filled him in on the Sampson twins, especially the male half. "We need to identify the gophers between Burke and Sampson."

"Well, so far our boy's been quiet as a mouse. Doesn't even say much to his dog, the poor beast. Dog's name is Rudy, by the way."

"Good to know in case we have to break in. How long are you staying there, Nicky? You sound beat."

"The night crew is coming on momentarily. I'm heading straight home to my beddy-bye."

"Your replacements have my number, right?"

"Yep, Regan, they've got your number."

CHAPTER SIXTY-FIVE

S HORTLY AFTER leaving Quantico, Regan noticed a black SUV behind her. She kept glancing in her rearview mirror; the vehicle continued to tail her, keeping a discreet distance.

She turned into a neighborhood, twisting back and forth through the quiet streets. The SUV followed.

Regan felt fear start to gnaw at her gut. Tiny streams of sweat trickled down her back.

She called Nick. "I'm being tailed."

"Where are you?" he said, his tone alert.

"King Street in Alexandria."

"Head to Fort Ward Park and drive around it until I get there. Don't make any stops and stay on well-traveled streets."

"Okay," she said, relieved to know he was on the way. She was on Seminary Road, just passing the hospital. As she turned on Howard Street, the SUV raced up alongside and slammed into her, tires screeching as they shoved her car to the side of the road.

Regan ducked down, hand trembling as she reached for her gun. Two shots blasted her car, one through the windshield and one through her side window, missing her by inches. She didn't dare peek up over the door; she crouched down further, hearing two more shots. Neither one hit her car, but she braced herself for another round when she heard the car squeal off.

A car door slammed. Nick screamed, "Regan!"

She jumped out of the car and ran to her partner. "Oh, Nick. Thank God." She was shaking badly. "Did you get any numbers on the plate?"

"The last three. Virginia plates. You okay?"

"I'm fine – just a little rattled. And my car's messed up." The Honda Accord had a dented front fender and two bullet holes.

"Were you able to get off a shot at all?"

She shook her head. "No. Did you?"

"Yeah, two. I don't think either of them hit the driver."

"You get a description?"

"No, it was too dark. We'll try running partial plates to see if anything matches, but don't hold your breath – there's about a million black Ford Explorers around here."

They leaned against Regan's car until her breathing returned to normal. "Well," she said, "we must be getting too close for *somebody's* comfort."

The first person that came to mind was Mac Holman.

THE NEXT morning, Nick was back on the stakeout, the brown van replaced by a newer white one parked further down on the same side of the street as Burke's townhouse. Undercover agents painted fire hydrants while the techs inside the van kept an ear on Burke.

Regan climbed into Nick's car, the smell of hot food and coffee wafting in with her. She handed him a paper-wrapped breakfast burrito. "I figure it's the least I can do since you saved my life."

"Hey, anytime," he said, grinning at her. "Doing okay?"

"So far, so good. Nobody's taken a shot at me yet, but it's only ten a.m. Heard anything interesting?"

"Yep," Nick said, taking a bite of burrito. He chewed and swallowed before answering. "I was just getting ready to call you. Our boy Charlie is taking a trip tomorrow. I heard him making the reservation."

"Where he's going?"

"Houston."

"Hmm, I wonder if he's going to visit a certain CEO."

"Might be." He took a swallow of coffee, followed by another bite of the burrito.

"Okay, Nick. If we can, let's maintain surveillance until he leaves. I'll grab a flight to Houston tonight."

"What about your meeting with the OPR?"

"I can get Al to extend my medical leave. I'll tell him I'm seeing double." She looked at Nick and crossed her eyes.

Nick tossed the half-eaten burrito back into the wrapping. "I'm going to Houston with you."

She thought about it a moment. "Right now I'm just following hunches, and they may not lead anyplace, Nick. Since I'm on leave, I don't have to take the time to clear it first. I think it's better if I go alone."

"I knew you were going to say that. But these are dangerous people, Regan. You found that out last night."

"I know. I'll be careful. I just want to see where Burke's going. I'll keep a safe distance and observe."

"What if Al finds out? You'll be in deep shit."

"Well, like I said before, I can always move back to Juneau."

Was she tempting fate on purpose, hoping for that outcome?

Nick was quiet a moment. "I guess in some ways I don't blame you. You could have a good life there – maybe get married and have a houseful of babies and a job that's a whole lot less stressful than this one." He turned to her. "But is that what you want?"

He was asking the very question she'd been asking herself over and over. "I don't know, Nick. Parts of it are certainly attractive. Jack is different than any guy I've ever met. But I love the FBI. So I just don't know."

"I get that. But if you choose to go back home, don't let it be because the Bureau kicked you out."

Regan reached over and squeezed his arm. "You're a good friend, Nick."

"And because I'm such a good friend, I'll get you the flight information on Burke." The FBI could access passenger manifests if there were "people of interest" traveling from one point to another.

She nodded and climbed out of the car. She heard him say, "Hey, Regan?"

She popped her head back in. "Yeah?"

"I mean it ... be careful, okay? And call me. I'll talk you through surveillance."

CHAPTER SIXTY-SIX

REGAN COULDN'T sleep, her mind buzzing with questions. Maybe a jog would help her sort things out.

The motel sat near other motels in a flat, sparsely populated area. She felt reasonably safe and would see anybody approaching.

As she ran in the dark, she formulated theories in her head. Would Carney be likely to have someone go directly to Charlie Burke to plan an operation? Someone like Mac? She didn't think so; it would be too easy to trace that contact. If Mac *was* involved, there had to be someone between him and Burke – at least one more layer of protection, if not more.

That individual would have to be someone highly skilled as well, but whose reputation wasn't tarnished. Someone connected enough to get things done. Carney – and maybe Ness – wouldn't trust an operation like this to anyone less.

The chain is only as strong as its weakest link.

From the little bits of conversation they had picked up in Burke's house, he seemed brusque and impatient. Not the sort to work with someone he didn't know and trust implicitly. The go-between was likely someone Burke had worked with before. Perhaps another former CIA agent.

Or maybe a *current* one. Could someone at the agency be working both sides of the fence as Burke had done?

She turned and jogged back toward the motel, her heart beating fast. She had a new thread to follow.

≈

BAGGAGE CLAIM was crowded and noisy with arriving passengers. Regan stood near the carousel for Burke's flight.

She spotted him. He was walking with another man, and the two were absorbed in conversation.

They moved to an empty spot right next to Regan. Burke looked at her and smiled.

She returned his smile and looked back at the luggage rotating in front of them. Burke's companion leaned over to grab his bag. As he lifted it off the carousel, Regan got a glimpse of his ID tag: John Berryton.

As the two men moved off with their bags, Regan stood with her hands on her hips and tried to appear frustrated. She made a show of looking at the suitcases other people had claimed, as though perhaps someone grabbed hers by mistake.

Hers was actually parked over by the metal divider that separated the carousels from the walkway. The two men exited onto the sidewalk; she grabbed the handle of her suitcase and hurried out the door behind them.

They continued their conversation, unaware of her standing nearby. They jumped into a cab. Regan moved to the curb, stepping in front of the woman who was next in the cab line.

"Sorry – I have an emergency," she said to the woman as she hopped into the waiting cab.

"Yeah, right," she heard the lady mutter as she slammed the door.

"Could you, uh, follow that cab?"

"Whatever you say, ma'am," said the driver, lurching away from the curb.

She called Nick. "I'm in a cab following Burke's cab."

"Gee, that's original."

"Fastest way to track him, smarty-pants."

"Yeah, as long as he doesn't see you," said Nick. "Remember, Burke's a pro. Don't let your cab driver slow down when the other cab drops him off, wherever that is."

"Okay. Hey, I need you to run a name for me. John Berryton."

"Sure thing, Reegs. I'll get back to you."

The cab in front pulled in at the Four Seasons.

"Keep going, please," said Regan. "Drive around for ten more minutes, then return to the hotel." She wanted Burke and Berryton to have time to check in before she got inside.

The cab driver shook his head and did as he was told. He mumbled something; it sounded an awful lot like, *It's your dime, crazy lady.*

CHAPTER SIXTY-SEVEN

R EGAN WASN'T used to such nice digs. Compared to last night's hotel, it was like stepping up from a hamburger to prime rib.

She pulled out a black linen pantsuit and an ivory silk shell. She gathered her hair into a bun at the nape of her neck and plopped a wide-brimmed, black hat on her head to mask her red hair.

Regan hoped the hat and sunglasses would keep Burke from recognizing her as the same woman he saw at the airport – if he happened to glance in her direction at all.

She sat in a corner of the lobby, flipping through a magazine and keeping an eye out for Burke and Berryton. An hour later, they appeared, moving to the front doors to wait. At one point, Burke glanced in her direction, but his look didn't linger.

A black limousine arrived and the two men stepped into the midday sun. As the car moved off, Regan hurried through the doors and to the parking lot where her rental car waited.

She zigzagged through traffic, soon getting the limousine in her sights. She followed it all the way to the corporate offices of Axis Oil.

Regan pulled into employee parking and watched as the two men got out of the limousine; she flattened herself on the car seat until they were inside the building.

She settled in to wait, her eyes riveted on the entrance. Why had she talked Nick out of coming? Nobody to talk to, no snacks to munch on. She gave an exaggerated sigh.

Regan picked up her phone and punched in a number.

"Jenesco."

"I'm bored, Nick."

"On surveillance, huh?"

"Yup. Sitting in the parking lot at Axis."

"How long you been watching him?"

"Uh —" Regan looked at her watch. "Seven minutes."

"*Seven* minutes? My God, Regan, you're such a baby. I knew I should've gone with you. Hey, I have something for you on Berryton. He's Burke's attorney."

"What firm is he with?"

"Banks, Berryton and Smythe. Mid-sized D.C. firm."

"What else do we know?"

"He represented Burke in the matter involving Tangiers International. I suspect he's Burke's counselor on all legal matters, but I'll have to dig a little more to confirm that."

"At least we know what his relationship with Burke is."

"Too bad you can't get in there and eavesdrop on that meeting."

"Yeah, but since I can't, I don't know if there's much point in sitting here staring at the building. I think I'll head back to the hotel and wait there."

"Here's a little surveillance tip, Regan. You go where the subject is, not wait for them to come to you."

"Okay, Nick. Point taken."

~

REGAN WHILED away the hours making phone calls. She got caught up with her mother, then she and Jack talked until her battery ran out. It left her feeling lit up like a Christmas tree.

That chief job is looking better and better.

Regan fished in her tote bag for the car charger and plugged her phone in. More calls to make; time to get her head back in the game.

"Hey, James, me again," said Regan.

"You decided to take me up on that glass of wine?"

"That would be kinda hard, since I'm not in Washington right now. No, I just had one more quick question for you."

"Another dinner with me then?"

He frustrated the hell out of her. "Never mind, James. I'll use my other CIA contact."

"You have another CIA contact? Who?"

"I'm not going to say. Now do you want to help or should I call him?"

"Okay," he said with a dejected sigh. "What do you need?"

"I need to know who worked with Charlie Burke when he was at the agency. Any loyal underlings who still work there?"

"I can tell you that without even looking anything up. His name is David Lancaster. He was a new operations officer that Charlie took under his wing. Charlie made sure Lancaster was always on his foreign intelligence team – like he was trying to create a clone of himself."

"If you don't mind my asking, James, how do you know that? It's not like the CIA is a little organization where everybody knows everybody."

"True, but like I told you a couple days ago, I play basketball with a bunch of guys. We go drink beer afterwards, and some of the guys like to brag about their exploits. Not me, of course."

"Of course not."

"Mainly because I don't have any exploits to brag about."

Regan laughed softly. "So is Lancaster part of that group?"

"No, but some guys he works with are. They gripe about the lucky breaks he got because of Charlie Burke. By the time Burke left the CIA, Lancaster had a solid foothold of his own."

"What's Lancaster's position now?"

"He's a senior operations officer. Stationed overseas someplace. Hang on – I can tell you where."

She heard James tapping on his keyboard.

"Looks like he's stationed in Saudi Arabia, but he's back here on temporary duty of some kind."

"Do you suppose Burke and Lancaster keep in touch?"

"I'd be surprised if they didn't. From what I heard, Charlie treated him like the son he never had."

Regan hung up, promising to buy James lunch when she got back. Show appreciation without making it seem like a date.

She had one more call to make. "Resa? It's Regan."

"Regan! How are ya, hon? Are you back in Houston?"

"Actually I am, but I'm not staying long. I just have a quick question for you."

"Let me send my limo to pick you up. I need some girl talk with all these big burly bodyguards around here. Too much testosterone, ya know what I mean?"

Too much for Resa? Regan never would've predicted that. "I'd love to but I'm working on the investigation. I need to stay put."

"Pooh," said Resa. "Okay, hon, what do you need to know?"

"Does your husband have a friend or associate by the name of Charlie Burke?"

"Charlie? Hell, yeah. We've been to his place in Tangier. I know they've done some deals together, but I don't know the particulars. I do know Charlie went with Bob on one of his trips to Bahrain, if that helps."

"What's your impression of Charlie?"

"Charlie's good-lookin', and he's really smart, but he doesn't say much. Guys like that make me nervous ... you always wonder what they're thinkin'. And with Charlie, I don't know, there's something in those eyes that makes you wonder if what he's thinkin' isn't always good. Know what I mean?"

"Uh huh," said Regan. "Thanks, Resa. Next time I'm in Houston, we'll get together for some girl talk. I promise."

"Lookin' forward to it, hon."

CHAPTER SIXTY-EIGHT

J ACK HUNG up the phone and smiled at Susie. "I like that girl," he told the dog. "I like her a lot."
Susie wagged her tail, ears pitched forward as she waited for the word *run*. Her favorite activity, hands down.

Jack didn't disappoint her. He needed to burn off some pent-up energy, too.

As he jogged along Fritz Cove Road, Susie zigzagging her way from the road through the ditch to the woods through the ditch to the road, Jack's mind was flooded with images of Regan. He'd been on pins and needles since she left, distracted from his job for the first time ever.

What if she didn't come back? What if their brief time together was all there was?

The thought of it made his chest ache.

Forest ranger jobs in Washington, if any, would hardly contribute to his research; besides, he was currently in the middle of a grant-funded research project. He couldn't just abandon it.

Jack looked up and saw a car coming down the middle of the road. His elderly neighbor, Frank, should've had his license pulled years ago. He honked and waved, veering dangerously close to Jack.

Up ahead, he saw Susie streaking from the ditch toward the road. Jack screamed, "Susie, stop!" He froze, arms bent, shoulders scrunched, bracing himself for the collision.

At the last second, Susie pivoted toward him. The big Buick missed her by a whisker.

It left him so shaken his eyes filled with tears. Jack moved over to the ditch and dropped down, waiting for his heart to stop pounding. Susie sniffed at the bushes nearby, intent on scaring up something to chase.

Finally, Jack stood. He turned and began walking back toward home. The dog, sensing his mood, ran to him and stayed close to his side.

I'm becoming an emotional wreck, thought Jack. He had to find a way to get Regan Manning out of his mind.

≈

REGAN WONDERED how the limo driver was killing time. It had been nearly three hours, and the car hadn't moved from its spot at the curb, just to the left of the front entrance.

He'd gotten out for a smoke a couple times, still wearing his uniform coat despite the oppressive heat and humidity. She had long since shed her jacket and hat.

At least it's beginning to cool off. She glanced at her watch: five-forty. She thumped her fingers on the steering wheel and considered calling Nick again, but he'd just mock her.

Clouds had moved in; she heard rumbles of thunder. The rain-cooled air would be a relief.

Her phone rang. It was Al.

Her heart started to race. "Hey, boss. What's up?"

"If you're feeling up to it, Regan, I'd like to meet with you first thing in the morning. I want to see where we are with the investigation."

The thunder rumbled.

Why didn't I let the call go to voicemail?

She turned the key in the ignition and rolled up her window. "Uh, I have an appointment first thing, but we could meet in the afternoon."

"Okay, that should work."

The storm was right overhead, setting off a loud crack of thunder as the lightning flashed.

"Where are you?" said Al, his voice suddenly suspicious. "There's not a cloud in the sky."

"I'm ... I'll tell you tomorrow, boss," she said, hanging up.

I think I may have just bought myself a one-way ticket back to Juneau.

She looked up to see the limo driving off.

CHAPTER SIXTY-NINE

REGAN PARKED and watched Burke and Berryton enter the hotel. A few minutes later, she followed them in. She glanced around the lobby but didn't see the two men anywhere.

Self-disgust blurred her thinking. Al was going to be really pissed, and this little clandestine jaunt hadn't even yielded anything particularly useful. Burke and his lawyer met with Carney – so what?

Was she turning into the epitome of an arrogant Fibbie, one who thought she had all the answers? The type local cops couldn't stand?

Regan headed for the lounge. There was a small table in the corner that was empty.

"What can I get for you?" said the perky young cocktail waitress.

"Drambuie, please. Straight up."

"You got it, sweetie." The girl sashayed off to get her drink.

Regan fiddled with the cocktail napkin and attempted to sort out her thoughts. Resa had confirmed that Carney planned the tanker explosion. Maybe Mac was one of his errand boys, just like Trevor. It would make sense, since the two men had been best friends. Maybe Mac's contact was Lancaster, and Lancaster's contact was Burke. Burke or Lancaster or somebody they hired paid a visit to Marty Sampson, who loaded them up with toys that made a loud bang when something bumped into them. Burke or Lancaster lined up the mercenaries to take the explosives to the Strait of Hormuz and plant them there, ready to surprise the *Seacat*.

The waitress plunked her drink down on the table along with a bowl of party mix and strode away.

She took a sip of the Drambuie, feeling the liqueur burn as it went down. She popped a peanut into her mouth and went back to her thoughts.

They designed the incident to look like the Islamic Revolutionary Guard was responsible. Or Iranian President Hossein Monshizadeh. So maybe they were trying to spark a confrontation, but why? If Monshizadeh —

"Is this seat taken?"

Regan looked up. Standing beside her table, smiling down at her, was Charlie Burke.

"Oh – I don't mean to be rude, but I'd just like to enjoy a quiet drink," she said.

He pulled out the chair and sat down anyway, still wearing an amused smile on his face. "We seem to be turning up in all the same places," he said.

She suppressed a shiver and gave him a questioning look.

"On my street in Georgetown, at the Houston airport, and now here. Call me paranoid, but it's starting to feel like you're following me."

Regan kept her face neutral, trying to mask her astonishment. He *saw her* in Georgetown?

"You flatter yourself, sir. I don't know you from Adam. And I'm certainly not following you. Now please leave."

"That's amazing. You have an identical twin then – with that same beautiful hair."

"Well, I ... I don't know what to say. There are lots of redheads, and *this* redhead has never been to Georgetown. You've obviously mistaken me for someone else. If you don't mind, I'd rather be alone." She gave him the sternest look she could muster in her current state of panic.

He observed her a moment longer, a half smile on his lips, his eyes matching Resa's description.

Finally, he stood. "Of course, ma'am. Sorry to offend. Your drink's on me." He gave a slight bow, which reminded her again of Sean Connery.

It had an effect on her; she was shaken *and* stirred.

❧

THOUGH SHE felt like running back to her room and locking herself inside, Regan forced herself to move through the lobby slowly, casually, stopping to peruse a rack of sightseeing brochures.

Finally, she moseyed to the elevator and pressed the button for the floor above hers.

When she got off the elevator, she hurried down the hall to the stairwell and descended one flight to her floor. She peeked out the stairwell door and sprinted to her room. Once inside, she double-locked the door and sat down on the bed, breathing deeply to calm down.

She couldn't believe Burke saw her that many times. *But why wouldn't he? He's former CIA, for godsakes.*

She called Nick. "You were right. Burke's good." She told him about her encounter with him in the bar. "Confirmed what I already suspected – I'm really shitty at surveillance."

"Regan, you need to come back. This is getting dangerous. If he saw you on his street in Georgetown, no doubt he saw me, too. He knows there's a stakeout, which is why he doesn't say much. He knows we're listening."

"I wonder if he ordered the hit on me two nights ago."

"Maybe so … and if that's the case, how did he know your identity?"

Regan felt a shiver go up her spine. This *was* getting dangerous.

"I'll be on a flight out first thing in the morning."

CHAPTER SEVENTY

F EW PEOPLE impressed Carney like Charlie Burke. The man was smooth, professional – and he could get his hands on anything or anybody.

The hotel project in Muharraq would move forward faster now that Burke was helping out. He would grease the palms that needed to be greased in order to make sure the causeway connecting the island to Juffair got built sooner rather than later.

That, along with Ness's little bit of assistance – which, as it turns out, he probably didn't need – meant RBC Enterprises was poised to explode in Bahrain. Carney needed to expedite his divorce so Resa couldn't get her grubby hands on any of it.

It wasn't that he was driven by money. Carney simply saw money as a tool for improving the world; if he was going to truly make a difference, he needed lots of the green stuff.

The Caspian deal was a case in point: the "investment" was all about the flow of oil, as vital to him as his own blood. The revenue it generated would allow more fields to be explored and tapped, thus guaranteeing America's way of life for years to come.

And soon he could shift funds back to the rotary steerable device, producing one more feather in the oil industry's cap.

Carney got up from his desk and moved over to his office bar. He poured a drink and gave himself a toast.

☙

REGAN SLEPT badly, her dreams a distressing jumble.

She stood at the edge of a mammoth canyon that stretched for miles. Jack was on the other side, but she couldn't get over to him.

Ella Vargas was at the bottom of the giant ravine, attempting to climb up the sheer wall face, repeatedly losing her foothold and tumbling back down. Regan was desperate to help her but couldn't figure out how without a rope or climbing tools.

A black and silver chopper suddenly appeared overhead, a rope dangling from the open door on the side. Was it for her or Vargas? Could she use it to get over to Jack?

Regan started to reach for the rope and felt a crushing sense of foreboding.

She came awake, heart pounding; her body, along with the sheets, were damp with perspiration. She crawled out of bed and into the shower.

She was in the lobby by six, still groggy as she checked out and headed for the airport.

Burke's flight back to Washington, according to Nick, was later in the morning. Regan had to get back to face the music with Al.

After returning her rental car, she sat in the lounge at her gate, sipping coffee and feeling out of sorts as she pondered her fate. Snippets of the dream kept coming back to her.

"We meet again."

She knew who it was before she even looked up.

"Will this be your first trip to Washington?" he said sarcastically.

She was in no mood to deal with Charlie Burke. She looked up at him with daggers in her eyes. "Listen, you son-of-a-bitch," she hissed, "I don't know who the hell you are, but get away from me or I will call airport security. Got it?"

Burke looked taken aback, like maybe he *had* mistaken her for someone else. He held up both hands in surrender and went to join John Berryton in the next row of chairs.

When they called the flight, the two men boarded as first-class passengers. Regan averted her eyes as she passed through first class on the way to her seat at the back. She was glad to be as far away from Charlie Burke as possible.

She couldn't shake the nagging sense that she, instead of Burke, was the one under surveillance.

CHAPTER SEVENTY-ONE

THAT WAS too close for comfort," said Nick.

Regan held the phone with her shoulder while she opened the frozen bag of bread and popped two slices into the toaster. "Yeah, tell me about it."

She pulled a stick of butter from her nearly bare refrigerator and sniffed it. "You should have seen the look on his face when I yelled at him, though." She giggled, pitching the butter across the kitchen into the wastebasket.

"You might conquer surveillance yet."

"Don't count on it. You're not supposed to get made. I don't know how you do it, Nick."

"So you're meeting with Al this afternoon?"

"Yep." She remembered what Nick had said about getting kicked out the Bureau, knew that was the last thing she wanted. "Wish me luck, partner."

"Good luck, Reegs." He didn't bother to sugarcoat things; he knew she was in trouble.

"Hey, Nick? Find out about David Lancaster. Skip the stakeout – Burke's probably alerted him that we're sniffing around. I'm sure ol' Charlie has figured out it's the FBI on his trail."

"Okay, I'll see what I can dig up on Lancaster," Nick said.

"Good. If I'm still an agent after today, I'll help you get him."

☙

AS USUAL, Al's face revealed nothing.

"So, Regan, been doing a little traveling?"

243

Should she say she was visiting her cousin in Texas? No, she couldn't lie. Even if she could, Al would never buy it.

She nodded.

"Discover anything useful?"

Regan filled him in on her excursion. She also furnished the details she'd learned from her CIA friend, James.

When she finished, Al was quiet.

She knew better than to prod him. She tamped down her anxiety and waited.

"Well, on the plus side," he said, "you've managed to accumulate a good bit of information on our friend Carney." She saw the photo Eric took in the open file in front of Al; he still didn't know Regan was on that Hanston chopper with Nick. Nor was she about to enlighten him.

"Your instincts about Carney, including his influence on Trevor Wolf's actions, appear to be dead-on." Al paused.

A tiny flicker of hope ignited in her gut.

"On the down side, however, you show signs of being a rogue agent. I can't risk that in my unit, Regan."

The tiny flicker snuffed itself out. She tensed, waiting for the official dismissal.

But how could she go without at least making an attempt to defend herself? "Can I just say one thing?"

Al pointed his hand at her, palm up, inviting her to go ahead.

"I'm not a rogue agent, Al. I understand the value of teamwork more than most people. And the thing that's always made me a valuable member of *any* team is what you just mentioned – my instincts. My ability to interpret behavior and anticipate what my adversary might do next."

The image of Burke standing next to her table in the bar flashed in her head. *Okay ... that was an exception.*

"I love the FBI," Regan continued. "I'm not ready to leave it. If you'll give me another chance, I promise not to overstep my bounds again. Please, Al – let me help you take down Carney."

"It may not be up to me, Regan. The OPR is waiting to meet with you as soon as we finish up here."

"If they clear me, will you?"

Al's gaze was steady. Slowly, he began to nod. "Like I told you before, you're the best agent I've got."

CHAPTER SEVENTY-TWO

YOU'LL SURVIVE the inquiry, Regan," said Jack. "You're too good at what you do for them to give you the boot."

It was their nightly conversation, a pattern that had evolved gradually and was the highlight of Regan's day. His steady encouragement buoyed her during the relentless scrutiny by the OPR; in turn, she learned the intricacies of Jack's research in tree genetics and forests' natural defense systems.

Lately she detected an undertone, though, a slight tempering of his affection. The spark between them in Juneau had been intense, unmistakable; perhaps for him, the memory of their time together was beginning to fade. Maybe Jack saw a relationship with her as simply too great a challenge.

But her memory of their time together hadn't dimmed at all. Though brief, it ignited the yearning for love and connection that she'd barricaded off for too long—removed the police tape that surrounded her heart.

She thought about Jack constantly, mentally transporting herself to his deck, where they sipped wine and talked about their day as they watched the seagulls in Fritz Cove. Or they slumped together on the leather couch, bodies touching, watching logs burn in the fireplace as Susie snoozed on the rug.

Regan held tight to one thing: as soon as the investigation was over, she planned to take some time off. She would be on the first plane to Juneau.

Why hadn't she told him that? No wonder he was slipping away from her – all he knew was how much she loved her job.

It was true – she *did* love the FBI. And she didn't want to be kicked out of it.

But maybe it was time to leave of her own accord.

৵

IT TOOK almost a week. In the end, OPR concluded Regan acted appropriately.

"Welcome back," said Al, clapping her on the shoulder in what was, for him, a gesture of extreme warmth. "We've got a lot of work to do."

Regan was relieved to be cleared, but it didn't stop her from ruminating over what would've happened if she'd flat-out refused to obey the secretary's orders to stay back. Would Vargas still be alive? Would Trevor have found a way to do Carney's bidding anyway?

The questions would plague her for a long time.

"Okay, boss, suited up and ready for duty. What would you like me to do?"

Nick had kept her in the loop; she knew what needed to be done, but she didn't dare get ahead of Al.

"First, Regan, it's time we took this further up the food chain. I've set up a meeting with the executive assistant director of law enforcement services – Neil Latham."

Yikes, thought Regan. *That's way the hell up the food chain.* "When?"

He looked at his watch. "Twenty minutes from now."

She was suddenly nervous. "You're coming, too, right?"

Al shook his head. "No, you'll meet with him alone."

"Without Nick?"

"Alone means just you, Regan. Not me, not Nick. When I contacted Latham about a possible meeting, he requested a one-on-one with you. I'm not one to argue with a higher-up." His face held a hint of amusement.

"Got it."

CHAPTER SEVENTY-THREE

I'VE HEARD some good things about you, Agent Manning," said Latham.

"Thank you, sir," said Regan, surprised. Her apprehension lessened a little.

"I know the Office of Professional Responsibility just completed an inquiry on your actions in Alaska. I'm pleased with their findings, as I'm sure you are." He smiled.

Regan looked down at her hands.

"You know, Agent Manning, the tough cases rarely turn out to be demonstrations of pure brilliance, no matter who the case agent is. We're forced to make decisions instantly and do what we can to keep people out of harm's way. You kept things under control under constantly changing, continually escalating conditions."

She met his eyes, said nothing.

"It is unfortunate that things turned out as they did for Secretary Vargas and her chief of staff – I'm certainly not minimizing that. But to pursue a hostage taker in a huge underground mine, with all its attendant pitfalls – well, that's gotta be a first. And I know it had to be scary as hell. From what I've been told, you didn't flinch."

"Frankly, sir, I wish I'd done more to head things off before they even got to the mine." *And you're wrong about the flinching.*

"According to the OPR report, the entire FBI team, along with others in attendance at Perseverance, heard Ella Vargas order you to stay back. The other agents indicated you only partially obeyed that order, that you followed at a discreet distance. You made the best of a bad situation."

She hoped that one day she'd see it that way, too.

"How are your injuries? Have you recovered fully?"

"Yes, thank you, sir." Except for the ribs, still protesting whenever she turned too quickly.

"Good. Glad to hear it. Now then, let's turn our attention to the ongoing investigation. Tell me what you know."

Regan relayed all the details to Latham; he listened without interrupting.

"Here's something you should know, though," she said softly. "I got made tailing Burke."

"From what I hear, you gave a convincing performance at the Houston airport."

So he'd already heard! Regan felt herself blush.

"But I agree it would better serve the investigation to use seasoned surveillance experts from now on."

"My partner, Nick Jenesco, is CIRG's best, sir."

"Noted. Now, I want to discuss a highly sensitive issue. Agent Manning, is there anything concrete to suggest Vice President Ness may have acted … inappropriately?"

"No, sir, nothing but the assertions of Robert Carney's estranged wife that the vice president may have received compensation for favors on Carney's behalf in Bahrain."

"What kind of favors?" Latham's brow was furrowed.

"Mrs. Carney claims that Vice President Ness talked to the commander of the Navy's Fifth Fleet in Bahrain to pave the way for Robert Carney to get a piece of the action in building infrastructure for the military. He's doing it under a separate company called RBC Enterprises. According to Resa Carney, her husband paid Ness to do that."

"I see," he said, leaning back in his chair and pressing his fingers together to form a tent. "I understand Ness and Carney go way back."

"All the way to Harvard," said Regan. "Frat brothers."

Latham smiled. "Those ties go deep. Almost makes you wonder why it was necessary to *pay* an old friend for his influence, if indeed that's what happened." He shook his head and leaned forward, perching his arms on his desk. "With regard to your conversation with Mac Holman, do you think he can be persuaded to provide evidence in exchange for his own protection?"

"To be honest, I'm not sure," said Regan. "What I picked up on the most was his pain and confusion. It was hard to read his intent. He may or may not have had something to do with the shots fired at me that night."

"Well, I'm going to have a conversation with the deputy director," he said. "I think it's possible he'll want to set up a meeting with the president's chief of staff to inform her of these allegations. Keep yourself available, just in case."

"Of course, sir. How would you like me to proceed in the meantime?"

"If you can, try to have another informal conversation with Mac Holman. Give him the chance again to assist in the investigation."

"Yes, sir."

"Apart from that, continue to follow your leads, but remain vigilant. If these guys detect the Bureau's interest in them, I don't have to tell you the amount of danger you could be in, Agent Manning."

CHAPTER SEVENTY-FOUR

THE PRESIDENT'S chief of staff? You're running with the big boys now," said Nick. He perched on the edge of her desk.

"Big *girls*, Jenesco. The president's chief of staff is a woman."

"Whatever. Maybe you'll get to meet with Eli himself."

"Yes, of course," said Regan. "I'm sure the president invites people at my pay grade over to the Oval Office for chats regularly. So give me the goods on Lancaster. What did you find?"

"Not much. His overseas exploits are pretty murky. We don't have the security clearance to dig very deep – but maybe you can have your new friend, the president's chief of staff, look into it for you."

"Very funny. So how's the Charlie Burke tail coming along?"

"Okay ... and by the way, thanks for the endorsement with the EAD. He told Al that I should head up surveillance on this entire investigation. Pretty impressive pull you have, Manning."

"Yes, it's all about me, of course. Has nothing to do with your surveillance record."

Nick's cell phone rang. "Jenesco. Right, I'm on my way." He hung up and said, "Gotta go. Burke is on the move."

&

SHE MANAGED to persuade Mac to meet her for lunch. He seemed determined to keep his guard up, but he looked like hell. The pallor in his face contrasted sharply with the dark circles under his eyes.

Regan attempted light conversation; Mac wasn't biting. Should she cut to the chase and ask him if he was the one who sent the hit men after her?

No, I want him to cooperate, not clam up.

"Mac, have you thought any more about our conversation? Are you willing to help us gather the facts surrounding Robert Carney's involvement in the oil tanker explosion?"

"You want me to betray the vice president?"

His answer startled her. "How exactly is that betraying the vice president?"

"Carney is his best friend."

"So you think they're in cahoots on something?"

"I didn't say that," he said quickly. "But taking down Carney would be personally devastating for the vice president." He crossed his arms and lifted his chin, physically trying to wrangle control of the conversation.

If he felt secure, he wouldn't be here.

Regan sighed loudly. "All right, Mac. Let's stop playing games. Either you agree to help us build a case against Carney or you don't. We will do it with you or without you. Our focus is *not* the vice president – unless, of course, we uncover something that points a finger at him and we have no choice. And let me remind you that if you possess knowledge of wrongdoing and don't disclose it, you could be charged with obstruction."

She hoped that would shake him loose.

He dropped his hands into his lap. "Okay, what do you want to know?"

"First, I have to ask you, Mac, have you done anything illegal?"

"Uh, I, no, I don't think so …"

"C'mon, you're an attorney. You know the law. Have you complied with it?" She wondered how much she could get him to admit.

"For the most part," he said.

"It's pretty black-and-white, Mac. Yes or no?"

He paused and chose his words carefully, being an attorney and all. "I figured out that Trevor was working for Carney. I didn't tell anybody because I thought I could handle it myself when he got back to Washington – thought I could talk some sense into him."

"What made you suspect Trevor's relationship with Carney?"

"Trevor's behavior had gotten a little weird – or weirder than usual, I should say. And then he said something that told me he had had a conversation with Carney after Bob left Alaska."

"Which was?"

"That the IRG might have been responsible for the tanker explosion. I was the one who told Carney that after we got some intel to that effect – but I never mentioned it to Trevor or anyone else. I mean besides the vice president, of course."

"But it wasn't the IRG, was it?"

Mac shook his head. "Carney wanted to stage the destruction of his tanker, the *Seacat*, so he could collect the insurance on it. Axis is making some extremely heavy investments right now – the development of the new drilling tool, the purchase of new double-hulled tankers to replace their old single-hulled ships, investments in renewable energy sources, overseas investments, things like that. He needs the cash."

"So he tried to pin it on the Iranian government – or the Revolutionary Guard – just so he could collect the money for his damaged ship," Regan said.

Mac shrugged and nodded.

"Seems like a pretty elaborate scheme just to get rid of a piece-of-crap tanker. After he paid everybody who helped him pull it off, there wouldn't be much left for his so-called 'investments.' Sorry, Mac, I'm not buying it." She crossed her arms and leaned back in her chair.

He looked down at the table, apparently trying to figure out how much he had to tell Regan to get her off his back. "Okay. Carney also asked for my help identifying some government officials in the Caspian region."

"For what?" She leaned forward.

He hesitated before answering. "He wants to shift the focus away from Persian Gulf oil. He wants Axis to control the pipeline transporting oil from the Tengiz field."

"So he planned to bribe certain government officials to make sure that happened."

Mac nodded.

"How much?"

"Sixty-five million."

Regan slumped back in her chair. "No wonder he was short of cash."

Mac had started to turn his coffee cup in circles, just like he had before when he talked about Trevor.

"How much did your boss know about this?"

"He knew nothing, I swear. Landry Ness is guilty only of being a bad judge of character. Of being too loyal to his friend."

Did Mac know about his boss being paid to help Carney in Bahrain? Had Resa possibly gotten it wrong?

"So what you're telling me is that the vice president has not broken any laws."

Mac met her gaze. "Absolutely not."

"Are you sure your boss hasn't been compensated in any way for providing assistance to Robert Carney?"

"Of course not!" he said indignantly.

"You mentioned intel on the tanker explosion. Did that come from the CIA?"

He gave her a wary look, followed by a single nod.

"Mac, did you hook Carney up with some of your CIA contacts?"

Mac looked like Regan had just whipped out a gun and pointed it at him.

"Like David Lancaster, maybe?" she said.

His eyes widened even more.

"And Charlie Burke?"

He nodded, dazed at her knowledge.

"Are they involved with Carney's projects in Bahrain?"

"I don't know. I didn't *want* to know. All I did was hook them up."

"Which still makes you culpable." They were going to need Mac to testify against Carney; Regan saw her chance. "Mac, I believe

Carney is responsible for the deaths of three people – your best friend along with Ella Vargas and Cory Winslow."

"Who's Cory Winslow?"

"A man Trevor apparently hired to plant bombs designed to scare Vargas so she'd abandon the energy plan and leave Juneau."

Mac shook his head, stunned. "I had no idea …"

Time to tighten the screws.

"But you *did* have an idea that Trevor had become mixed up in some questionable activities – and yet you did nothing to stop him. And you knew of Carney's intention to bribe officials in the Caspian. I believe you're familiar with the Foreign Corrupt Practices Act?"

Mac nodded miserably.

"At the very least, you helped Carney commit a felonious act. I think you know as well as I do that you're looking at some jail time."

Mac's eyes filled. "I told you what I know …"

"I want you to agree to testify against Carney."

"He'll have me killed," he said, his voice trembling. "You don't know how powerful he is."

"We'll protect you."

"The way you protected Secretary Vargas? And Trevor?"

His words stung.

"We will make sure you are protected, Mac."

"Sorry, but I need more assurance than just your word."

"I can have someone higher up in the Bureau contact you. Will that be adequate?"

He nodded glumly.

Regan couldn't help but feel sorry for him. She reached across the table and touched his hand. "I know this is hard, Mac. But look at it this way: you're doing it for Trevor."

CHAPTER SEVENTY-FIVE

ONCE AGAIN, the hour was late as Regan left the office and headed for Alexandria. She watched to be sure no one tailed her this time.

Traffic was light; as she drove, her thoughts drifted to Jack. She couldn't wait to call him the minute she got home.

She pulled into the parking lot in her apartment complex, glancing around, as usual, to be sure no one lurked in the shadows.

Just as she reached the stairs leading to the second floor, a hand came from behind and slapped a cloth over her nose and mouth. She dug her fingernails into her attacker's hand and flailed her other arm up over her head, trying to grab his hair.

Her ribs screamed in protest; she tried to keep her focus there, to keep from slipping away.

The next thing to enter her consciousness was the wicked headache. How long had she been out?

Regan opened her eyes a crack and saw a familiar face.

"Welcome back, Agent Manning," said Burke.

She tried glaring at him, but it hurt too much. She peered around; they appeared to be in some type of warehouse arranged with a sitting area. She rested on an old sofa; Burke sat nearby in a high-backed office chair. A man she didn't know perched on a wooden stool. She glimpsed two other men standing in the shadows – presumably her attackers.

The thought of the men staring at her while she slept creeped her out. She noticed the top two buttons of her blouse were open; she hoped that meant they checked for a wire and nothing else.

"Where am I?" she said hoarsely.

"You're here with us. Once again, you and I seem to be frequenting the same spots."

The man on the stool smiled. He was about her age with dark hair and dark eyes. Extremely good-looking. David Lancaster.

"Agent Manning. We meet at last," he said with a smile.

She remained silent, waiting to see what was next on their agenda.

"Suppose you fill us in on why you've become so intrigued with us," said Lancaster.

Had Mac sold her out?

She sat up and was immediately socked with dizziness. She closed her eyes to let it pass, then she looked at Lancaster. "Ten days ago, I chased Trevor Wolf and his hostage, the energy secretary of the United States, through an abandoned goldmine. Ella Vargas wound up dead, and I ended up on a ledge in a rotten mine shaft, badly injured, wondering if my fate would be the same as the secretary's. You might just say I have a peculiar interest in finding out what prompted Mr. Wolf to go off the deep end." She wrapped her arms around her aching ribs.

Burke and Lancaster watched her intently. Lancaster said, "And have you determined why that was?"

She chose her words carefully. After all, they were in league with Carney, the mastermind behind all of this. "Robert Carney used Trevor to eliminate his longtime adversary."

"You seem to think you know an awful lot about Robert Carney," said Burke.

She didn't answer. He hadn't asked a question.

"So, out of professional courtesy, we're going to give you a warning. But just this one time. Understood?"

They didn't know she knew about the bribe. Otherwise, those two men in the shadows would have slit her throat instead of chloroforming her.

She nodded. Her head felt like it was about to split open.

"Back off," said Lancaster. "Stay away from Carney, stay away from us. Otherwise, your pal in Juneau – Jack Landis, I believe? – will have a freak accident while he's out there talking to the trees. Do I make myself clear?"

∂

THE TWO shadowy goons drove her back home. They pulled into the parking lot and yanked her from the car, then they sped off.

Back in her apartment, she burst into tears. *Please, not Jack … don't hurt Jack …*

He answered on the first ring. He knew immediately something was wrong. "Regan? What is it?"

"Nothing. I – I just really want to see you."

"Are you okay?" There was alarm in his voice.

"Yeah … I think the investigation is just getting to me a little." She wiped away the tears on her cheeks. "Just be really careful when you're out working, okay?"

"I will." He paused. "And Regan? I really want to see you, too. More than you can possibly imagine."

∂

MAC WAS still in his office when Regan called.

"The deal is off. You're on your own, Mac."

"Wait – no, I was just scared! They saw us together today."

"Who contacted you?"

"Lancaster. He threatened to have me killed if I didn't tell him about our conversation. I didn't tell them everything you knew."

Mac had the good sense to know that if he had, he would've likely contributed to yet another death.

"Okay, I need to see how the Bureau wants to handle this. In the meantime, Mac, I suggest you keep your head down."

CHAPTER SEVENTY-SIX

NEIL LATHAM looked extremely unhappy. "Lancaster is active CIA. He's pretty damn cocky, kidnapping and threatening one of my agents. Obviously he believes we can't tie him to Carney."

"But can't we link him to Carney though Charlie Burke?"

"Not if we don't have physical evidence," said Latham. "These guys are CIA, Regan. They know what they're doing."

"What about Mac?" she said.

"I'm having him picked up for questioning. We'll hold his feet so close to the fire he won't be able to walk for a week."

"Good," said Regan. "I think he's getting close to the breaking point."

"I've set up a meeting with the president's chief of staff, Belinda Griffith," said Latham. "I want you to relay the details of the investigation to her firsthand."

"Okay," said Regan. "When?"

"This afternoon at two. Let's meet back here a little after one-thirty. The deputy director will be coming along, too."

෯

REGAN WAS decked out in her best suit – an emerald green straight skirt and jacket that accentuated her eyes. Her auburn hair fell in soft curls to her shoulders, and she'd even taken the time to file her nails and apply a coat of clear polish.

She sat with Latham and the deputy director outside Belinda Griffith's office, fidgeting in her chair. Fortunately it was only a few minutes before an assistant showed them in.

The chief of staff greeted them. She pointed them to a sitting area; once they were all settled, she turned to Regan.

"Well, Agent Manning. I'm delighted to finally meet you. You've had an interesting few weeks, to say the least." She smiled warmly.

"Yes, I have," Regan replied, her body stiff with nerves.

"I'd like to hear about it."

Regan relayed the pertinent details of her story, beginning with the bomb blast heralding their arrival in Juneau. When she was finished, Belinda asked her several questions, then invited Regan's bosses to comment. The diciest bit was the vice president's potential involvement; they couldn't afford to get it wrong.

Belinda stood. "If you could all wait just a moment, I'll be right back." She left the office.

After a few minutes, she reappeared. "Okay, the president would like a few minutes with you. Come with me, please."

Regan thought of Nick; he would faint if he saw where she was now, heading for the Oval Office. She felt a little lightheaded herself.

Eli Sanford was even more handsome and charismatic in person than he was on TV. Regan was completely star-struck. She gazed around, trying to take it all in. After all, this was a one-shot deal.

The walls were a creamy ivory; cerulean blue embossed satin curtains framed the Rose Garden. The paintings that adorned the walls were mostly landscapes of America's diverse geography.

On the credenza behind the president's huge desk sat framed pictures of his wife and children, as well as his parents, who still lived in Iowa.

Taped to one wall, just beneath a painted landscape depicting a wheat field and a windmill, was a crudely drawn picture of a pink house with blue trees around it. The artist's chosen medium was crayon. At the top, it said, "To Daddy." She felt like hugging him for his fatherly departure from Oval Office decorum.

Sanford was a warm and friendly man, skilled at putting people at ease. Once again, she told her story. With each telling it sounded more surreal, even to her.

"You've confirmed my suspicions, Agent Manning. We've attempted to connect the dots but there were still too many missing pieces – even with some of the help we had. Belinda?"

She opened the door and said, "You can come in now."

In walked Charlie Burke.

CHAPTER SEVENTY-SEVEN

BURKE SMILED at Regan's stunned face. "You stumbled into the middle of an undercover sting."

Regan slowly recovered. "So you weren't let go from the CIA," she said. "That was a ruse. What about David Lancaster? Is he in on this, too?"

She suddenly remembered where she was. "Oh, I'm sorry, Mr. President. Please, go ahead."

"Not at all, Agent Manning. Feel free to ask Agent Burke anything you like." The other two FBI men watched the whole scene with astonishment.

"Who shot at my car?" Regan asked Burke. "Who was trying to kill me? I thought it was you."

"Mac told Carney about his conversation with you, and Carney sent two men to eliminate you. Seems he's grown quite fond of having people bumped off when they get in his way."

"Keeping his own hands clean, of course," said Regan.

"Of course. He employs skilled hit men to do it for him. Lucky for you your partner got there in time."

Regan shook her head, dazed to think how close she'd come to being murdered.

"And to answer your question about Agent Lancaster, he has lost his way, unfortunately." Burke's tone was full of regret. "He had the skill and the intelligence to go far in the agency. But he got tied up with Robert Carney. The oil baron is the master he serves, not the CIA, despite his continued affiliation with us."

"So Lancaster believes you're a CIA outcast," said Regan. "He's using you to get what he needs to do Carney's bidding, and you're using Lancaster to get to Carney."

"That's right," said Burke.

"What about in Houston? You already knew who I was, didn't you?"

Burke nodded. "But I couldn't reveal my identity until I figured out what you were up to – saw how much you knew."

Regan suddenly saw how this was going to play out. She was about to join Charlie Burke undercover.

"As you know, Agent Burke, I'm not the best at undercover surveillance." She gave him a self-conscious smile.

"To the contrary, Agent Manning. Your little display of anger at the Houston airport gave me pause. I thought we *had* made a mistake."

She laughed. "I was particularly grumpy that morning."

The president broke in. "You two will need to move quickly. We won't be able to hold Mac Holman for questioning very long, but while he's in FBI custody, Ness's information source is cut off. He'll have to go directly to Carney for an update, and we're ready to capture any such conversation." Sanford had a grave look on his face. "We'll know soon if the vice president is truly involved."

A STRAND of red hair popped loose from her ponytail. She tucked it behind her ear and boarded the Houston-bound flight, pretending not to notice the two men sitting on the other side of the departure lounge who occasionally cast a glance in her direction.

The flight was bumpy; she couldn't help but wonder if that was an indication of things to come.

She'd brought a carry-on bag, so she skipped baggage claim and headed straight outside to hail a cab. As they blended into traffic, she spoke to her driver. "Excuse me, is there a cab following us with two men in the back seat?"

He glanced in the rearview mirror. "Yes, ma'am."

Good.

They pulled up to the intercom in front of the gate to Resa Carney's house. The cab following them passed by and continued on down the road.

She rolled down the back window and said, "Regan Manning here to see Mrs. Carney."

The gate slowly opened and the taxi drove forward, depositing her in the circle drive. She paid the driver and ran up the front steps.

Resa greeted her at the door. "Nice to meet you, Lindsay. Regan tells me you're not a *true* redhead like us – but you sure coulda fooled me, hon."

CHAPTER SEVENTY-EIGHT

HANSTON OIL called a press conference to make an important announcement.

The CEO stood at the podium, a distinguished gentleman who had worked his way up through the ranks over the past four decades. He planned to retire soon, and this announcement would certainly add sparkle to his legacy.

"Ladies and gentlemen, it gives me great pleasure to inform you that Hanston Oil is in the process of developing a tool that will change the face of the oil drilling industry ..."

At the back of the room, Eric and Fish exchanged a high-five.

CARNEY'S ASSISTANT burst into his office. "Boss! You have to see this!"

He frantically grabbed the remote and aimed it at the plasma screen on Carney's office wall. The Hanston CEO's face filled the screen.

"... a drilling device that will allow us to penetrate layers of rock heretofore impenetrable. Domestic oil fields believed to be depleted will yield additional crude oil ..."

"What the hell?" screamed Carney. "There's *no fucking way!* I'll sue them! Get Ness on the phone."

A minute later, Ness was on the line.

"What the hell is going on, Landry?" he screeched.

"What are you talking about?"

"Hanston just announced development of the extraction tool. You promised me exclusive —"

"I don't know what's going on, Bob. Mac hasn't been in today and I can't find him. Let me talk to Eli's people and find out what's happening."

"We had a deal, Landry. The balance in your offshore account *proves* it." He probably shouldn't have said that out loud – someone could be listening. But then again, he paid people handsomely to make sure that didn't happen.

"I'll get back to you," the vice president said, hanging up.

Carney slammed the phone into its cradle. His assistant said, "Mr. Carney, there's one more thing …"

"What?" barked Carney, his tan face suffused with rage.

"That FBI agent, Regan Manning, arrived at your wife's house a short time ago. We've set up surveillance."

"Resa's been spilling her guts to the FBI," he growled.

"According to the chauffeur, this isn't that agent's first visit, either."

Carney looked up; the expression on his face was deadly.

"Have the house set on fire – and make sure they're in it," he said.

He felt a twinge of regret. He'd always liked that house.

CHAPTER SEVENTY-NINE

REGAN AND Burke pulled up in front of Axis and jumped out, guns drawn. Police cruisers pulled in behind them, lights flashing.

The police chief ran up to them. "Agents, I just got word that Carney's house is on fire."

Regan felt a surge of panic. "Did the occupants get out?"

"Haven't heard yet. I'll keep you posted."

Regan turned to Burke. "Let's get this bastard, Charlie."

Burke raised his arm and gave the signal. A horde of officers stormed the Axis headquarters, sealing off the exits.

The two agents jumped on the elevator and headed for the top floor. They stayed close to the wall as they crept toward Carney's office.

Regan peeked through the window, saw Carney's hand reach for the phone on his desk. She nodded at Burke.

They burst into the office. Regan bellowed, "Robert Carney, FBI! You're under arrest!"

They were staring into the frantic eyes of Carney's assistant. "He ... he's not here ..." His hands were in the air, shaking badly.

"Where is he?"

He pointed toward the window. In the direction of the hangars.

Regan turned to one of the police officers. "Take this man into custody." She and Burke sprinted from the office.

༅

CARNEY RAN up the airplane steps. He could see the flashing red-and-blue lights on the other side of the trees and knew he had only seconds.

Good thing he'd called the pilot ahead and told him to get the plane ready.

"Take it up!" he screamed. "Let's go!"

The idling engines ramped up and the plane rolled toward the runway.

Carney shook his head slowly back and forth, overwhelmed with disbelief. How had things gone so wrong?

It had to be that agent. Manning.

But she'd be dead by now. Along with that bimbo he never should've married in the first place. He never seemed to learn.

He'd lay low for awhile in Tangier. Bunk with Charlie Burke until things blew over.

Carney glanced out the window and saw two people running toward his plane, guns drawn. He leaned closer, scarcely able to believe his eyes.

The last two people on earth he expected to see. Especially together.

Regan Manning and Charlie Burke.

ふ

REGAN WATCHED with chagrin as the plane lifted off.

Burke was already on the phone. "Get the Air Force to scramble fighter jets immediately. The tail number on Carney's plane is ..."

As he read off the tail number, Regan dialed Lindsay's cell phone and held her breath.

"Pryor."

Regan exhaled loudly. "Thank God you're okay, Lindsay. Did Resa get out safely, too?"

"Yep. All of us, including her pack of Dobies, escaped through a tunnel. Good thing Carney was as paranoid as he was when he built that house. Did you get him?"

"Not yet. He took off in his plane, but some F-16's will convince him he doesn't want to go anywhere today."

Lindsay laughed. "What do you want me to do now?"

"I want you and Resa to meet Charlie and me at Houston Hobby. Our turboprop is waiting there to take us all back to Washington."

"Awesome," said Lindsay. "I have a friend there I'd like to see."

CHAPTER EIGHTY

H E'S IN custody," said Burke. "We can go ahead and take off."

"Hallelujah," said Resa. "Thanks to that madman, I have nothing to wear but the clothes on my back. And this isn't even one of my favorite outfits."

Resa didn't seem especially perturbed that she'd just lost her house and had to leave her precious Dobies in the care of her bodyguards. Or maybe it was the other way around.

Besides, Resa and Carney weren't divorced. She'd end up with everything, including the insurance settlement on the still-smoldering house.

Regan called Nick. "Pick up Lancaster."

"You got Carney?"

"We got Carney."

"Good. How'd Lindsay do?"

"Excellent."

Nick didn't know that in a couple hours he'd be able to ask the Anchorage agent face-to-face.

ༀ

SHE WATCHED Burke season the steaks, then glanced toward the sliding glass doors leading out to the patio. Nick and Lindsay sat side-by-side at the table, under the umbrella, happily engrossed in conversation.

Regan recalled her partner's reaction when he saw who followed her off the plane; she'd never seen Nick so flustered. Or so pleased.

"Can I help, Charlie?"

"Know how to make a salad?"

"You mean tear up lettuce and chop a tomato? Sure, I think I can handle that."

"Great. The makings are right there, wooden salad bowl's in that cupboard." He pointed without looking. "I'll go slap these on the grill."

His dog, Rudy, followed him outside.

When he came back in, the dog on his heels, Regan said, "You know, Charlie, when we first started surveilling you, when we bugged your house, we felt bad for Rudy because you never talked to him."

Burke gave a loud, hearty laugh. "We talk, don't we, buddy?"

The German Shepherd barked and wagged his tail.

"See there?"

Regan laughed. "So you were just being quiet for our benefit?"

"Of course." He bent down and stroked the dog's sides. "I didn't want you snoops listening in on our business. Me and Rudy talk about some serious stuff."

Regan wondered if Charlie talked important business with some of the women who came for a visit, too.

"Just so you know," said Burke, "I found that first bug in less than five minutes. I have to admit, though, that one in the magazine you guys left in the door ..." He smiled. "That was good."

"Thank you. We Fibbies are pretty brilliant."

Burke made a face. "No comment."

"So ... now that the investigation's over, are you heading off to Tangier for a little R & R?"

"Nah. I don't really like the place. It was just a front."

"Well, if you're up for some fishing in Alaska, I know someone with a fancy boat."

A smile lit up his face. "Now you're talkin'."

"Hey, Charlie, there's something I've wondered about."

"What's that?" He took a sip of his wine.

"How did the captain of the *Seacat* know the explosion was coming?"

"I alerted him," he said. "I was in Saudi Arabia with David when the men planted the mines. I told him I was taking a helicopter out over Abu Musa Island to make sure the operation got carried out as it was supposed to."

"That didn't raise his suspicions?"

"Not at all. He knew how much money those mercenaries were being paid. He also knows what an untrusting S.O.B. I am. Anyway, I radioed the captain from the helicopter and told him I had sensors picking up something in the water. He said their own sensors didn't seem to be working, but he slowed down enough that they just hit the one mine."

"So if you hadn't alerted the captain, they could have sustained heavy loss of life. Would Carney actually have allowed the crew of his tanker to be killed?"

"Absolutely. He has an almost total disregard for human life – especially if it gets in the way of his goals."

"Wow, he's even more psychopathic than I thought. I bet a lot of politicians will be scrambling to return the campaign contributions he gave them."

"Yep, I expect so. I sure would." Burke absently rubbed Rudy's ears.

"So it looks like Axis will ultimately survive under new leadership, even though things are going to be bumpy for awhile," said Regan.

"The shareholders will take a hit for the next few quarters, that's for sure. But it's a big company, and I imagine they'll get back on track eventually," Burke said. "Now that Sanford has shifted project leader status in ANWR to Hanston, Axis is going to have to learn to play nicely with others again."

"That William Fisher is something else, isn't he?" said Regan. "I still can't believe he came up with a new design for the tool and produced preliminary schematics that fast."

"Yeah, I bet Fish gets a nice, fat bonus this year. So … what do you say, shall we head outside and break up that private party?"

"Let's do," she replied. "It's getting way too serious."

⮧

"LADIES AND gentlemen, I have a statement to make."

Regan and Burke sat in Belinda's office, watching the president on TV as he spoke from the White House press room.

"It causes me profound sorrow to report that Vice President Landry Ness has been taken into custody and charged with corruption in a scheme involving Axis Oil CEO Robert Carney."

An audible gasp escaped members of the press gathered before him in the room.

"Mr. Carney is also in federal custody, charged with bribing a public official, insurance fraud, and conspiracy to commit murder, along with a number of other charges. A third arrest, that of CIA Agent David Lancaster, was made this morning in conjunction with the scheme, and formal charges are pending." He didn't mention Mac, who was considering a plea deal in exchange for his testimony.

"Just think," said Regan, "because of us, Ness and Carney might get to be roomies again. Leavenworth this time instead of Harvard."

Burke nodded. "Nothing like a little greed to keep friends close."

They went back to watching the president. Regan noticed the lines in Sanford's face, knew how troubled he was over the actions of Landry Ness, whom he'd long admired as a talented statesman. The events of the last twenty-four hours also renewed the grief he felt over the death of his energy secretary.

"The arrests are the culmination of an extensive probe by agents with the Federal Bureau of Investigation and the Central Intelligence Agency. We owe them a debt of gratitude for their dedication and courage, without which these egregious deeds may have gone unpunished."

Regan looked at Charlie and smiled. "He's sayin' we rock, dude." She started to reach out her hand.

Burke held his hands up. "Whoa, you're not gonna do one of those complicated hand-bump things, are you? I'm an old boot – I don't know that stuff."

Regan laughed. "Don't worry, old boot, I was just going to shake your hand."

They turned back to the TV.

"I am confident," said the president, "that these arrests will bring to justice those responsible for the death of Energy Secretary Ella Vargas. For more than a decade, she campaigned tirelessly for alternative energy, and I intend to work with Congress to ensure that her efforts will not be wasted."

I just might be able to help with that, thought Regan.

☙

REGAN PULLED into the circle drive and parked. She admired the landscaping that surrounded the red brick Georgetown home as she made her way to the front door.

An attractive, dark-haired woman met her at the door. "Come in, Agent Manning. My husband is in here."

Regan moved through the spacious foyer and into the living room where Congressman Slade waited. He stood.

"Hello, Congressman. Thank you for seeing me."

His eyes held more curiosity than contempt. "Of course," he said.

"I know this is somewhat awkward," said Regan.

"Please, have a seat," said Slade. He sat down and leaned forward, arms perched on his knees. A surprisingly open, unguarded posture.

"Up in Alaska," Regan began, "Secretary Vargas told me how much she planned to rely on you to shepherd her energy plan through Congress. She said no one else had your command of the issues involved – or your level of commitment to them. Apart from her, that is." She smiled; Slade smiled back.

"So here's my dilemma. I want Secretary Vargas to get her wish – to have you be the one to see that her plan has a decent shot at getting passed."

Slade looked down at his clasped hands, taking a moment to respond. "I understand your dilemma, Agent Manning. The aggravated assault charge against me makes it harder for me to play such a visible role with the Vargas plan."

Regan shot a quick glance at Mrs. Slade to gauge her reaction.

"It's okay," said Slade. "Marilyn and I have talked about everything at length. I finally took the advice she's been giving me for twenty years to get help with my anger. It's appalling to realize that I'd become my father."

Those dads, they do have a lingering effect.

"Good," she said. "I'm really glad to hear that."

"I'm no longer involved with Kate, nor will I ever cheat on my wife again."

Regan hoped he meant it, but time would tell.

"And I'm prepared to take whatever's coming to me for my actions – including the loss of my political career." He blinked when he said that part; he may be prepared, but that didn't mean he wouldn't cry like a baby.

"Well then, Congressman, here's what I'm proposing." Regan proceeded to lay it all out.

She hoped she wasn't being naïve in getting the charges reduced to simple assault in exchange for his work on the energy plan. Regan personally wanted a victory for Vargas, yes, but now she also wanted to believe Slade was, indeed, a changed man.

Sometimes you just have to go with your gut.

CHAPTER EIGHTY-ONE

REGAN STOLE the ball and launched a three-pointer. *Swish.*

"I see you haven't lost your competitive edge, Rocket," Ally said breathlessly. She grabbed the ball and raced in for a layup.

"Neither have you, Oop," said Regan, wiping the sweat off her brow with her shirt.

Their laughter echoed in the empty gym.

Regan tucked the ball under her arm and looked around. "Wow, remember this place? We used to have it rockin' to the rafters."

"Best time of my life," said Ally, her expression wistful. Her gaze shifted to the gym doors; she broke into a smile. "I think somebody's looking for you." She dropped her voice to a whisper. "Somebody hotter than hell."

Regan turned. Jack stood in the doorway, Susie peeking around his legs. "Gotta go," she said. "My ride's here."

She ran over and kissed Jack, feeling like a schoolgirl again. "Hi, Jack. Hi, Susie Woozy."

"Hi, yourself. You hungry?"

"I'm starved. But I need a shower first."

"You can shower while I make lunch. Then we'll head over to the airport."

"Sounds perfect," she said, taking his hand. "I can't wait to see Charlie."

৯

"MAN, I think I've died and gone to heaven," said Burke, the wind whipping his hair.

"You and me both," said Regan. They gazed at the ultramarine water as the boat leaped over the waves, Jack at the helm.

Susie stood on one of the benches, front legs perched on the boat's port side. "Won't she fall in?" said Burke.

"That's what I thought the first time I came for a boat ride with them," said Regan. "I kept wanting to hold on to one of her hind legs. But no, that old Susie's a salty sailor." The alliteration made her laugh.

Susie turned her head and looked at them, mouth open in a wide grin.

"Wait'll you see the brown bears on Admiralty Island, Charlie," Jack shouted over the noise of the engine. "Pretty impressive sight."

"We won't be getting real close, will we Jack?"

"See, what did I tell ya?" said Regan. "CIA guys are big fat wimps."

"Uh oh," said Jack. "I hope I'm not gonna spark an inter-agency fed fight."

"Nah, we're good," said Burke. "Just make sure she doesn't try to shove me toward one of those brownies."

Regan couldn't imagine ever feeling happier than she did right now. If she came back here for good, would it always feel like this?

She looked at Jack, watched him as he surveyed the scene from behind his Ray-Bans. She'd never met anyone so comfortable residing in that space between man and nature, who didn't require much human interaction but could nurture a relationship with the deftness of a maestro.

Because of him, the closed-off tunnels of her soul had begun to open. She felt herself slowly coming into balance.

The chief was waiting for an answer. Her dad wanted her to take the job.

Right now, though, the fish were biting.

CHAPTER EIGHTY-TWO

"THIS PLACE agrees with you," said Burke. They'd ridden the tram back down and stopped for a beer at the Red Dog Saloon.

"You think?" said Regan, her voice competing with the honky-tonk piano.

Burke nodded. "You seem content." He grabbed a handful of peanuts and began cracking them open.

"I am, Charlie. Jack's ... well, he's ..."

"Perfect for you, it looks like. I mean, I haven't known you that long, or him either, but you two seem to belong together."

"I think so, too. And the chief of police job ... that's a pretty plum deal."

"Would you miss the D.C. action?"

"Sure, a little, but I'm ready for some balance in my life. All work and no play makes Regan a ball-busting bitch."

They both laughed.

"I know what you mean, though," said Burke. "Sometimes it seems like agents aren't expected to have a personal life. I was married to a good woman once, but I was a bigamist – married to the agency at the same time. My biggest regret in life."

Regan nodded, understanding completely. Tomorrow, after she dropped Charlie off at the airport, she would go see the chief.

❧

THE AIRPORT bar was dim, but not enough to hide the redness in her eyes. They sat side-by-side in silence, hands clasped tightly, bodies touching.

278

"I'm not sure about this, Jack," Regan said quietly.

"I am," he replied, his own eyes sparkling with tears. "You're still on an upward trajectory in the Bureau, Regan. You have to see where it takes you."

Regan had put off her visit with the chief for a few days, giving herself more time. When she announced to Jack that she had made up her mind, planned to take the chief's job, he reminded her of the thing they shared most, apart from their blossoming love for each other: passion for their work. He couldn't stand by and watch her take a job she didn't really want. Even if – *especially* if – she was doing it for him.

She knew he was right, but that didn't make it hurt any less. "We'll be three thousand miles apart."

"Think of all the frequent flyer miles we're gonna rack up," said Jack, squeezing her hand.

She turned and looked at him, studied his face as though she were imprinting it on her brain.

"I'll be here, Regan," he said. "I'll wait."